"**GREAT !! BOOK** Lynda McDaniel can write. This is one fine read. READ THIS ONE." ~Wooley, Amazon Vine Voice Reviewer.

"**FIVE STARS!** Lynda McDaniel has that wonderfully appealing way of weaving a story, much in the manner of Fannie Flagg. The tale immediately drew me in, into the town, into the intriguing mystery, and into the people. [This mystery is] a real treat to read and made me anticipate meeting the characters in yet another installment." ~Deb, Amazon Hall of Fame Top 100 Reviewer

"*A Life for a Life* **is one of the most satisfying books I've read this year.** Everything about the book delighted me. *A Life for a Life* has also been compared to *To Kill a Mockingbird*. Both are character-driven and back a strong message of forgiveness, redemption and acceptance." ~Ana Manwaring, writer, blogger

"**Thoroughly enjoyable and intriguing** with descriptive powers and beautiful mountain scenery. Intense family and friend dynamics with character vulnerabilities and complex relationships that steal the reader's heart and make this mystery a must-read." ~Pam Franklin, international bestselling author

"The most satisfying mystery I've read in ages."
~Joan Nienhuis, book blogger

"The story has a wonderful balance of drama, mystery, and suspense that easily left me wanting more. What made the story that much more appealing is that it is more than a just a cozy mystery, as the author interweaves Della's personal journey of self-discovery and sense of community that she finds along the way in the small Appalachian town." ~Kathleen Higgins-Anderson, Jersey Girl Book Reviews

"Marvelous read! A compelling story told through the eyes and voice of two remarkable narrators [who] possess the same hopes and dreams for a new life. They describe their home life in such great detail that you feel like you have been transported to a small mountain town and are fortunate enough to catch a stunning glimpse into living and working in the deep woods." ~Yvette Klobuchar, author of *Brides Unveiled*

"McDaniel's mystery novel delivers a pair of unforgettable crime-solving characters. Using her keen knowledge of the charm (and less than charming features) of life in the North Carolina mountains, she lured me into her story and kept me there. I hope Della, Abit, and the gang will be back!" ~Virginia McCullough, award-winning author of *Amber Light*

Your free book is "Waiting for You"

Get your free copy of the prequel, *Waiting for You* and meet the stars of the Appalachian Mountain Mysteries series—Abit Bradshaw and Della Kincaid.

I've pulled back the curtain on their lives before they met in Laurel Falls—between 1981 and 1984. You'll discover how Abit lost hope of ever having a meaningful life and why Della had to leave Washington, D.C.

If you haven't started the series yet, *Waiting for You* will get you started in style.

Get your free copy of *Waiting for You* here:
https://www.lyndamcdanielbooks.com/free

A Life for a Life

A Mystery Novel

Lynda McDaniel

*Dedicated to all the Appalachian people who
changed my life for the better.*

September 2004

Prologue: Abit

My life was saved by a murder. At the time, of course, I didn't understand that. I just knew I was having the best year of my life. Given all the terrible things that happened, I should be ashamed to say it, but that year was a blessing for me.

I'd just turned 15 when Della Kincaid bought Daddy's store. At first nothing much changed. Daddy was still around a lot, getting odd jobs as a handyman and farming enough to sell what Mama couldn't put by. And we still lived in the house next door, though Mama banned me from going inside the store. She said she didn't want me to be a nuisance, but I think she was jealous of "that woman from Washington, D.C."

So I just sat out front like I always did when Daddy owned it, killing time, chatting with a few friendly customers or other bench-sitters like me. I never wanted to go inside while Daddy had the store, not because he might have asked me to help, but because he thought I *couldn't* help. Oh sure, I'd go in for a Coca-Cola or Dr. Pepper, but, for the most part, I just sat there, reared back with my chair resting against the outside wall, my legs dangling. Just like my life.

I never forgot how crazy it all played out. I *had* forgotten about the two diaries I'd kept that year. I discovered them while cleaning out our family home after Mama died in April. (Daddy had passed two years earlier, to the day.) They weren't like a girl's diary (at least that's what I told myself, when I worried about such things). They were notes I'd imagined a reporter like Della would make, capturing the times.

I'd already cleaned out most of the house, saving my room for last. I boxed up my hubcaps, picking out my favorites from the ones still hanging on my bedroom walls. (We'd long ago sold the collection in the barn.) I tackled the shelves with all my odd keepsakes: a deer jaw, two dusty geodes, other rocks I'd found that caught my eye, like the heart-shaped reddish one. When I gathered a shelf-full of books in my arms, I saw the battered shoebox where I'd stashed those diaries behind the books. I sat on my old bed, the plaid spread dusty and faded, and started to read. The pages had yellowed, but they stirred up fresh memories, all the same. That's when I called Della (I still looked for any excuse to talk with her), and we arranged a couple of afternoons to go over the diaries together.

We sat at her kitchen table and talked. And talked. After a time or two recollecting over the diaries, I told Della we should write a book about that year. She agreed. We were both a little surprised that, even after all these years, we didn't have any trouble recalling that spring.

April 1985

Chapter 1: Della

I heard my dog, Jake, whimpering as I sank into the couch. I'd closed him in the bedroom while the sheriff and his gang of four were in my apartment. Jake kept bringing toys over for them to throw, and I could see how irritated they were getting. I didn't want to give them reason to be even more unpleasant about what had happened earlier in the day.

"Hi there, boy," I said as I opened the door. "Sorry about that, buddy." He sprang from the room and grabbed his stuffed rabbit. I scratched his ears and threw the toy, then reclaimed the couch. "Why didn't we stay in today, like I wanted?"

That morning, I'd thought about skipping our usual hike. It was my only day off, and I wanted to read last Sunday's *Washington Post*. (I was always a week behind since I had to have the papers mailed to me.) But Jake sat by the door and whined softly, and I sensed how cooped up he'd been with all the early spring rains.

Besides, those walks did me more good than Jake. When I first moved to Laurel Falls, the natural world frightened me. Growing up in Washington, D.C. hadn't prepared me for that kind of wild. But gradually, I got more comfortable and started to recognize some of the birds and trees. And wildflowers. Something about their delicate beauty made the woods more welcoming. Trilliums, pink lady's slippers, and fringed phacelia beckoned, encouraging me to venture deeper.

Of course, it didn't help that my neighbors and customers carried on about the perils of taking long hikes by myself. "You could be murdered," they cried. "At the very least you could be raped," warned Mildred Bradshaw, normally a quiet, prim woman. "And what about perverts?" she'd add, exasperated that I wasn't listening to her.

Sometimes Mildred's chant "You're so alone out there" nagged at me in a reactive loop as Jake and I walked in the woods. But that was one of the reasons I moved to North Carolina. I *wanted* to be alone. I longed to get away from deadlines and noise and people. And memories. Besides, I'd argue with myself, hadn't I lived safely in D.C. for years? I'd walked dark streets, sat face-to-face with felons, been robbed at gunpoint, but I still went out whenever I wanted, at least before midnight. You couldn't live there and worry too much about crime, be it violent, white-collar, or political; that city would grind to a halt if people thought that way.

As Jake and I wound our way, the bright green tree buds and wildflowers soothed my dark thoughts. I breathed in that intoxicating smell of spring: not one thing in particular, but a mix of fragrances floating on soft breezes, signaling winter's retreat. The birds were louder too, chittering and chattering in the warmer temperatures. I was lost in my reverie when Jake stopped so fast I almost tripped over him. He stood still, ears alert.

"What is it, boy?" He looked up at me, then resumed his exploration of rotten squirrels and decaying stumps.

I didn't just love that dog, I admired him. He was unafraid of his surroundings, plowing through tall fields of hay or dense forests without any idea where he was headed, not the least bit perturbed by bugs flying into his eyes or seeds up his nose. He'd just sneeze and keep going.

We walked a while longer and came to a favorite lunch spot. I nestled against a broad beech tree, its smooth bark gentler against my back than the alligator bark of red oak or locust. Jake fixated on a line of ants carrying off remnants from a picnic earlier that day, rooting under leaves and exploring new smells since his last visit. But mostly he slept. He found a sunspot and made a nest thick with leaves, turning round and round until everything was just right.

Jake came to live with me a year and a half ago when a neighbor committed suicide, a few months before I moved south. We both struggled at first, but when we settled here, the past for him seemed forgotten. Sure, he still ran in circles when I brushed against his old leash hanging in the coat closet, but otherwise, he was officially a mountain dog. I was the one still working on leaving the past behind.

I'd bought the store on a whim after a week's stay in a log cabin in the Black Mountains. To prolong the trip, I took backroads home. As I drove through Laurel Falls, I spotted the boarded-up store sporting a For Sale sign. I stopped, jotted down the listed phone number, and called. Within a week, I owned it. The store was in shambles, both physically and financially, but something about its bones had appealed to me. And I could afford the extensive remodeling it needed because the asking price was so low.

Back in my D.C. condo, I realized how much I wanted a change in my life. I had no family to miss. I was an only child, and my parents had died in an alcoholic daze, their car wrapped around a tree, not long after I left for college. And all those editors and deadlines, big city hassles, and a failed marriage? I was eager to trade them in for a tiny town and a dilapidated store called Coburn's General Store. (Nobody knew who Coburn was—that was just what it had always been called, though most of the time it was simply Coburn's. Even if I'd renamed it, no one would've used that name.)

In addition to the store, the deal included an apartment upstairs that, during its ninety-year history, had likely housed more critters than humans. Plus a vintage 1950 Chevy pickup truck with wraparound rear windows that still ran just fine. And a bonus I didn't know about when I signed the papers: a living, breathing griffon to guard me and the store—Abit Bradshaw, Mildred's teenage son.

I'd lived there almost a year, and I treasured my days away from the store, especially once it was spring again. Some folks complained that I wasn't open Sundays (blue laws a distant memory, even though they were repealed only a few years earlier), but I couldn't work every day, and I couldn't afford to hire help, except now and again.

While Jake and I sat under that tree, the sun broke through the canopy and warmed my face and shoulders. I watched Jake's muzzle twitch (he was already lost in a dream), and chuckled when he sprang to life at the first crinkle of wax paper. I shooed him away as I unwrapped my lunch. On his way back to his nest, he stopped and stared down the dell, his back hairs spiking into a Mohawk.

"Get over it, boy. I don't need you scaring me as bad as Mildred. Settle down now," I gently scolded as I laid out a chunk of Gruyere I'd whittled the hard edges off, an almost-out-of-date salami, and a sourdough roll I'd rescued from the store. I'd been called a food snob, but these sad leftovers from a struggling store sure couldn't support that claim. Besides, out here the food didn't matter so much. It was all about the pileated woodpecker trumpeting its jungle call or the tiny golden-crowned kinglet flitting from branch to branch. And the waterfall in the distance, playing its soothing continuo, day and night. These walks kept me sane. The giant trees reminded me I was just a player in a much bigger game, a willing refugee from a crowded, over-planned life.

I crumpled the lunch wrappings, threw Jake a piece of roll, and found a sunnier spot. I hadn't closed my eyes for a minute when Jake gave another low growl. He was sitting upright, nose twitching, looking at me for advice. "Sorry, pal. You started it. I don't hear anything," I told him. He gave another face-saving low growl and put his head back down.

"You crazy old hound." I patted his warm, golden fur. Early on, I wondered what kind of mix he was— maybe some retriever and beagle, bringing his size down to medium. I'd asked the vet to hazard a guess. He wouldn't. Or couldn't. It didn't matter.

I poured myself a cup of hot coffee, white with steamed milk, appreciating the magic of a thermos, even if the contents always tasted vaguely of vegetable soup. That aroma took me back to the woods of my childhood, just two vacant lots really, a few blocks from my home in D.C.'s Cleveland Park. I played there for hours, stocked with sandwiches and a thermos of hot chocolate. I guess that's where I first thought of becoming a reporter; I sat in the cold and wrote up everything that passed by—from birds and salamanders to postmen taking a shortcut and high schoolers sneaking out for a smoke.

A deeper growl from Jake pulled me back. As I turned to share his view, I saw a man running toward us. "Dammit, Mildred," I swore, as though the intruder were her fault. The man looked angry, pushing branches out of his way as he charged toward us. Jake barked furiously as I grabbed his collar and held tight. Even though the scene was unfolding just as my neighbor had warned, I wasn't afraid. Maybe it was the Madras sport shirt, so out of place on a man with a bushy beard and long ponytail. *For God's sake*, I thought, *how could anyone set out in the morning dressed like that and plan to do harm*? A hint of a tattoo—a Celtic cross?—peeked below his shirt sleeve, adding to his unlikely appearance.

As he neared, I could see his face wasn't so much angry as pained, drained of color.

"There's some ... one," his voice cracked. He put his hands on his thighs and tried to catch his breath. As he did, his graying ponytail fell across his chest.

"What? Who?"

"A body. Somebody over there," he said, pointing toward the creek. "Not far, it's ..." he stopped again to breathe.

"Where?"

"I don't know. Cross ... creek." He started to run.

"Wait! Don't go!" I shouted, but all I could see was the back of his stupid shirt as he ran. "Hey! At least call for help. There's an emergency call box down that road, at the car park. Call Gregg O'Donnell at the Forest Service. I'll go see if there's anything I can do."

He shouted, "There's nothing you can do," and kept running.

Jake led the way as we crashed through the forest, branches whipping our faces. I felt the creek's icy chill, in defiance of the day's warmth, as I missed the smaller stepping stones and soaked my feet. Why didn't I ask the stranger more details, or have him show me where to find the person? And what did "across the creek" mean in an eleven-thousand-acre wilderness area? When I stopped to get my bearings, I began to shiver, my feet numb. Jake stopped with me, sensing the seriousness of our romp in the woods; he even ignored a squirrel.

We were a pack of two, running together, the forest silent except for our heavy breathing and the rustle we made crossing the decaying carpet beneath our feet. Jake barked at something, startling me, but it was just the crack of a branch I'd broken to clear the way. We were both spooked.

I stopped to rest on a fallen tree as Jake ran ahead, then back and to the right. Confused, he stopped and looked at me. "I don't know which way either, boy." We were just responding to a deep, instinctual urge to help. "You go on, Jake. You'll find it before I will."

And he did.

Chapter 2: Abit

Four cop cars blocked our driveway.

I thought I might've dreamed it, since I'd fallen asleep on the couch, watching TV. But after I rubbed my eyes, all four cars was still there. Seeing four black-and-whites in a town with only one could throw you.

All I could think was *what did I do wrong*? I ran through my day real quick-like, and I couldn't come up with anything that would get me more than a backhand from Daddy.

I watched a cop walking in front of the store next door, which we shared a driveway with. As long as I could remember, that store hadn't never had four cars out front at the same time, let alone four *cop* cars. I stepped outside, quietly closing our front door. The sun was getting low, and I hoped Mama wudn't about to call me in to supper.

I headed down our stone steps to see for myself. Our house sat on a hill above the store, which made it close enough that Daddy, when he still owned the store, could run down the steps (twenty of 'em, mossy and slick after a rain) if, say, a customer drove up while he was home having his midday dinner. But of an evening, those same steps seemed to keep people from pestering him to open up, as Daddy put it, "to sell some fool thing they could live without 'til the next morning."

I was just about halfway down when the cop looked my way. "Don't trouble yourself over this, Abit. Nothing to see here." That was Lonnie Parker, the county's deputy sheriff.

"What do you mean nothin' to see here? I ain't seen four cop cars all in one place in my whole life."

"You don't need to worry about this."

"I'm not worried," I said. "I'm curious."

"You're curious all right." He turned and spat something dark onto the dirt drive, a mix of tobacco and hate.

That's how it always went. People talked to me like I was an idiot. Okay, I knew I wudn't as smart as others. Something happened when Mama had me (she was pretty old by then), and I had trouble making my words just right sometimes. But inside, I worked better than most people thought. I used to go to school, but I had trouble keeping up, and that made Daddy feel bad. I wudn't sure if he felt bad for me or him. Anyways, they took me out of school when I was twelve, which meant I spent my days watching TV and hanging out. And being bored. I could read, but it took me a while. The bookmobile swung by every few weeks, and I'd get a new book each time. And I watched the news and stuff like that to try to learn.

I was named after Daddy – Vester Bradshaw Jr. – but everyone called me Abit. I heard the name Abbott mentioned on the TV and asked Mama if that was the same as mine. She said it were different but pronounced about the same. She wouldn't call me that, but Daddy were fine with it. A few year ago, I overheard him explaining how I came by it.

"I didn't want him called the same as me," Daddy told a group of men killing time outside the store. He was a good storyteller, and he was enjoying the attention. "He's a retard. When he come home from the hospital, and people asked how he was doin', I'd tell 'em, 'he's a bit slow.' I wanted to just say it outright to cut out all the gossip. I told that story enough that someone started calling him Abit, and it stuck."

Some jerk then asked if my middle name were "Slow," and everybody laughed. That hurt me at the time, but with the choice between Abit and Vester, I reckoned my name wudn't so bad, after all. Daddy could have his stupid name.

Anyways, I wudn't going to have Lonnie Parker run me off my own property (or nearabout my property), so I folded my arms and leaned against the rock wall.

I grabbed a long blade of grass and chewed. While I waited, I checked out the hubcaps on the cars—nothing exciting, just the routine sort of government caps. Too bad, 'cause a black-and-white would've looked really cool with Mercury chrome hubcaps. I had one in my collection in the barn back of the house, so I knew what I was talkin' about.

I heard some loud voices coming from upstairs, the apartment above the store, where Della lived with Jake, some kind of mixed hound that came to live with her when she lived in Washington, D.C. I couldn't imagine what Della'd done wrong. She was about the nicest person I'd ever met. I loved Mama, but Della was easier to be round. She just let me be.

Ever since Daddy sold the store, Mama wouldn't let me go inside it anymore. I knew she was jealous of Della. To be honest, I thought a lot of people were jealous a lot of the time and that was why they did so many stupid things. I saw it all the time. Sitting out front of the store most days, I'd hear them gossiping or even making stuff up about people. I bet they said things about me, too, when I wudn't there, off having my dinner or taking a nap.

But lately, something else was going on with Mama. Oncet I turned 15 year old, she started snooping and worrying. I'd seen something about that on TV, so I knew it were true: People thought that any guy who was kinda slow was a sex maniac. They figured since we weren't one-hundred percent "normal," we walked round with boners all the time and couldn't control ourselves. I couldn't speak for others, but that just weren't true for me. I remembered the first one I got, and it sure surprised me. But I'd done my experimenting, and I knew it wouldn't lead to no harm. Mama had nothin' to worry about, but still, she kept a close eye on me.

Of course, it was true that Della was real nice looking—tall and thin, but not skinny. She had a way about her—smart, but not stuck up. And her hair was real pretty—kinda curly and reddish gold, cut just below her ears. But she coulda been my mother, for heaven's sake.

After a while, Gregg from the Forest Service and the sheriff, along with some other cops, started making their way down Della's steps to their cars.

"Abit, you get on home, son," Sheriff Brower said. "Don't go bothering Ms. Kincaid right now."

"Go to hell, Brower. I don't need your stupid advice." Okay, that was just what I *wanted* to say. What I really said was, "I don't plan on bothering Della." I used her first name to piss him off; kids were supposed to use grownups' last names. Then I added, "And I don't bother her. She likes me."

But he was already churning dust in the driveway, speeding on to the road.

That evening, all I could think about was Della and what them cops had been doing up in her apartment. Four cars and six men. I wudn't even hungry for supper. Mama looked at me funny; she knew I usually didn't have no trouble putting away four of her biscuits covered in gravy.

"Eat your supper, son. What's wrong with you?" she scolded, like I were 8 year old. Well, what did she think? Like we'd ever had a day like that before. I asked to be excused, and Daddy nodded at her. I couldn't figure out why they weren't more curious about everything.

"Do you know what's going on?" I asked.

Daddy just told me to run along. Okay, fine. That was my idea in the first place.

Even though the store were closed, I headed to my chair. A couple of year ago, I'd found a butt-sprung caned chair thrown behind the store. I fixed it with woven strips of inner tube, which made it real comfortable-like, especially when I'd lean against the wall. I worried when Daddy sold the store that the new owner would gussy everything up and get rid of my chair. But Della told me I was welcome to lean on her wall any day, any time. Then she smiled at me and asked me to stop calling her Mrs. Kincaid; I was welcome to call her Della.

I liked sitting there 'cause I could visit with folks, and not everyone talked down to me like Lonnie and the sheriff. Take Della's best friend, Cleva Hall, who came by at least oncet a week. She insisted on calling me Vester, which was kind of weird since I wudn't used to it. At first, I reckoned she was talking about Daddy. But then I figured she had trouble calling me Abit, which was pretty nice when I thought about it.

I'd been on my own most of my life. Mama and Daddy kinda ignored me, when they weren't worried I was getting up to no good. And I didn't fit in with other folks. Della didn't neither, but she seemed okay with that. She chatted with customers and acted polite, but I could tell she weren't worried about being accepted. Which was good, since folks *hadn't* accepted her. Sure, they bought her food and beer, but that was mostly 'cause the big grocery store was a good ten or more mile away out on the highway. They'd act okay to her face, but they didn't really like her 'cause "she wudn't from here." Truth be told, I liked her extra 'cause she wudn't from here.

I couldn't understand why Della *chose* to live in our town. It weren't much, though I hadn't never been out of the county, so how would I have known whether it was good or not? I had to admit that the falls were pretty to look at, and even Daddy said we was lucky to live near them. And we did have a bank, a real estate and law office combined, a dry goods store, Adam's Rib and few other restaurants (though we never ate out as a family). And some kinda new art store. But there wudn't a library or gas station or grocery store—except for Della's store, which sat two mile outside of town on the road to the falls.

After supper, I felt kinda stupid sitting out front with the store closed and all, but I hoped Della would hear me tapping the chair against the wall and come down to talk with me. Mama didn't like me to be out of an evenin', though I told her I was getting too old for that. It was funny—Mama was a Bible-readin' Christian, but she always thought the worst things. Especially at night. She never told me this, but I figured she thought demons came out then. (Not that she weren't worried about demons during the day, too.) I hated to think of the things that went through her head. Maybe I was slow, but so be it if that meant I didn't have to wrestle with all that.

I looked up at Della's big window but couldn't see nothin'. I wanted to know if she was all right—and, sure, I wanted to find out what was going on, too. Then a light went on in Della's kitchen. "Oh, please, please come downstairs," I said out loud. But just as fast, the light went out.

Chapter 3: Della

I switched off the kitchen light and limped back to the couch. No aspirin in the bedside table or in the bathroom or kitchen cabinets. Good thing I lived above a store.

Earlier in the woods, I'd twisted my ankle as I scrambled over a mass of tangled limbs trying to get to the open space where Jake waited, barking. Under the towering canopy of giant oaks, little grew, creating a hushed, cathedral-like space. Usually. Jake finally quit barking when he saw me, but he began a strange primal dance, crouching from side to side as he bared his teeth and emitted ugly guttural sounds. I closed my eyes, trying to will away what I knew lay ahead.

A young woman leaned against a fallen tree trunk blanketed in moss. Her head flopped to one side, long black hair covering half her face, though not enough to hide the vomit that pooled on her left shoulder and down her sleeve. She looked vaguely familiar; I'd probably seen her at the store.

I edged closer and reached out to feel her neck. Cold and silent. She looked up at me with the penetrating stare of the dead; I resisted the urge to close her eyes.

The woman, her skin smooth and clear, seemed no older than twenty or so, but her face was locked in a terrible grimace. Pain would do that, possibly the last sensation she'd felt. Just below her left hand lay an empty syringe. I thought about drug overdose or possible suicide. I'd seen both before.

I knew it wouldn't be long before the sun slipped behind the mountains and took the day's warmth with it. We needed help, soon. I held out little hope that Madras Man would call Gregg. And yet, for some reason, I didn't want to leave the young woman alone.

For the first time in what felt like hours, I thought about the store, which really wasn't that far away, as the crow flies. And Abit, who was usually around, even on a day the store was closed. I looked at Jake and recalled how he somehow knew the command, "Go home." I had no idea how he'd learned it, but he'd built an impressive reputation on it. Not long after we moved to Laurel Falls, Vester ordered Jake off his porch. (Leave it to Jake to find the sunniest spot to lie in.) He told him, "Go home, Jake." And he did. He stood up, combed his hair (that all-over body shaking dogs do), and trotted down to the store, scratching on the door for me to let him in. The men hanging out on the benches started laughing and calling him Rin Tin Tin, admiring his smarts.

I searched through my pack for something to write on, but it offered only keys, wallet, and remnants of lunch. I looked at the woman's backpack. *No, I couldn't*, I told myself. But as long shadows blanketed the mountains, I opened a side compartment and rifled through it. I found a small, blank notebook with an attached pen, tore out a sheet, and wrote a note describing the location, best I could. I wiped my prints off the pen and notebook, and put them back in the pack. The note went inside the bread bag I'd stashed in my pocket after lunch; I tied it to Jake's collar.

"Go home, Jake. Go home!" It was a longshot, but worth a try. His brown eyes looked sad, but then they always did. "Go home, Jake. Be a good boy."

The third time I said it, he turned and ran, though not down the path we'd taken. *God, I hope he knows where he's going*, I thought, as he raced up the creek bank. And I prayed Mildred hadn't called Abit inside.

I watched Jake climb the steep trail and head over the ridge. When the last of his golden fur disappeared below the horizon, I laid back against the red oak, avoiding the stare of the dead woman. It would be at least an hour before anyone could get there.

I tried to rest, but when my eyes closed, unwelcomed memories rushed to mind. I reopened them. That's when I saw the dead woman turn her head toward me. I screamed, but quickly felt foolish. It was just the wind blowing her long hair.

I knew not to touch anything. I'd been involved in several police investigations in D.C. and watched enough television shows to know the drill. But eventually, curiosity won out. I crawled over to her, pulled my sleeve over my hand to avoid fingerprints, and began carefully rummaging through the backpack again, trying to find out who she was and where she'd come from.

Her wallet contained twenty-six dollars and a few coins, but all the slots normally bulging with credit cards and driver's license were empty. I also found a syringe case, the kind diabetics carry with them. Otherwise, the pack held only an apple and a scarf. No keys or identifiers of any kind.

I was getting stiff, so I stood, stretched, and started pacing. From a different angle, I noticed a corner of white barely sticking out of the left pocket of her flannel shirt. I pulled down my sleeve again and removed the note. I clumsily opened the handwritten note with my makeshift gloved hand.

I'm tired of so much sorrow. My life or death doesn't matter. L.

I struggled to refold the note and slip it back into the pocket. I knew I didn't have any connection to this death, unlike a tragedy I witnessed in D.C., but my nerves felt raw. I kept walking. I started to shiver from the cold, but wouldn't allow myself to borrow anything from her stash. I found another smooth beech tree surrounded by brush that sheltered me from the wind, scrunched down, and waited.

My thoughts drifted back to my home and office near Dupont Circle, where I wrote for a variety of magazines and newspapers. I had a nickname among colleagues—Ghoulfriend—because I somehow kept getting assignments for sad and even violent stories. I was good at it, maybe because I took the time to understand both the backstory and the current story. I covered unimaginable situations, except by those who'd suffered them. Men who passed as loving fathers during the workday but turned into monsters in the basements of their family homes. Women who grew up with abuse and perpetuated that pattern on to another generation. Men so troubled by wars that it seemed only natural to kill—including themselves, either intentionally or through the slow death of drugs and alcohol. I recalled the relief I always felt when I'd hear about their passing, and how I still grappled with that. It seemed wrong to be glad someone died, but when their suffering never stopped, it was hard *not* to be thankful they'd finally been released from so much pain.

I stood again and paced around the natural enclosure. I noticed some British soldiers, the green matchstick lichen with bright red "hats," standing at attention atop a huge fallen trunk, its center hollowed out by rain and time and animals seeking shelter. The birds were singing again—or was I just hearing them again? Two nuthatches flittered through a nearby stand of white pines. A cluster of spring beauty eased my mind, until I saw they were growing inside the skull of an opossum. I kept moving.

As I paced, I noticed that her youthful face was pretty in the way that most young people are. I couldn't imagine why her life had to end that way. I knew features were superficial, that the urge to kill yourself garnered energy from dark places deep within, but she didn't look tired or drained like the other victims I'd seen. No telltale lines that broadcast an unbearable hurt. But who really knew?

I shivered in my light jacket and waited. Finally, I heard Jake's bark over the grinding gears of a four-wheel drive.

My throbbing ankle brought me back to my apartment. When I stepped out onto the landing, I noticed the sun had dropped behind the mountains, carving the sky with angry slashes of purple. Swallows swooped through the air, as though they were drawing a curtain on the day.

I limped down the long wooden staircase that hugged the outside of the building, leading down to the driveway. Only the promise of aspirin inside the store kept me moving. As I turned toward the front door, I saw Abit craning his neck to see me. Jake had run ahead and jumped in Abit's lap, threatening to topple him from his chair. I couldn't help but smile at my makeshift family.

I recalled the first time I saw Abit, a lanky kid nervously pacing around the front of the store, afraid the new owner would throw out his chair and ban him from his perch near the door. He'd reminded me of a teenaged Opie Taylor, sporting a cowlick and overalls. Still did.

"Howdy, Mister. I suspect you'd like to come in." I'd started calling him that to avoid using his mean-spirited nickname, though that was hard to stick to since almost everyone called him Abit. Over the years, it seemed to have morphed into just another name, no more peculiar than Cletus or Enos; I hoped it had lost its sting for him. When he looked over his shoulder toward his house, I added, "I don't think your mother will mind today. Besides, it's after hours. You can't bother the customers, can you? Why don't you pick out something to drink, and we'll talk."

Chapter 4: Abit

I was so glad to see Della I almost fell over, what with Jake jumping up and licking my face and making my chair wobble. Della gave me a big hug when I stood up and let me have a Dr. Pepper on the house. I started rattling on about how I'd seen the cop cars and how boring the hubcaps were. I finally slowed down and asked, "How are you?"

"Well, something really serious happened," she said, "and I want to tell you and your parents at the same time. I don't think it's right for me to tell you something like this alone."

"I'm not a baby."

"I know, but let's do this the right way. I've got what I came for. Grab your drink and let's go up to the house."

"They already know. Daddy talked with the sheriff," I said, trying to stall.

"Oh, I'm sure they've heard a lot through the grapevine, but you know how that goes. Lots of wrong information gets passed on. And I can't tell this story again. I've already told it a couple of times to Sheriff Brower."

"He's an asshole!" I said, and Della kinda laughed, though not for long. I liked to make her laugh, but she was hurtin', and I didn't want to make things worse.

"Come on," she said, patting my back, "you lead the way." We started toward the steps, but then she stopped.

"Oh, wait, one more thing before we go up. I wanted you to know that I thought Jake would run home to you. I knew you'd get the help I needed."

I wudn't sure what she was talking about, so I didn't know what to say. But I was happy that she'd thought about me during her time of need.

"So based on the note, it appears to be a suicide," Della said, finishing up the day's events. "I don't think Brower plans to do much investigating. He seems content to let it go at that."

"Well, isn't that about right?" Mama added. Daddy just nodded. He hadn't said a word since we first came in. He wudn't real comfortable round women, especially someone like Della.

"I suppose so," Della said, though she wudn't very convincing, if you asked me. Mama didn't pick up on that. She just said something to me about not bothering Della.

"He's not a bother," Della told her before draining her glass of water. When we first got to the house, she asked Mama for some water and swallowed what seemed like a handful of aspirin. "You know, I like hearing his chair tapping against the wall. I feel as though someone is watching over me."

Mama frowned, imagining something that wudn't. Her acting like that drove me crazy. But I reckoned deep down she appreciated that someone liked me besides her. I'd have added "and Daddy," but I didn't think that were true.

Chapter 5: Della

Jake grabbed a spot at the foot of the bed. We were finally alone. I'd told my story for the last time (at least for that day), but that didn't stop me from replaying it over and over. I kept hearing Brower barking orders at the clearing.

He'd swaggered around the scene, looking at me with suspicion and telling Gregg O'Donnell to stay out of his way. His head shaved in classic jarhead fashion, Brower was one of those former Marines who never got over it. He treated everyone in the county as though we were inexperienced recruits in need of a dose of Semper Fi.

"Back off, Brower," Gregg said for no specific reason, other than because someone needed to rein him in. Gregg was usually cool-headed, but Brower could've made a coma patient angry. "Cleva Hall called me because she didn't know what else to do. None of us knew what had happened—or where. We all thought this happened on Forest Service land."

Gregg was being kind, not mentioning that I'd written Laurel Falls Wilderness on the note Jake delivered. That's how he got involved. How was I to know I'd wandered into land owned by the state? That made it Brower's responsibility. He hadn't dealt with a real crime since Adam's Rib was robbed, and he was enjoying himself. Never mind a young woman was dead.

Actually, I was glad I hadn't known. I was grateful it was Gregg who arrived first. He got out of his truck and threw his arms around me, holding me tight while I tried, unsuccessfully, not to cry. He told me Jake had stopped at Cleva's—her land lay on his path home—and barked for her to come to the door. I looked back at Jake, closed up in Gregg's truck so he wouldn't disturb the scene, and blew him a kiss.

While we waited on the sheriff, Gregg tucked me inside his truck, next to Jake. He handed me an army-green blanket and cranked the heater to high. I started to thaw. I put my arm around Jake and rubbed my face against his, his dog breath like life-affirming perfume.

It took Brower only twenty minutes to show. He grilled me as though I were a suspect, asking me what I was doing that deep in the woods by myself, as though he'd been hanging out with Mildred and her buddies. We went through all the particulars, and he abruptly concluded my interview. "I'm done with you for now. Oh, one more thing. You didn't touch anything, did you?"

"Just her carotid," I lied. "I needed to see if she were alive."

"And just what would you have done if she were?" Brower asked, his lip curling.

"CP frigging R."

Brower glared. He never liked me, mostly because I'd bought Coburn's. I'm sure he and his father (who owned the SuperMart out on the highway) had been rubbing their hands together as Coburn's faltered. By the time it went on the market, the store was a dusty relic of its glory days, not unlike the old tractor slowly returning to the earth outside of Vester's barn. Brower's father put in a bid on the store, but Vester chose mine. And since I'd begun to draw customers back, Brower must have figured I was a threat to his inheritance. I wished.

"One of my men will drive you home," Brower said. "I'll be there in about an hour, so don't go anywhere."

"I'll take her," Gregg said, climbing into the truck and slamming the door. When I joined him, he took a few deep breaths to check his anger and began driving slowly over the bumpy old logging road. We were both quiet as we made our way out of the forest. Gregg was first to break the silence. "Sorry you had to experience that, Della."

"Me too," I said, my voice shaking, his kindness harder to take than Brower's bravado. I started to cry again.

Gregg pulled the truck into a turnout and stopped. Jake whimpered and tried to lick my face, but I pushed him away. God, his breath smelled horrible; so much for its life-affirming qualities. Then I remembered he was a hero and hugged him. He tried again, and I let him lick away.

"Well, that helped," I said, wiping my face and smearing dirt through the tears. I stroked Jake and added, "He's some dog, isn't he?"

"That he is. You're lucky he's so damn smart. By the way, when I got to Cleva's, she had him resting on the sofa by the fire, feeding him homemade biscuits." Gregg looked at his watch. "Speaking of which, would you like to get something to eat? It's getting on to suppertime."

"I'm not very hungry. Besides, I've got to be back for Brower."

"To hell with Brower. You need something to eat. You got a bad chill out there." He looked over, his mouth twitching with the beginnings of a smile. "And I have to admit, I'm starving." He drove us to Geri Cantwell's— one of the best diners in North Carolina, just outside the park perimeter. It made all the guidebooks and rarely disappointed. I was starting to look forward to some of her homemade chicken soup when I saw all the cars in her parking lot.

I couldn't face all the questions. "Do you think people know about this by now?"

"Does a wild bear shit in the woods? They knew a couple of hours ago, I'm sure," Gregg said. "Jake's antics are legendary. Word of that alone spread fast. Add in a dead body, and it reached the speed of light. How about we get it to go? You can lie on the seat so no one sees you."

"What will you tell everyone?"

"Oh, that I took you home, that Brower froze me out, and they'll have to pester him with their questions. That'll shut 'em up." He did smile that time.

Somehow I got Jake to hunker down in the floor of the cab, while I stretched across the wide vinyl seat of Gregg's government-issue Ford Ranger. Next thing I knew, Jake's bark startled me awake. I peeked over the dash as Gregg approached with a large brown bag. Jake must have been spooked because Gregg was one of his favorites. No one in the diner seemed to notice, though, and we eased out the driveway and headed toward home.

As Gregg pulled in the store's driveway, he cleared his throat. "Do you mind if I come up and wait with you?" he said. "I know Brower doesn't want me around, but I'd like to make sure this goes the way it should. I don't trust him."

"I'd love it. Oh, and let me pay you for the soup."

He scowled so hard I felt the tug of a smile myself. "That's a good sign," Gregg said. As he opened my door, he added, "Oh, and just FYI, Brower may be better than the alternative. If the girl had died on Forest Service land—and it was deemed a crime—the FBI would be called in. Hard as it may be to believe, you might have an easier time with our sheriff."

I nodded, though I couldn't imagine that. The three of us headed up the stairs, Jake happy to be out of the truck and back home. Me, too, even if a long evening lay ahead.

"Well, Jake, that's one for the record books," I said, as I turned out the light on my bedside table. But he was already asleep after his heroic day. I was hoping to join him, but I stared at the ceiling for hours.

Chapter 6: Abit

I barely slept that night. Too much going on, most of which I wudn't privy to. I just knew that things weren't going to be the same for a while. I liked our regular routine—eat breakfast, head down to the store, and sit in my chair. Della'd open up round eight o'clock (which lots of folks thought was too late), and I'd get to see everyone and say howdy till dinnertime. Afterwards, I'd watch a little TV or take a nap (though no one made me do that anymore—it just felt good after one of Mama's big dinners). Later, I'd mosey down to the store again, and things pretty much repeated themselves till suppertime.

The next morning, I ate later than usual (Mama let me sleep in after our big night), so I was feeling jumpy. I wanted to get downstairs as the folks started to show up. I knew our town—people would suddenly need a quart of milk or a six-pack of Pabst. It was pushing eight o'clock when I finished breakfast; I wiped my mouth with my napkin and scooted my chair out.

"Son, why don't you stay home today? Your mother could use your help in the garden."

"Yeah, and she could use your help making her feel special, not a draft horse." Well, I just thought that. What I said was, "Daddy, not *today*. I mean I *will* help her, but not *this* morning. I want to get down to the store and see what's happening."

He nodded. He could barely make eye contact with me, which was okay that time 'cause he gave up real quick-like.

I hurried down the steps and saw four people already waiting for Della to open. Two were regulars, on their way to the t-shirt plant, but two had never shopped at the store before, at least that I could recall. I hoped they'd at least buy something. More people were coming round to the store again, like the days before Daddy gave up.

I had to ask one of the new people to get up from my chair. I figured he didn't know no better, but I think I scared him. People were afraid of me 'cause I was pretty big for my age and my words came out different sometimes. Mama said I sounded kinda gruff. The man jumped right up and knocked over the chair. He set it right, and I smiled at him to let him know no hard feelings, but that seemed to make things worse.

Just before eight o'clock, Della limped down the stairs, waved at me, and opened up. Pretty soon I heard her cash register ringing, so I knew it would be a good day. Not that she wouldn't've given it all back if she could've made things different for that poor girl.

I looked in on her during one lull about midday, and she just blew her bangs out of her eyes with a slow, deep breathe. I looked both ways to make sure Mama wudn't looking and stepped inside. I pulled a Dr. Pepper out of the cooler and dug round in my pocket for my change.

"That's on the house, Mister."

"No, you can't give me these for free all the time. I've got the money right here." I plunked a handful of pennies and nickels and dimes on the counter.

"Okay, then," she said, "how much do you owe me?"

"Thirty-five cent, plus tax. Just take it out of these coins."

"I can, but you can, too."

Della thought I could do better than most people did. Daddy always took over for me, which made me worry I might lose some of the schooling I'd had. I really missed going to school. Most kids wouldn't never say that, but I reckoned they didn't know how much they'd miss it— and their friends. I hadn't exactly had friends, but I did get to hang out with other kids.

I picked out three dimes and one nickel. I knew I was short on the tax, but I wanted to see what she'd say.

"I'll take one more penny, Mister, but just put it in the penny jar to help someone else who needs one, okay?"

I picked up the rest of my change and stuffed it in my pocket. "How's it going?"

"Well, you've seen the parade of curiosity seekers. I just wish they'd care as much about the young woman as the juicy crime story. She didn't have any ID on her, and no one's identified her yet. I finally remembered why I'd seen her at the store. She asked me to order some kind of bread she liked and gave me the money in advance. But she wouldn't give me her name or a way to reach her when it came in—just said she'd be back for it."

"What kind of bread?"

"I've put a couple of loaves in the freezer over there. Some kind of healthy loaf. I'll probably end up eating it myself."

I wandered over to the freezer and saw what looked like a couple of brown bricks with seeds glued all over them. I'd stick to Mama's biscuits. "I'd better scoot. Mama will have a fit if she sees me here."

"What time is it?" Della asked, looking at her watch. "Oh, hell, I've got to go see Brower in a few minutes. He wants me to sign something. You want to know the truth? I'm almost looking forward to Brower instead of all these questions here at the store, over and over again."

I musta looked at her like she were crazy, 'cause she kinda laughed. "Yeah, I guess that was over the top. I'll just be glad for a little break. I won't be long." She patted my back as we walked to the door, then taped a "Sorry I'm Closed" sign on the door, locked up, and drove off.

I went home for dinner, which was my favorite— chicken and dumplings, green beans that Mama put up last season, and fresh rhubarb pie, first of the year. Afterwards, I started to head down to the store, where a couple of folks were sitting in their cars, waiting for a heavy rainstorm to move out. But Daddy called out and told me to clean up my mess in the barn. That's what he called my hubcap collection. My mess.

Chapter 7: Della

"Lonnie, get me that damn file. And is that Kincaid woman here yet?"

Deputy Lonnie Parker flashed an embarrassed look my way. Brower was never known as a cheerful guy, but his mood seemed particularly rank. Lonnie hesitated, then grabbed the file and headed into his boss's office. I could hear a mumbled discussion before Lonnie returned with his head bowed.

"He said he'll see you in ten minutes. He's got to make some phone calls first."

"That's fine, Lonnie. I'm in no hurry to relive yesterday."

"Man, that musta been hard on you. I've never been involved in anything like that."

I just nodded, as I flashed on the similar incidents I'd seen in D.C. But I didn't want to relive those either—or get into one-downmanship with the deputy. He and the sheriff lived in Laurel Falls (Lonnie with his mother, Brower with his ego), but their county office was about ten miles from the store. I mostly knew them by reputation and, of course, through the rumor mill.

Lonnie had always been courteous to me, though I knew he could pick on Abit as badly as the rest. While I watched him go back to typing a report, I couldn't help but feel a pang of pity. He lived in a culture that expected him to be tough, but he didn't seem well suited to that role. He was just the flunky of a hard man, and together they played out the old kick-the-dog routine. Brower got dumped on by his boss, he took it out on Lonnie, who made fun of Abit, and so on. Except it seemed to stop with Abit. He just absorbed the jabs, as though he deserved them.

"Coffee?" Lonnie asked as he pulled the report from his typewriter.

"Thanks, but I'll hold off on any more. I've had plenty today."

"You just don't want the sludge we serve," he said, as he walked to the kitchen. He came back with a drip-stained mug that made me doubly glad about my decision.

"Kincaid!" Brower shouted through the office door. When I opened the door, I noticed that his face sagged with fatigue, and his shirt, buttons straining over his belly, looked as though he'd slept in it.

"Good morning, Sheriff."

He motioned to the chair. "Okay, let's go over this again. What were you doing in the woods yesterday?"

"Having lunch with Jake."

"Why that area?"

I sighed. I'd gone over all this last night. "It's a favorite spot."

Brower smiled. "Not any longer, I bet."

I waited; I knew he was baiting me. I hadn't left Abit's house till about ten o'clock, and after that, I'd had trouble winding down. I thought about a glass of wine, but alcohol had never been a good relaxer for me—I'd fall asleep, then wake up a few hours later with jarring thoughts made worse in the dark. As it turned out, that would have been better than lying awake most of the night.

"So did you recognize this girl?"

Brower called every woman a girl, but that time he wasn't off by much. "She'd come by the store once. That's where I see most people, and I knew there was something vaguely familiar about her face."

"So, you *did* know her?"

I ignored that. "Have you identified her yet?" I asked. I didn't mean anything by that comment, but he took offense.

"Nothing from her prints," he said, then added, "We're doing the best we can. It's not easy on our limited resources." Brower moved on to other details we'd gone over last night. I didn't understand why we were doing it all over again. Where was the damned typed statement I was supposed to sign?

Finally, he slid a sheet of paper over with a pen. "I better not find out you messed with anything. It's bad enough you touched the body, but under the circumstances, I'll let that pass. You sure you didn't mess with anything else?"

I just looked at him.

"Okay, that's it for now. Looks like suicide. We'll get the tox screen in a couple of weeks. Meanwhile, as they say, don't leave town."

I dug my fingernails into my palm to keep from saying something snide. I tried to think that somewhere inside him, deep down, there was something that would allow me to feel compassion for him, but at the moment, it alluded me. I stood and turned to leave his office.

"By the way, that's a damn fine dog you've got. I never went much for mongrels, but I believe he got all the best features from his mixed parentage," Brower said. "Let me know if you ever want to give him away."

"Sure, Sheriff. I'll put you at the top of the list" ... *of bastards*, I thought to myself.

"Listen, Missy, no one invited you to move here. Lose the bitch attitude if you want to stay in business."

I turned, my hand still on the door knob. "What did you say?"

"You heard me. I've always wondered why you came here. Running from something back there in the crime capital of this fine country?"

"This fine country, Brower, let's people move wherever they want."

"So why here?"

"I bought that store fair and square. I fixed it up, and now people want to come there because it's more convenient, and because, well, it doesn't have your ornery father in it."

Brower stood, his face burning red. "Get out."

As I closed the door behind me, I knew I'd gone too far, taking a slap at Brower because I was tired and couldn't stop myself. Lonnie kept his head down and typed a line or two on what looked like a blank sheet of paper.

On the way back to the store, I stopped off to see Kitt Scanlon and check out what was showing in her gallery. Kitt had become one of my best customers, her taste in food and wine similar to mine. About the same time I bought Coburn's, she'd moved to Laurel Falls from somewhere east of here. Raleigh, I believe she told me. Rumor had it she and Brower had something going on.

I should have rushed back to the store, but I needed to shake off that experience with the sheriff. And I wanted to support her new venture—if only with goodwill. I didn't have money right now for art, not to mention the art was more edgy than my taste. It must have cost a fortune to redo the old gas station and add the moveable gallery walls and track lighting, but she'd done it right.

When I opened the door, she had her back to me, hanging a cumbersome piece of wall sculpture. She looked the part of gallery owner—tall, slim, black leather boots over tight designer jeans, a gorgeous purple silk top, and long blond hair, perfectly highlighted. A guy magnet. No wonder those rumors were flying about Brower, though I couldn't imagine what she saw in him.

"Hey, do you need a hand with that?" She jumped. "Oh, sorry, I didn't mean to startle you," I added. "I just came from a meeting with Brower, and I wanted to stop by and see what was new."

She set the sculpture on the floor and wiped her hands on her fancy pants. "Oh, Della. That must have been so rough—finding that girl and then having to deal with our sheriff. I bet you need to get the taste of *that* experience out of your mouth."

I wondered if her last statement was more about her own experience with Brower than yesterday's tragedy. "He thinks it's a suicide, but I'm not so sure."

"Really? I thought it was a done deal."

"Well, yeah, Brower would like it that way."

"Wonder who that poor girl was?" Kitt asked.

"No one seems to know. Maybe just a tourist passing through."

"Strange. Someone looking for a beautiful place to kill herself." She shivered, and we were both quiet for a moment. "Well, if I were you, I'd try to get that scene out of my mind. Take a look at the art," she added, sweeping her arm through the air. "That always makes me feel better."

I glanced at the tortured sheet metal sculpture splashed with red paint and quickly said, "I will another time. I've got to get back to the store. Just wanted to say hi. Oh, and I've got a new sheep's milk cheese I think you'd like. Come down some evening at closing time, and we'll open a bottle of wine and give it a try."

"Eating up your profits? Sounds irresistible. I'll pick up some things while I'm there." Kitt held out her hand, performing some elaborate shake she must have brought from her hip art community. "See you soon, sister."

Chapter 8: Della

Two people were sitting in their cars when I got back to the store, waiting for a storm to blow through. And, of course, waiting for me. I tried to get help from Billie, a local woman who enjoyed time away from her three demanding kids, but she needed to take one of her passel to the pediatrician in Boone. I parked as close to the store as possible, ran from my truck, unlocked the front door, and tore off the Sorry sign. As they hurried in, dripping wet, I made my apologies. I felt better when one nodded and the other even smiled, seeming to understand the circumstances.

I knew I shouldn't dread customers, but at that moment, all I wanted to do was brew some coffee and grab something to eat. Besides, if they were like the parade so far that week, they were mostly in the market for a firsthand report on the biggest news since Jimmy Carter campaigned in town six years ago.

"Hey, honey," a third customer warbled as she came through the door, her sensible plastic rain bonnet and long yellow slicker keeping her dry. "How're doing?"

Dammit, what a cynic I've turned into, I said to myself. Myrtle and Roy Ledford, her husband of fifty-two years, were some of my best customers. And early on, they'd welcomed me into their home, where I'd sampled my first—and last—moonshine. Something interesting always happened there. One evening, Roy pulled out his grandfather's wax-canister phonograph and played a recording of a tinny voice singing, "I thought you were a dream, but you were just an old string bean." Another time, they regaled me with stories of Roy's bootleg days, right out of *Thunder Road*. He'd gotten caught and sent to the federal prison in Ohio. Ever since, thirty some years later, locals still referred to him as "Roy He-Went-Up-the-River Ledford."

I always returned from their home laden with gifts— canned peaches and freshly baked bread, honey and jam, biscuits and pies. Until folks got to know you, being new could generate suspicion. But others wanted to be the first to entertain you, sometimes so they could one-up their neighbors, but mostly out of genuine kindness.

Myrtle's voice sounded as though she had Parkinson's, but she was as healthy at seventy-one as I was some twenty some years behind her. She'd suffered from the lousy medical care at the local hospital, when the slip of a scalpel during a simple procedure had damaged her vocal cords. "You sure had a rough day yesterday," she added, piling groceries into her basket.

"You was lucky you had that old dog with you," Roy added.

"I was, Roy. In fact, I'm lucky to have Jake any day."

The mention of his name sent Jake howling upstairs. He'd turned out to be the perfect shop dog. The first day he joined me in the store, he just naturally knew how to behave when strangers came and went. He held strong opinions about being part of the scene.

"Speaking of the devil," I said. "I'll be right back."

The rain had let up, so I didn't have to rush up the stairs. Good thing. My ankle felt better, but it still bothered me enough to cause a limp. I'd barely opened the door before Jake flew past me, down the steps. I followed, and as I rounded the corner, I saw him pressing his nose against the door where it met the frame, willing it to open. Roy obliged, so I took advantage of the moment and sat on one of the benches out front under the overhang, where the seats were dry. The sun was out again, and the fresh spring air carried the sweet scent of the hyacinths blooming nearby.

I looked over at Abit's empty chair. Where was he? I should've been glad he was off doing something more constructive, but I liked knowing he was nearby. I cracked the front door and asked, "Everybody doing okay?" Jake looked up sheepishly as Roy rubbed him behind his ears. He broke away and started running around the store, sussing out smells and possible rodents; he was better than any cat. "I want to check on Abit."

"You go ahead, honey. We've got a good bit of shopping to do," Myrtle answered for everyone.

I took my time up the long flight of stone stairs to Vester and Mildred's front porch. As I approached the house, I could see Abit sitting at the table, talking to his mother, finishing off a piece of apple pie.

"Hey, Della, how'd it go?"

"Well, as good as could be expected. I wanted to let you know I'm back."

Mildred didn't frown, like she often did when I made a fuss over Abit. She had a prim mouth that said more about her thoughts than the few words that came out of it. I worried that she didn't trust me, or maybe she didn't like sharing her son's attention. "Mildred, thanks for last night. It was good to talk to all of you."

"I know that was mighty hard on you," Mildred said. Looking down at the cars pulling up in front of the store, she added, "And I know you'll be busy for the next few days with shoppers and gossipers. Why don't you stop by for supper tomorrow evening? I'm cooking a fresh ham."

Mildred's cooking was better than some four-star restaurants in D.C. I flashed on a table laden with homemade biscuits and beans and corn pudding and probably another fresh pie. "Sounds great, and I could use some company. It's harder at night." When I squeezed Abit's shoulder, he spoke through a mouthful of pie, something that sounded remotely like, "I'll be down in a minute."

Three more cars were lined up, with another pulling in as I headed down their steps. Lately, it felt as though all I did was go up and down stairs. Some days, especially before June when the tourists came, maybe only ten people shopped all day, and I was wishing for one of those now. Then I remembered my bank balance and quickened my step, best I could.

Chapter 9: Abit

I was enjoying all the people coming and going that week. More cops—different departments and duties—and even some guy up from Asheville. That reporter from our local newspaper was coming by a lot, too. Earlier, Della had made a joke about the *Mountain Weakly*, but I didn't get it. When she explained it to me, I snorted so hard, I got some Coca-Cola up my nose.

That babe from the new gallery stopped by at closing time on Wednesday. Della told me she was coming for some wine and cheese and chitchat, and I could see them inside when I had to go home to Mama.

We still didn't know who that dead girl was—just that her name began with L, but nothin' else. Not a peep from anyone after the articles in the newspaper and even some news stories on TV. And nobody knew who the guy was who ran through the woods and told Della about the body. Brower said in one of the articles that he was probably just some tourist out for a nice walk in the woods. "That'll be a walk he doesn't forget any time soon," Brower told the reporter. What a jerk.

So, all kinds of gossip was flying. Brower and those other cops stuck with suicide. Della told me too many things seemed off to just leave it at that, but she admitted that we didn't have any evidence that L was murdered, either. Of course, that didn't stop two local thugs who didn't have nothin' better to do than to get stinkin' drunk and do mean things. I'd seen 'em come by the store for beer, but I went to bed too early to know what they was up to, late at night, cruising the county and acting up.

When I came down to the store the next morning, though, I found big red painted letters on Della's picture window: MUIDEIEI. It was real scary looking, like blood with lots of drips. I figured it was a word I hadn't learned yet. Whatever it meant, I knew it was no good, so I got some blades from Daddy's toolbox and started scraping. I was still on the letter U when Della came downstairs. Jake was jumping round all happy to see me, like we hadn't just seen each other the day before.

"What does MUIDEIEI mean, Della?"

"MURDERER, honey, but the R's dripped into one big slug of a letter—those three letters that look like I? Someone was writing MURDERER on my store." I barely heard her, her voice so low.

"There's no 'someone' about it. You know it's got to be them drunks Buddy and Donnie. Don't pay them no mind." I went back to scraping. "And besides, ain't no way *you* done the murder, even if she were killed. Why in the world would they write that on your store?"

Della just stood there a while before asking, "Do you have another one of those razor blades?"

Chapter 10: Della

Not long after Abit and I finished cleaning the window, Tony Benedict, the reporter from the *Mountain Weekly,* walked in. His shirt was buttoned wrong, and coffee stains made a peculiar pattern down the front. Over the past twenty-five years, I'd seen a world of sloppy reporters. It was a hard life, and once you got engrossed in a story, personal hygiene could take a hit.

Ever since I'd found the dead woman, it seemed Tony couldn't stay away from the store. No one at his paper had given Coburn's as much as a new-business listing when I first opened. Not that I cared all that much, but I couldn't understand why Dockery Real Estate got a half-page spread and Coburn's didn't merit a mention. Well, I knew, but I couldn't change that.

"Mornin', Miss," he said, as if he didn't know my name. I nodded. "Just wanted to let you know that we're running the memorial service notice, the one Father Max has planned for next Wednesday. I got it in just before the deadline for this week, so it's in today's paper."

"Well, I'm sure your readership will be up this week. People seem to be, well, enjoying this tragedy. How many pages this week?"

He looked surprised and answered, "Twenty-four."

"From twelve? Wow. You *are* doing good."

"Hey, we're not trying to milk this or anything. We think it's important to keep people informed."

"Okay. Now let's hope all those curiosity seekers make time to pay their respects to L."

"Who?"

"The woman who died. What kind of reporter are you?" I snapped, and just as quickly regretted it. No doubt their meager outpost of the Fourth Estate was doing the best it could. And I liked journalists. I used to like them a lot. My ex had been one of the best at the *Washington Post*.

"Oh, right. Sorry. I forgot her initial from the suicide note," he said, unfazed by my rudeness. "Anyway, I just wanted to see if you'd like to carry some extra copies of the paper in your store."

"Sure, why not? Bill me?"

He nodded and headed out to his car, returning with a thick stack.

The rest of the day saw a steady stream of customers, with a few gossipers on the prowl for inside information. And Emmett McCallum, one of our bread deliverymen (not the good stuff from Asheville but Bunny Bread, which most customers preferred), brought a couple dozen loaves. Even better, he solved a different mystery for me when he said, as he was leaving, "Well, let's go deliver bread."

For months, I'd been making my excuses when folks said in parting, "Let's go to the house." Truth be known, I was surprised so many people were inviting me to their homes, and frankly, I didn't want to go with them. When Emmett invited me to join him on his bread route, it finally dawned on me that was just a colorful way of saying goodbye. I laughed at myself and imagined how puzzled folks must have been by all my excuses. They didn't want me tagging along to their homes, either.

About quarter to six, I closed early. If folks were desperate, they'd honk. As I climbed the stairs, I could hear Jake snuffling at the door. I hadn't let him come to the store as much lately, what with all the strangers streaming in and out. Inside, I scratched his chest and behind his ears, and we went downstairs again so he could romp around behind the store. The traffic was heavy enough that I needed to keep an eye on him; I'd seen too many dead animals on the road. I watched as he worked his way through the tall grass and deeper into the back woods. After twenty minutes or so, he came flying when I called out, "Dinner!"

I was too tired to cook, so I poured a glass of merlot and fell into my favorite chair. I loved my sanctuary above the store. No one had lived there for a couple of decades—except squirrels and raccoons—and Vester had used it only for storage for years. When I bought it, the whole building was so derelict I couldn't move in until some of the most basic work was completed. That period between responsibilities, while I was waiting on the remodel, turned out to be one of the best times of my life.

I stayed at the Falls Inn just off the Blue Ridge Parkway for a couple of months and lived simply, with only a kitchenette, bed, dresser, table, and two chairs. I'd sold all my furniture before moving south and played out the fantasy of being a drifter—reading, sleeping, hiking, and taking drives into Asheville, the largest town in the region. Other than overseeing the construction, there wasn't much I could do. After the long hours and deadline-filled years as a journalist, I just did what I felt like doing, when I felt like doing it.

The apartment sat high enough above the store that its front windows captured the tops of the Unaka Mountains piercing the horizon to the west. Like most dwellings around here, the view hadn't been a consideration. These mountains were wallpaper to folks who'd lived among their beauty—and considerable hardship—for generations. The kitchen, which commandeered the front of the apartment, originally had only two small windows, side by side. I'd thought about moving the kitchen and turning that area into my living room and dining area, but the cost was prohibitive. Instead, I had the windows torn out and filled the space above the counters with large plate-glass windows. While sitting in the living room, just behind the kitchen, I could see only endless mountains and sky.

The two identical bedrooms in the other half of the apartment had been reconfigured. My carpenter moved their shared wall, expanding one room for my bedroom and saving the remaining space for an office/guest room.

I did the best I could with the rudimentary bathroom, adding a claw-foot tub under the shower head and a batik curtain encircling the tub.

On the couch, gazing out those windows, I could forget I sat above a country store, until someone honked or knocked, treating me like an all-night convenience store. Early on, I made some folks mad when I wouldn't answer, but they soon got over it. I hadn't always been so good at protecting my space, but servitude was no longer an option, especially given how much time I already spent inside Coburn's.

I must have dozed off because the telephone jerked me awake. I hoped like hell it wasn't another call from Brower.

"Hello?"

"Della, honey, I just wanted to check on you."

I sighed, grateful it was my friend Cleva Hall. "Thanks, Cleva, but they really aren't *my* troubles. No one knows whose they are. Brower has no ID on that poor woman yet."

"Well, don't put on such a brave face. It must have been terrible to find that girl. You sure you're doing okay?"

"Well, yeah. I haven't been sleeping great, but all in all, I'm fine. And thanks for calling Gregg when ol' Jake arrived at your doorstep."

"He's a pretty smart cookie, though I know better than to use that word in front of him. If you weren't so fond of him, I might just steal him."

"I'm sorry I didn't call you—I've been kind of busy with Brower and all the looky-loos. Gregg said he'd let you know I was okay."

"He sure did. And don't give that a thought. If I had to spend time with our sheriff, I might just start drinking again." I sipped my wine in agreement. "How about you come out my way tonight? Spend the night, we'll catch up, and maybe you'll sleep better out in the quiet."

I smiled at her comment. Local folks sure had a different idea of quiet. Compared to D.C., there was nothing but quiet, but those who lived out of town thought the decibel level in Laurel Falls ranked just shy of Grand Central Station. Cleva lived about five miles from town, where the air was sweeter and the wildlife even more plentiful. Her home perched on a ridge, not far from the falls, the rush and rumble of its waters a continuous backdrop. I'd missed Cleva lately and looked forward to sharing her company.

"I'd love that, Cleva. Can I bring something?"

"Just Jake and yourself. How's he holding up?"

"He's had his dinner and evening romp. Now he's curled up on the bed. But he'll be delighted to get up and come see you."

When I first moved to Laurel Falls, I found Cleva by getting lost. Jake and I were out hiking, and we walked what felt like miles before I realized the sound from the falls had gotten louder—though we'd planned to hike in the opposite direction. I was getting cold and parched (our water gone after Jake accidentally knocked the canteen from my hands) when I saw a farmhouse on the ridge. I'd always been shy about going up to strangers' homes, but I needed help.

As Jake and I neared the house, I could see someone waving. "Howdy stranger," the woman called. "I've been meaning to come down and meet you. Glad you beat me to it."

Who is this person who seems to know me? I thought. As we walked toward her, I recalled the mountain logic—anyone new to town was already "known" because they knew you were the only person they didn't know. I first experienced that phenomenon when a friend from D.C. got lost and stopped in a café to ask if anyone knew me. The café owner said he, "didn't know no Della Kincaid." Offering her thanks, my friend turned to leave, when he added, "But I can tell you how to find her."

Once Jake and I arrived at her porch, Cleva stuck out her hand. "Cleva Hall. Pleased to meet you, Della Kincaid." As we shook hands, she chuckled at my surprise that she knew my name. "Oh, you know how we are," she said, opening her screen door and motioning me inside. "You're looking a bit bedraggled. Come on in, and after a visit, I'll run you home in the Jeep."

I stepped into a knotty-pine paneled living room where a wood heater belched welcomed heat. Comfortable chairs surrounded it. I was looking at a picture of Jesus on the wall when Cleva said, "Don't worry, honey. He means the world to me, but I'm not like those folks at the Church of God."

I laughed at her reading my mind. I was about to comment when Cleva asked if I'd like some coffee to warm up. Recalling the coffee at the sheriff's, I paused, then nodded. Anything hot would feel good, even just as a hand warmer.

Cleva and Jake headed to the kitchen, and I could hear her offering him a treat. I saw no signs of a dog, so I was hoping she wasn't giving him a chunk of fatback. I stood by the heater and rubbed my raw hands. A photograph of a man with Franklin D. Roosevelt hung to the left of the heater; otherwise the walls were bare. The real artwork lay outside, through an oversized window facing the mountain vista behind her house. I recognized the handiwork of the same man who'd worked on my apartment. It was a small town.

A coffee grinder buzzed in the kitchen. Jake wandered back into the living room with a large Milk Bone. When he'd polished that off, he nosed around the hardwood floors, never missing a chance to hoover crumbs. Before long, the aroma of strong, fresh coffee wafted into the room as Cleva came in with a pot and two cups. And a plate of homemade cinnamon rolls.

"I bet you thought you were going to have to swallow some of that wee-wee water they claim is coffee 'round here," Cleva said, chuckling.

I hadn't said more than three words since I'd first seen her waving at me. And she seemed to read my mind.

"I knew what you were thinking," Cleva continued. "I used to drink that bilge water myself. But I had a cousin move to Oregon, and that whole Pacific Northwest is filled with good coffee roasters. When I went for a visit, I got converted."

The coffee was strong and rich. I added some thick, fresh cream.

"And take one of Peg's rolls," Cleva said. "Have you had the pleasure of meeting Peg Parker, Lonnie's mother? Best baker 'round the falls." I nodded, my mouth full of the flakey roll, sticky with sourwood honey and cinnamon.

"Now, tell me about yourself," Cleva said, content to listen once she'd taken care of her hospitality duties. We talked like old friends till the sun went down. Cleva repeated her offer for a ride home and patted my shoulder. "I've enjoyed this, honey. I'm glad things turned in a fashion that led you to my home."

I'd enjoyed it too. I told things about myself I rarely shared, in part because Cleva, it turned out, was a good listener. And storyteller. She was a strong, independent woman who'd never married, though she had a huge family that benefited from her generous spirit. And she'd done more than her share of nurturing as a teacher, and later principal, in the local schools.

We'd been friends for almost a year now. In fact, Cleva was my only adult friend living close by. Kitt Scanlon seemed like a potential friend, though we'd only visited at each other's stores. The women I met through the store were nice enough, but I'd learned that they saw me as their shopkeeper, a distinction that had never entered my mind until a customer hinted at it one day.

Jake licked my hand and brought me out of my reverie. I rubbed his ears for a while before heading downstairs to pack the truck. After hitching him in with his makeshift seatbelt, I eased the truck out of the driveway and onto Hanging Dog Road. A car racing into my parking lot made me swerve, its driver beeping the horn and flashing the lights.

Chapter 11: Della

I threw my truck into park and got out. Jake tried to join me. "Stay, boy. This won't take a minute."

At first, I didn't recognize the driver, but when I got closer, I saw that she was a regular, Mary Lou Dockery. Her face was bruised and her lip bleeding. She'd have a black eye come morning.

"I need some Band-Aids, Mrs. Kincaid," she said, as though she'd just skinned her knees.

"You sure do, Mary Lou. Let me open up for you." We walked to the store in silence. I didn't want to pry, and Mary Lou didn't look as though she had the energy to answer questions. "You sit there, and I'll round up some supplies for you." I quickly gathered the Band-Aids, alcohol, and gauze. "Do you need any tissues," I hollered from the back of the store.

"No, we've got them." I brought the supplies to the checkout. "And I won't need the gauze, Mrs. Kincaid," Mary Lou mumbled.

"Okay, sure. Anything else?"

"Well, I could do with a quart of milk as long as I'm here. And Duane wants some Pabst."

Good God. She was picking up beer for the son of a bitch who beat her. "Mary Lou, if you ever want to talk, I'm here by myself most of the time …"

"Nothing to talk about. This is how it goes around here. One man is like the next."

I wasn't going to launch into my feminist diatribe. Mary Lou had four kids and no reasonable way to extricate herself from her marriage. "Hey, talk is free. Maybe ways to cope with the reality of the situation. I'm not trying to put you out on the street."

Mary Lou tried for a smile, but didn't quite make it, only managing to crack her lip open again. We settled up. I slipped a small box of Belgian chocolates into her bag and hoped she wouldn't give them to her kids. Hershey's was good enough for them. I watched her drive off, lost in thoughts about the havoc men can wreak.

As I pulled into Cleva's long driveway, the sky was scorched with pink and purple streaks that reminded me of Mary Lou. Jake steadied himself on the truck's dashboard, whimpering a happy tune that broke the spell of that sorrow. No doubt he was anticipating the extra helpings of treats at Cleva's. Once sated, he'd get to run free for a while to chase rabbits and opossums across the nearby meadows.

"Honey, how're you doing?" Cleva asked, hugging so hard I couldn't answer. My extra-long hug back said it all.

Dinner already filled the table: a mountain of fried chicken surrounded by bowls of fresh peas, cauliflower au gratin, and asparagus. Plus three-inch high biscuits and an apple crumble. We enjoyed the meal without mentioning L's death. The grapevine had brought Cleva up to date, and that night, I was grateful for its unceasing buzz. Instead, we talked about our travels over the years, and I shared how much the natural beauty was feeding my life. "But it still doesn't feel like home," I confessed. "I keep expecting to pack up from a long vacation and head out."

"Well, it takes time. Folks around here can be standoffish, but you've got me and Jake and Vester Junior. That's a good start." Cleva paused and added, "You look as though you could use an early night. Ready to turn in?"

She was right about that, and about my sleeping better away from town. But I still had disturbing dreams. Not surprisingly, I was working hard to escape from somewhere; when I awoke, I felt as though I'd been running all night. I couldn't blame it all on The Day. It was just a new iteration of a recurring dream I'd had for years.

Jake had had his own troubles settling down—he must have heard different noises in the night and probably smelled a skunk or other critters wandering near the house—but he eventually joined me on the bed, sleeping deeply without any audible dreams. The next morning, we came downstairs to another feast—fresh biscuits, sausage, grits, and scrambled eggs. *Good thing I don't live here*, I thought, as I felt my waistband pinch. But that didn't stop me from tucking into the spread and loving every morsel.

"I wanted this to be a good break for you, Della," Cleva said as we scraped the plates into her compost bucket under the sink. "But I also wanted to show you this note I got from that dead girl. She sure was polite. She wrote me after I gave her a lift back to her campsite. She was staying by the river, no one around for miles, and I saw her wandering down the highway with that pack on her back. It was coming up on dusk, and I was afraid she wouldn't make it before dark. I just had to stop."

I held up the note. "Did you show this to Brower? A normal sheriff would consider it evidence."

"Well, he's not normal—I can't stand that man. And you said he'd closed the case."

"Well, he's waiting for the tox screen, but he's likely to close as fast as possible." She looked so forlorn, I added, "I'll make a copy and give him the original. You don't have to deal with him."

When I read the note, I could see it was written with the same precise, yet somewhat childish scrawl, I'd seen in the woods. A sweet note, saying that a favor from a stranger had a special quality to it, for which she was grateful. She added that she hoped she could do a favor for Cleva someday soon and signed it, Lucy. Finally we knew her first name.

"Doesn't sound like someone fixin' to leave this earth, does it?" Cleva said.

"It can be hard to see a suicide coming," I said, setting the note down on the table. "I've known people to commit suicide while a cake baked in the oven. And she probably *did* want to do you a favor. Her emotions were on her sleeve. At her age, everything seems so wonderful and horrible." I shivered remembering another suicide I'd witnessed. I sure hadn't seen that one coming.

"You cold, honey? The sun hasn't come full up. I could put on some heat."

"No, I'm fine," I said, looking at my watch. "Though I need to get to the store. I wish I could sit here all day."

Chapter 12: Abit

It'd been a little over two weeks since The Day, as Della was calling it. Things were calming down—except for the rains, which had been blowing like crazy. Good thing the store's roof had an overhang, so I could sit out front, rain or shine. I liked feeling protected.

But there weren't much going on, and it was kinda boring again. Not that I wanted someone else to die to spice things up, but it'd been special having so many people coming in and out of the store. Even when Daddy ran it that never happened. To tell you the truth, that's why he sold it. Della came along at just the right time, for Daddy, anyways.

I really liked it inside the store since Della got it all cleaned up. The fresh coffee and bakery bread and even those stinky cheeses she liked (I reckoned she was the only one who ate them) mixed together for a good smell. I couldn't imagine what that store woulda been like if Sheriff Brower's father had bought it like he'd said he was gonna do. I was glad Daddy decided different. That was a good thing he did, I had to give him that.

One night last week we did have a little dustup. From our living room, I heard some tires screeching in front of the store. Mary Lou Dockery came flying up into the driveway just as Della and Jake were leaving. I knew without seeing that Duane had beat up on her again. And

I hated to think about what Della musta thought of the men round here.

I'll grant you they could be rough. They'd get to drinking, and while that was supposed to make them feel happy, it just seemed to let all their frustrations and sorrows well up and pour out. I felt that sometimes—not from drinking, but from too many thoughts and feelings racing round inside. Like when I'd be on the playground, getting teased, and next thing I knew, my arms would just start swinging away. A visiting nurse at school taught me to beat up on my bed pillow, which I had to admit was a lot better than on Bobby McKeever. Bobby thought so, too (though he was still an asshole).

I'd lost more feathers than you'd think could come out of one pillow. Mama even noticed. "What're you doing in the night, son? Having a pillow fight in your dreams?" she'd ask. Funny thing was, the more I'd hit that pillow, the less I felt I needed to, not just then but down the road when something else pissed me off. I wanted to run down and tell Mary Lou to let Duane know about pillows, but they'd all driven off by the time I could've made it outside.

It was kinda weird, too, because Duane was real nice to me when he stopped by the store. He'd take time to ask about me or my hubcaps or something he knew I liked. He even brought me a hubcap he'd found beside the road. Daddy would never've hit Mama, but he'd never ask me nothin' about my day, neither. Things like that confused me.

And Gregg O'Donnell came by one night. He carried a big bouquet of flowers that didn't look like they came from no garden round here. Besides, Gregg lived at the ranger quarters, and they didn't have a garden, so he musta bought them somewhere. He stayed way longer than usual. I got called home before he left, but I paid attention and heard truck doors opening and closing just after ten o'clock.

But otherwise, I was just sitting round, whittling on a piece of walnut Duane gave me. I was aiming for a little bear, and it was starting to take shape. While I took a little more off its butt (bears have big ones, but not *that* big), I was replaying what Della had told me about The Day. She'd described Tattoo Man to some folks, but no one claimed to know him. And we still didn't know nothin' about the dead girl, except her first name. Not a soul had called Sheriff Brower to report someone was missing. That made me so sad. As sorry as my life was at times, at least Mama and Daddy would've been looking for me!

The guy down in Asheville who cut up dead bodies—I forgot what he was called—said she had the sugar, but it weren't too much insulin that killed her but the poison hemlock in her body. Man, that stuff was bad news. Mama warned me about that when I was just little. We'd go out looking for wild foods like purslane and watercress, and along the way, she'd point out what hemlock looked like. She'd wag her finger at me and tell me to stay away from that stuff.

Oh, and that priest guy, Father Max, showed up the other evening. Della told me later that they'd finished planning a service for Lucy. I heard them upstairs in her apartment; the windows were all open 'cause we were having a hot spell, odd for April. I saw the notice in the newspaper and asked Mama if I could go to the funeral. She told me, "Well, I'm not leaving you here all alone!"

Even though the store was closed on Sundays, I liked sitting there better than at home. Just before eleven o'clock, Della came down the steps all dressed up for church. She'd just started doing that on Sunday mornings—usually she'd be upstairs with a newspaper and coffee and music like I'd never heard before. She said it was box music, or something like that.

Her leaving meant Jake got to hang out with me. She'd started asking me to look after him when she had to leave for a while, but I had to promise to keep him behind the store, not out front. He was small enough I could handle him all right. She paid me one dollar for each time, which was great for both of us, 'cause then I had money to buy more in her store.

Chapter 13: Della

After the Sunday service, Father Max was busy greeting his small congregation, so I walked to the parking lot to head home. As I opened my truck door, I heard him call out, "The service is all set, I believe." We'd already worked out the details, so I figured he just needed to talk.

"Do you think anyone will come?" I asked.

"Sadly, yes." I raised an eyebrow. "Sadly," he explained, "because they'll come not to honor a life but to see who else shows up. Maybe a mystery relative will appear, bereft and distraught. That should be good for a few weeks of gossip."

He looked so down, I gave him a quick hug, even though we didn't know each other well. He'd been to the store on several occasions, but until the plans for Lucy's service, our conversations never ventured beyond manchego or cheddar. Cleva told me he'd once led a prominent Episcopal church in Savannah, Georgia, but after a mid-life lapse of judgment involving a parishioner, he was banished to our far-flung outpost. She added that at least he, unlike his Catholic brethren, had chosen an adult.

Quaint Episcopal churches, with their familiar red doors and white exteriors, dotted the mountains of North Carolina. They were vestiges from the days before air conditioning, when low-country families turned a season into a verb and summered here, fleeing the hot coastal areas and bringing their churches with them. Laurel Falls was lucky to have Max Perkins. Generous with his time and comfort, he brought a Christian civility not found in the pulpits of the Church of God and Southern Baptist churches.

"I'll be at the service," I assured him. "Thanks for hosting it. Some of the other churches are vilifying Lucy for her habitual drug use, but she was diabetic, for Christ's sake!" I would have apologized for my slip, but nothing seemed to faze Max.

He just nodded. "We're both getting a little too cynical, I'm afraid."

"I prefer to call it 'world weary.' That implies having come by it naturally."

"Say, I've been meaning to ask," Max said, changing the subject, "when you found Lucy, did you see the note she wrote?"

I wondered why he wanted to know—maybe for his homily at the service—but I couldn't tell even Father Max that I'd read the note. I just shook my head, rationalizing that somehow that wasn't lying. "Brower's not giving out much information. I did hear that someone at the courthouse leaked what the note said," I added to cover myself. "Something like 'I'm tired and full of sorrow.'"

"That doesn't say much, does it? I mean, who couldn't say that?"

"I'm not sure who it was written to. The world?"

"I wonder who has the note now," he said.

"I think the SBI, you know, the State Bureau of Investigation, collected all the evidence and took it to Asheville." He made no comment, looking lost in thought. "Doesn't it seem odd to be a stranger to this area and come here to die? But then, maybe she came as a kid with her family, had fond memories, and wanted to die among the beauty?"

"Makes as much sense as anything," he said, waving goodbye as he headed toward to the church. With his shoulders stooped and head bowed, he looked as though he were praying for all the lost souls, himself included.

I was leery of do-gooders—to me, most were just wearing a mask of piety. (Maybe Father Max was right about my cynicism.) But he seemed to be the real deal. His hard times stripped him of pretention and showmanship. And, of course, he drank. I seemed to attract a lot of alcoholics into my life. I used to think it was unfinished business, the legacy of two drunken parents, but I'd spent loads of time exploring that. I finally understood that I no longer attracted alcoholics, they were just everywhere. It would be hard *not* to run into one.

And Father Max was a gentle drunk, like those I saw in D.C. who fed pigeons and saved bread for squirrels and ducks. As their lives bore down on them, they drank spirits to feed their spirit, even if the respite lasted only a short time.

When I pulled out of the church parking lot, I saw Max disappcar behind the church's red doors, undoubtedly headed toward the remains of the communion wine. And I felt a flicker of concern about why he wanted to know about Lucy's note.

Chapter 14: Abit

"Sometimes things show up when you're not thinking so hard," Della said when she came down Monday morning to open up.

She looked wore out, so I wasn't surprised when she headed straight to the coffeemaker. She said she didn't want to say anything more just then. But before long, she came out with a mug of coffee and settled in a sunny spot on the bench. The mornings were still cool enough to need a little fire, from time to time, but the sun was getting stronger every day.

That's when she told me she had some kind of relevation. She said she saw something in her mind's eye that made her start awake in the night, and she couldn't get back to sleep. Mama had visions too, so I wudn't surprised when Della told me about hers. She saw the two notes—Lucy's suicide note and her note to Cleva— side by side, just as sure as if they was laid out on a desk in real life. That was when she knew something was wrong. The writing didn't look the same. It was real close, but something weren't right.

"Yeah, but if I were writing something at a desk at school, and something in my lap out in the woods, they'd look different," I told her. "Or maybe she wrote it real careful-like before heading into the wilderness."

"Good points, Mister. But the fact this made itself known to me, rather than my mind working on it, adds weight to my concern. That's what I meant about not thinking so hard."

I told her I knew exactly what she meant. "Like the time I knew something was wrong with our beagle, Fuzzy. I told Daddy, but he waved me off. Then Fuzzy passed on within the week. There'd been something wrong with his baying, and I heard it, but I couldn't put words to it."

"You keep paying attention to those messages," Della said. "It's hard for some people to accept them, but don't let that stop you from giving them the respect they deserve."

That's how Monday started. Later that day, when Della came back from seeing Brower again, she was really upset. I figured from what she'd said earlier, she musta asked him to see the note, the one from the woods, and he'd said no.

Brower was like that. Mean-spirited. The story goes that some six or seven year ago he'd taken up with some girl, but then he dumped her. Just like that. She'd moved to be with him and everything, but when he got into the school where sheriffs and cops go, and he became a lawman and a born again Christian, all at the same time, he left her behind. When he moved back two year later, everyone was all, "Ain't he a fine man?" just 'cause he was claiming to be born again and wearing a tin star. I bet that girl he dumped woulda had somethin' different to say.

But over time, I'd noticed that things balanced out. I couldn't say it always worked that way, but I'd seen it happen plenty of times. Like Tuesday morning, when I was coming down our steps toward the store and saw Lonnie Parker drive off in a hurry. He didn't see me, but I could tell he was hepped up about something. I sat down in my chair, reared back, and that's when I saw the envelope sticking out just a tad under the door. I couldn't wait till Della came down and found it.

Later that day, something even better happened. Della got a big delivery for the store 'cause business had picked up. She was trying to get everything inside before it rained again, and she asked me to help and that she'd pay me. Cash—not even trade. I checked with Mama, and she nodded, maybe even smiled. So I made five dollars helping Della, which was as good as being paid five dollars to eat ice cream. She said if business kept getting better, maybe I could even work a couple of afternoons each week, regular-like.

Chapter 15: Della

A crowd filed into the small Episcopal church, even more than I'd expected. Father Max caught my eye and shook his head. It was hard not to be cynical when you saw the likes of Roger Turpin, a tie tight around his bulging neck and tucked behind his Sunday-best overalls. He sat sprawled across the end of the pew, where delicate carvings seemed to cower under the weight of his thighs. Or Wayne Burnett sitting in the front of a church—probably the first church he'd been in since he was baptized. For them, I imagined the service wasn't much different from the Saturday night auction behind Junior's Automotive: a spectacle not to be missed.

I took a seat next to Abit and his parents, nodding hello. I almost didn't recognize Abit—he looked so grownup in his shirt and tie, his hair slicked down with Brylcreem. I was worried I'd been short with him earlier in the day when he'd asked if I needed help with any chores that week. He was beside himself with enthusiasm, looking forward to having honest work, but I just couldn't talk about the store at that moment.

Billie and her brood were in the row in front of us, and from the row behind, Cleva patted me on the back with that reassuring way of hers. I'd been in the church only three or four times, most of those since The Day, three weeks ago. Of course, the topic of church had been broached ever since I'd moved to the area, whenever I met someone for the first time. In these parts, there were two seasonal questions: "How's your garden?" (summer) and "Do you have plenty of wood?" (winter) and two perennial questions: "Do you have good water?" and "Where do you go to church?"

Invariably, I'd stumble and stutter until someone said, "Well, you'll just have to come to Bethany with us" (a Baptist church ten miles south) or "We've got the friendliest congregation at New Hope" (a Church of God group that met in the local VFW Hall and seemed to hate everyone, in all likelihood even one another). A couple of times I gave in, but found the sermons and announcements disturbing and decided I was better off staying home with Jake.

As the church filled, someone edged his way into our pew, scrunching in next to me. To make room, I scooted over closer to Abit and gave him a hug to ease any hurt feelings. He gave me that crooked smile that just killed me.

"Della?" the man who'd just settled next to me whispered, placing a hand on my arm.

I turned, then jerked my arm back as though it had been burned. I leaned so close to Abit I was practically in his lap. At first Abit thought I was playing around, but he looked at my face and knew something was wrong. I didn't dare look over at Mildred.

"What is it, Della?" Abit asked. I shook my head.

I panicked. I couldn't get out, I was so squeezed into the pew. I turned back to the man and growled, "What are *you* doing here?"

"I was worried about you. Rotten luck finding the girl."

"How did you even *know* about the girl, er, young woman? Or this service?"

He shrugged. "I started a subscription to the *Mountain Weekly* after you moved here."

God, it was just like him. Alex Covington, my ex-husband, Mr. Hotshot at the *Post*, once upon a time. I thought about our local rag and felt embarrassed, but he'd had the good grace not to comment. (And I hoped he didn't know about its wicked moniker). I was getting madder by the moment until I noticed Abit craning his neck so hard he was about to need traction. I almost laughed.

"Abit, meet Alex. Alex, meet Abit. Abit is my best friend at the store." Abit's face blushed as he stuck out his hand to shake. He had better manners than the educated prick next to me. The music stopped and Father Max stepped to the pulpit.

I barely heard the service. I kept thinking about Alex showing up, stealing my focus. Just like him to take over. I'd let him do that in our life together—and he was having a go at it in our life apart.

It still stung to think about how critical of me and my writing he'd always been. He became so toxic that I quit showing him my writing and ignored his comments once my articles were published. Eventually, his status was shot all to hell, but that just created new problems. When he started drowning his troubles with drink and other women, I moved out. Alex thought I was being "rash," which only reminded me of the one I got thanks to his indiscretions.

Lost in my thoughts, I felt Abit nudging me. "It's over Della. Let's get out of here and go back to the store," he said, tugging at his tie. I heard the Doxology. Time to go deal with the living.

As we filed out, I caught a glimpse of a familiar face—or more to the point, an arm. The same tattoo that had peeked beneath the hem of his Madras shirtsleeve in the woods on The Day. He'd cut his hair and shaved his beard, but he was the same guy. I started forcing my way into the crowd, struggling to get through the maze of people. They were pulling back and glaring at me, and I didn't blame them. I must have looked crazed after seeing Alex, suffering through a funeral, and pushing my way toward Madras Man, aka Tattoo Man. But by the time I got to the front door, he was gone.

Chapter 16: Abit

I didn't know what to make of that Alex guy. And I couldn't figure out how Della felt about him, either. Her face looked like one of them flip books Mama oncet gave me for Christmas—changing from sad to glad to mad in a flash. I knew one thing: he sure had a cool car. Didn't see many like that round here. I wanted to steal one of his hubcaps, but Della would've known who done it.

His plates said D.C., so she probably knew him from up there. When she first moved here, I overhead a phone call one day. Della was upset so her voice really carried (plus I had my ear to the door). Seemed like he'd been drinking a bunch after losing his job, and then she caught him in bed with someone he worked with. Sounded like one of Mama's soaps on TV. Della almost started crying on the phone. I knew 'cause she was talking the way I did when I was trying not to cry.

That sure confused me after the service, the way she ran out of the church. I thought she was chasing Alex, but then I saw him standing beside the pew, looking lost. I was working my way out—the crowd was just standing in the aisles, making it hard—and by the time I finally got outside, she was walking to her car. Alex must've pushed harder'n me, 'cause he'd caught up with her, and they talked some. Then they both headed off, like I weren't even there. But I was used to that—though I had to admit, this time my feelings were hurt.

And he spent the night! I'd already fallen asleep when I heard Jake barking, so I got outa bed to see what was goin' on. The moon was really bright, and I could see them standing round outside while Jake romped in the back meadow. The next morning, Della and Alex musta been down in the store early on, because I saw them head back upstairs just as I was coming down to sit in my chair, ready for another day of watching other people's lives.

Chapter 17: Della

As Alex took off in his noisy Mercedes, I couldn't help thinking how stupid that car looked in our hardscrabble community. Add in the diesel racket, and it was embarrassing. Abit, of course, thought it was a marvelous car. Ever since Alex arrived, I felt him watching my every move, trying to pick up signals about how any given detail might affect his world.

He was sitting in his chair, taking in the farewell scene. "Howdy, Mister," I said, ruffling his hair. It was a little sticky from the Brylcreem his mother made him use yesterday.

"Howdy. How was your evening?"

I laughed. "You've been waiting all morning to ask me that." I unlocked the door and went inside.

Abit could be as transparent as that plate-glass window he was looking through. I waved for him to come in—he was developing a taste for coffee, and I couldn't wait to get it brewing. Abit looked up at his house and shook his head. I got the day's cash out of the empty tub of chocolate ice cream in the freezer, flipped on the lights, and brought the sandwich board to the door.

"I'll trade you coffee for putting this out next to the road."

"Done!"

I watched him drag the heavy sign to the road and felt happy to know him. He was different, and not in the derisive way some people meant that. He had something special going on inside that head of his. Once he placed the sign near the driveway and turned back, he gave me a smile and wave, as though we hadn't just spoken.

"I'll get you that coffee," I whispered, just in case Mildred had ears as keen as her eyes. She probably didn't approve of his drinking coffee, but who knew? Country kids grew up fast, which was why I wanted to talk with him that morning. He was weaned on gossip and soap operas and had likely drawn the wrong conclusion.

When I handed him a half cup of coffee, I told him. "Abit, Alex is my ex-husband. I was surprised by his visit, as I believe you already realized. And he slept on my couch."

His neck turned red first, then it crawled up to his face. His freckles even disappeared. He carefully sipped the hot coffee, stalling for time to compose an answer. "I hope he wudn't mean to you," he finally said.

"No, not last night," I said, smiling at my loyal friend. But I didn't want to discuss Alex, so I headed back inside.

After Lucy's service, Alex had asked for a tour of my store and apartment. The day had turned sunny, and bright light streamed in my upstairs windows. The trees waved at us with their new green leaves while the mountain vista rolled on forever. I could tell Alex was impressed.

"That looks like the sky," he said, commenting on the walls of the kitchen, living room, and dining room. I'd painted them with a wash of cream over light blue and was pleased that I'd achieved the desired effect. "That plus the large windows makes me feel as though we're aloft in the trees," he added.

When I motioned for him to sit on the couch, he starting laughing, pointing at the large velour recliner. "What's that?"

"My Barcalounger."

"You said you'd never be caught dead in something like that. I remember wanting one at our home."

"Well, when in Rome. Actually, they're required here. You should get yourself one. I didn't know what I was missing."

"Where's the mini-fridge and massager?"

"They were out of stock, so I took the floor model." To demonstrate its finer qualities, I reclined at four different angles. Midway I stopped. "This is my favorite. I look due west across the mountains and watch the sunset when the days get longer."

Tires crunched in the driveway, and I remembered I had a store to run. I told Alex to make himself at home and went back to work. Business was good with folks swinging by after the funeral. Just before closing time, I started to smell an intoxicating mix of garlic, onions, and tomato. I'd missed Alex's cooking skills, and I was looking forward to being treated to a home-cooked meal—in my own home. His Bolognese sauce was perfect, made even better with some fresh pasta I brought up from the store, along with odds and ends for a spring salad. We polished off a bottle of excellent Chianti and finished with coffee and port.

After dinner, we talked more (me on the couch, Alex in the Barcalounger, which he'd taken to, as Cleva would've said, like a pig to a puddle). I'd had enough wine to feel relaxed, so I was comfortable talking about The Day. I also decided to take advantage of Alex's investigative mind. I showed him the two notes—the one Cleva had given me and the copy Lonnie Parker had slipped under the store's front door. They were a close match, but something felt wrong to me. Alex couldn't see it—told me I was just playing "Dragnet." Then he gave me a hug, and I remembered how dismissive those used to feel.

When the conversation ran out, our silence grew awkward. I pried myself off the couch, gathered bed linens and towels, placed them on Alex's lap, and told him goodnight. I chose not to let him use the guest room; I didn't want him to feel too comfortable. It seemed odd to be such strangers to one another, but that was how our lives had played out.

The next morning, we ate breakfast in the store, early enough even Abit wasn't out front yet. Alex sat in one of the rocking chairs circling the wood stove—which I'd lit, as the morning was cool (and to be honest, I wanted to show off my fire-making skills).

I watched as he took in all the provisions neatly stacked on wooden shelves, the barrels of flour and coffee beans underneath. I could tell he appreciated how much of myself I'd put into the store, a mix of practicality and comfort. He sniped about the lemon curd and salt-cured capers, adding his editorial opinion that few people would enjoy such things. He was right in part—I'd eaten a fair share of poor choices in inventory (which was okay with me, up to a point). But Alex was also painfully provincial, thinking no one could enjoy good food unless they ran in elite circles, preferable within the Beltway.

"I bet your friends enjoy visiting here," Alex said, as he munched on the last crumbs of a croissant. "You've got a gorgeous home above a well-stocked store—a hard-to-beat combination."

No mention of their wanting to visit with me, I noticed. "I did have one friend come up from D.C., but friends at our age are harder to make—and keep."

"But you do have friends, right?"

I smiled, thinking of my motley new family. "Yes, I do."

Alex seemed flummoxed by my smile. Knowing him, he'd imagined I'd found a boyfriend or whatever you call them at our age. Gregg O'Donnell had stopped by the other night, a couple of weeks after The Day. He was a good-looking guy, and at fifty-two, he was as fit as a ranger half his age. But I wasn't ready for that kind of attention. Besides, I was still dealing with the emotional turmoil of our divorce. I thought about how my real boyfriend was Abit, and smiled again. Alex had a serious frown going when we were both startled by an insistent rapping on the front door. I unlocked the door.

"Mornin' ma'am," a rugged-looking man said, tipping his Caterpillar cap.

"Mornin', Dexter."

"You got any liniment in here?" he asked, craning his neck as though he were afraid to come in.

"Is it for you or Geneva?"

"Geneva. She's doing poorly. Gone lame."

"That's because she's working too hard," I said, walking toward the back shelves.

He continued to stand at the door. "I know, I know, but there's too much to do right now getting the ground ready and tending to the calving."

"Here're a couple of choices, but this one sells a lot faster."

"Yes ma'am, thank you."

We headed back to the register. "I hope this liniment helps, and please tell Geneva I hope she feels better soon. Take care, Dexter." When he was out the door, I relocked it and pulled the shade down before anyone else showed up early.

"Yessir, it's over thar amongst the roots and berries," Alex mugged.

"Don't make fun. They think you sound pretty weird with your clipped speech."

"I'm not making fun of *them*—just *you*. Where'd you pick that up?"

"Where do you think? Here. I've made a point of talking at least a little more like the locals. It's called communication. I don't overdo it, but it helps. I used to see real fear in their eyes when I spoke. Fear of me and fear of being seen as ignorant. Like the time I marveled at the forsythia blooms, and my neighbor Mildred looked terrified. I later realized they call them yellow bells. She seemed really intimidated, so I've trained myself to stop and substitute a word here and there."

"Okay, okay, sorry. As usual, you're a better person than I am," he said, his eyes sparkling with amusement.

After breakfast, he packed his car—he'd bought a case of Billie's homemade preserves and a country ham—and headed out the drive toward home.

I could feel my mood sour as the day went on. Too much pressure from the murder, the store, and Alex. I took a break after a particularly difficult customer and sat on the bench outside. When I was through griping, Abit asked, "Do you like *anyone* here?"

"What do you mean?" I stalled. I knew exactly what he meant.

"Well, you complain about everyone."

"Not everyone."

"Well, maybe not Cleva. You don't like your customers, and you hate Brower. And I've heard you mumble under your breath about Mama and Daddy. I know you're trying to take my side, but it still kinda hurts." I couldn't speak. I just sat there, not knowing what to say. Then he added, "Do you even like *me*?"

That stung so badly I had to go back inside. I cursed Alex, thinking Abit and I were both out of sorts because of his surprise visit, but I knew that was only part of the problem. I messed around in the back storeroom for a while, until that wretched day was finally over. When I locked the front door, I noticed Abit wasn't in his chair. Same thing the next morning. I felt bad enough to entertain the notion of turning around and going back to bed, but I managed to open up and do some business. I checked at noon, still no Abit. I skipped lunch.

As customers came in, I made an effort to be more like what I imagined they wanted me to be. Even so, most just mumbled about what they needed, paid, and left. "Howdy," "goodbye," and sometimes, "Thankee, ma'am," but without any real warmth. There was a disconnect, a distance between us, especially when I was the shopkeeper. I didn't get it, and I couldn't fake it. I could sense that they didn't *not* like me, but our interactions came down to that impersonal give-and-take that had fueled economies for millennia.

The next morning, about ten o'clock, I heard tap, tap, tap, and my heart skipped. I didn't get my hopes up, but I opened the door. Abit just stared straight ahead. I went out and sat on the bench.

"I'm sorry," I said.

"What for? I'm the one who should be sorry," he said, both sad and petulant at the same time.

"No, Mister, it's all on me. I moved here, and I laid my expectations on a community that didn't invite me, or even want me. I get that. So thank you for making it crystal clear."

He just shook his head as he continued to tap against the store. We sat there, silent, until Mary Lou Dockery drove up. For once, there didn't appear to be any bruises. I helped her find a few things, rang her up, said goodbye.

She turned to leave, then stopped. "Thank you for the other night."

"What?"

"When you opened up for me. And gave me them chocolates." She smiled and added, "I didn't let the kids have a one."

I walked her out, and when she'd driven away, I sat down on the bench.

"You was smiling when you came out," he said, still looking straight ahead. At nothing in particular.

"Yeah. I spent a lot of time last night thinking about what you said, and it may sound odd, but I feel better about living here than I have since that first week, before I opened the store."

"Before you had to wait on us?"

"Hey, not fair. Well, not completely fair. I do like some folks here. Especially you."

When he starting blushing, I couldn't help but wonder about the crazy lives we all lived, begging for attention and then hiding—or even running—when we got it. Or moving somewhere new and complaining about it being different.

"I'm not finished thinking about what you said," I went on. "And I plan to live here and take advantage of this opportunity. Maybe it was a wild hair that made me move down here, but you and Cleva, Mary Lou, the Ledfords, and other folks to come, make me want to learn more about why I chose to live here."

"I cain't imagine why you'd list me among your friends after the way I talked to you yesterday. All I can figure is I was jealous of Alex."

"Well, no need for that," I said, ruffling his hair. "Besides, you were just being honest. And maybe a little crabby, like I was. Do your parents ever argue?"

"Not much. Mama just gives in to Daddy."

"Okay, not a good example. What about when you were at school. Did you ever get in arguments with kids but then you were playing just fine the next day?"

"No one ever played with me much."

"Man, I'm striking out here," I said.

"But I've seen it on TV," he said. "You know, people who love each other get mad, and then they seem to love each other more when they get over it. Like they learned something that made a difference."

I looked at him and thought, *nothing wrong with that brain—and heart.* I waited a beat and added, "Well, that's how I feel about us. We just learned some things about each other—and now we know each other even better. And I'm going to try to live into that. Okay?"

He smiled for the first time since yesterday. "I'm definitely okay, especially if you're okay."

"Okay." I wanted to give him a hug, but all things considered, I settled on bringing him a Dr. Pepper and going back to work. As I closed the door, I heard Abit ask, "Does this mean I still get to work here?" I chuckled and gave him a reassuring wave.

May 1985

Chapter 18: Abit

Della left! I saw her cleaning out her truck, and she told me she was going back to D.C.—just for a few days. I wudn't so sure. She'd been awfully upset lately, and I hadn't helped matters. She had dark circles under her eyes and seemed grumpy, though she'd been better since our talk.

Della told me Billie would keep the store open, and I was supposed to help her with big boxes and such and look after Jake. She handed me a twenty dollar bill and said that should cover things. I was happy about Jake, but I didn't much like Billie, and she didn't know what to make of me. Her kids treated me pretty bad at school, so I didn't really want to help her. But I knew Della would be mad if I didn't, and besides, I'd accepted her money.

After Della came down with her suitcase, she gave me the key to her apartment so I could let Jake out during the day. I wished I could stay with him up in that cool place of hers, but Mama would never've let me. I knew she'd think I'd go through Della's closet and check out her underwears. I wished Mama didn't think like that. I saw a TV show where some guy said that people who thought a lot of awful things about others really felt bad about themselves. That was the first time I'd heard it spelled out like that. It made me sad to think Mama might have been having a hard time herself.

I couldn't remember how I passed the time before Della bought the store. I knew I was bored a lot, especially after Daddy took me out of school. School days were good days, even with all the teasing. I'd always been big for my age—I was up to six feet and a little more. Kids joked about my high-water pants, but I couldn't help it. I kept growing out of them, and we couldn't just order a new pair whenever we wanted, even with Daddy's store account. And for some reason they made fun of my red hair. It was like Daddy's, back when he had enough to notice. I had his freckles too. They told me I was the spitting image of Great Uncle Rory in Ireland, when he was my age.

I sure hoped Della wouldn't be gone long, though to be honest, I was just hoping she'd come back at all.

Chapter 19: Della

"Oh my! Hello, hello, hello," Nigel Steadman said as he opened his apartment door, impeccably dressed in a three-piece suit featuring an apricot velvet waistcoat. I couldn't imagine wearing that in the heat—D.C. was already steamy in May—but that was his uniform. His weathered face cracked with a wide smile.

As he kissed both my cheeks, I could smell a faint, familiar hint of lavender aftershave. "Come in, come in, my dear. I've just made my tea. Have a seat. Oh, lovely to see you. I'll just pop downstairs to Firehook for a few of those tasty scones you like. One of the pleasures of living above such a fine bakery—not to mention the aroma of butter and cinnamon wafting through my abode."

"I won't say no, Nigel. I'm touched you remembered."

I had met a lot of people in my life as a reporter. I'd gotten to know many of them on a deeper level, as they let me delve into intimate details of their lives to flesh out the story. And they often grabbed my heart. I found myself outraged if they'd been wronged or bereft if they'd suffered a tragedy. I was in it with them, and I let these emotions fuel my writing, working to deliver the best possible story. Afterwards, they went on with their lives, of course, but I always felt as though I'd lost a close friend. Eventually, I couldn't do it anymore. That and other things conspired to make me call that realtor listed on Coburn's for sale sign.

Nigel was the exception. As I waited on the Victorian settee (more velvet, wine colored), I thought about the series of articles he helped me with after our initial collaboration. Funny fellow—so meticulous in everything, including his storytelling and forgery.

A British subject, Nigel married an American woman, and they settled in D.C. not long after World War II. Early on, he became a U.S. citizen and enjoyed dual citizenship. They split, but he stayed on in this apartment, where he earned a handsome living from expert forgery. I didn't interview him until after his second—and last—conviction. (Not a bad record, really, for a man who'd lived well off his penmanship for thirty years.)

That first time, I was working on a story about a white-collar crime ring, and he'd agreed to contribute, anonymously. We had to meet at his home, because he was under house arrest at the time. I'll never forget when he opened his front door. I was accustomed to the sometimes ragged, usually weary, look of many of the people I interviewed, but Nigel greeted me in sartorial splendor. I hadn't seen a velvet waistcoat since I'd spent my junior year studying in England.

Nigel had specifically asked me to come in the late afternoon. "Let's say four o'clock, dear?" Teatime, of course. We enjoyed some good cuppas together, even after the article ran. That first session together was almost five years ago, and Nigel's hair—still combed back in the sophisticated style of Claude Rains or Fred Astaire—had turned completely silver.

"Here we go, my dear," Nigel said, racing through his front door with a white baker's box tied with string. "Tea's up!" He darted into the kitchen and came back carrying a silver tray laden with scones, clotted cream, lemon curd, and the accouterments of tea. A brass clock delicately chimed four times, followed by a cuckoo clock adding its four calls a beat later. Expensive bric-a-brac filled every shelf, mantle, and table top, all without a speck of dust. I thought about what they'd look like in my store, under the patina of wood smoke.

As I sipped from my favorite bone china cup (a spray of violets splashed across its interior), I chuckled. "You do lead the good life, Nigel. What's your secret these days?"

"You know all my secrets, dear."

"All?"

"Well, almost all," he added with a wry smile.

"Are you back in business?"

"Direct as ever, I see. Well, yes and no. Do you recall how that agent from the Treasury Department started calling on me? You were afraid I was going to go to the slammer again, but he actually hired me."

I had a mouthful of scone and almost swallowed wrong. I made the universal motion with my hand for "keep talking!"

"Nothing really to report—I now work for The Man. I help them better understand the art of forgery. I rather like being respected for my expertise."

I looked around his expensive apartment. It would take more than a few government jobs to pay for such good taste. "Well, that's good, but surely the Feds aren't paying for all of this." Just then, the grandfather clock struck four—like a lot of grandfathers, a little behind the times.

"Good heavens, no! I've been lucky with my investments. A few stocks, bonds," he said, waving his hand this way and that.

"Let me guess. You're also on a first-name basis with a banker in the sunny Caymans?"

"No, my dear. Actually, I've always been partial to the Swiss."

We both laughed, and then I tucked into another scone. I carried some fresh baked goods at the store, but nothing like these. I'd missed them.

Nigel took a big bite of scone heaped with lemon curd and drained his teacup before adding, "Your visit is welcomed, yet unexpected. How long has it been? Most unfortunate turn of events that led to your leaving our fair city. So, what brings you back?"

I dug into my purse. "I have some handwriting I'd like you to compare. This is very important to me, and I needed someone I could trust."

Nigel chuckled. "Good heavens! I never expected you to need *my* services. Sounds delicious, though. Someone passing bad checks at your outpost canteen?"

"No, I have a copy of a thank-you note and the suicide note. I need to know if the same hand wrote them. We know who wrote the thank-you note, but we need your advice about the other one."

"Oh dear, I apologize for the inappropriate humor. Let me get my loupe."

Nigel stepped into his office. "You do realize there are many variables," he called out from the other room. "If someone were taking drugs, for example, or experiencing the shakes or writing on a difficult surface."

I didn't say anything. Let him decide. He came back with his jeweler's loupe around his head and sat down near a window. While he spent a quarter of an hour poring over the notes, I finished my tea and ate another half of a scone, as much out of nervousness as hunger. Finally, Nigel took off the loupe.

"I'm grateful that you didn't indicate which way you hoped my decision would go. I want to be as accurate and impartial as possible."

"And?"

"This is a forgery," he said, holding up the copy of the suicide note. "Mind you, a *very good* forgery. I could have used an assistant like this." He glanced at my face and immediately looked penitent again. He couldn't help himself, sometimes. "I am sorry, dear. I can see this is a very sensitive matter. Does it mean what I think it does?"

"Oh, hell," I said. "I really was hoping I was wrong."

"What tipped you off? This is quite good, you know."

"I'm not sure. I went to sleep one night, and in a dream, I saw both notes, side by side. They disturbed me enough to wake me. It was more like I *felt* something different in them than saw anything different."

"Oh, thank heavens your courts don't allow intuitives like you to testify. I'd be in the slammer with the likes of you on the stand." He smiled at me. "You were right on target."

"Are you sure? I mean what if she wrote it in her lap? It was found out in the woods, so it's not like writing at a desk."

"No, there are certain qualities that wouldn't be affected by that."

"Bloody hell!"

"Hey, that's my line. Can you stay a bit longer? I'll make some fresh tea. Always good to settle the nerves."

I looked at my watch. I had somewhere to be in a little over an hour, and I hadn't checked into my hotel. But I was enjoying Nigel's company too much to leave. I nodded.

"Well now," he said, his face serious and concerned. "This rather disrupts your whole getaway from life as you knew it, doesn't it?"

"Now look who's being as direct as ever. But you're right. I don't want to get involved. I've had enough of this kind of investigative work. I like my store and its simpler, daily routines."

"I know you don't want to get involved, but I know you will. Assuming your Wyatt Earp doesn't solve the case. You do have a sheriff down there in them thar hills, don't you? Turn it over to him."

Thinking of Brower, I must have made a face.

"That bad, eh?" he said, patting my hand before standing and heading into the kitchen to refresh our teapot. We drank more tea and visited for a while longer. His daughter lived in the Maryland suburbs, and he and his ex-wife were on better terms so that visits with the kids and grandkids were more enjoyable. He'd become more of a family man than a paperhanger—a term for forgers he despised. "It's an art form," he once admonished.

As I headed back to my hotel, I thought about what Nigel had shared, and I hoped Brower would listen. Of course, I couldn't mention Nigel by name—he'd made that clear as we'd said goodbye. And dammit, I couldn't show Brower the two notes side by side because he'd know Lonnie had slipped me that copy. But I'd think of something later. I needed to change and get over to Georgetown. Ah, hailing taxicabs. One of the finer activities of city life.

Sitting in the cab, I realized how exciting it felt to be back in D.C. Possibility thrummed throughout the city and woke up something within me that, though I hadn't realized it before, had gone dormant. And the comfort of sitting with an old friend, who knew my tastes and shared them, was exhilarating. As I was leaving Nigel's, a sorrow swept over me when he asked, "Do you think you'll be coming home again, Della?"

"This isn't my home now, Nigel. I miss its better features, but I'm not a part of it any longer. Besides, other than you, I really don't have any friends here anymore."

"Well, what about the museums, the theaters, the restaurants?" he said, waving his hand in the general direction of the National Mall. "Don't you miss them?"

Instead of answering, I gave him a big hug. Nigel closed the door behind me as I headed down the steps, then quickly reopened it.

"It really was good seeing you again!" He flashed a smile that took a decade off his face. "You will keep me abreast, won't you? I'd love a report from time to time." Then I heard him mumble something that sounded like, "I miss you."

I turned back to agree, but he'd already closed the door. As I hurried to find a cab, I wondered just what I'd have to report next time.

Chapter 20: Abit

Sure was quiet with Della gone. Except for them young'uns of Billie's. They was noisy and made a mess of the yard with their toys all over the place. I even caught one of them sitting in my chair. I'd been told I didn't have a poker face, which made sense since I'd never played the game and didn't think I ever could. I'd seen men play it, though, on reruns like "Gunsmoke" and "Big Country." Anyways, I gave that kid a look, and he jumped out of that seat like it were on fire.

Della called Billie yesterday to tell her she was coming home on Friday. Then she asked Billie to get me on the phone. Billie stretched the cord so I could stand outside and talk. I didn't know if she was being nice, on account of Mama, or she didn't want me in the store for her own reasons. But she just stood close by, until I had to give her a look, too. She headed back to the register.

When Della told me she had some news to share, I felt my knees turn kinda rubbery. I hoped she weren't going back to her ex-husband, but that kind of thing happened all the time, even round here. I was just thinking he seemed kind of stuck up and not worth it when I heard her say the news was about the girl, Lucy. That really confused me, 'cause how in the world did she find anything out about that up in D.C.? I started wondering if she'd gone to the FBI or something. Before she hung up, she said she counted me as someone she could confide in.

Chapter 21: Della

I was already at La Taberna when Alex arrived. I could see him cornered near the front door, the ever-ebullient host, Anastasia, laying a big Euro kiss on him. She was dressed in a designer black sheath, perhaps even more low cut than the last time I'd seen her. Josu, the maître d', oozing with professional courtesy, escorted Alex into the dining room. I'd gotten good at lip-reading during my reporter days, and I could just make out their conversation.

"Good evening, Josu. I see our table is ready—and waiting."

"Yes, madam arrived a little time ago. It was very good to see her again, if I may speak so directly." I saw a raised eyebrow, and loved him for it. The implication was as strong as his Spanish accent that Alex had brought women whom Josu *didn't* like. "But she doesn't seem to be herself," he added.

"She's been dealing with some serious stuff."

"When was she not, sir?" Josu said, sotto voce.

Alex nodded, as Josu pulled back his chair.

"I'm glad you shed your country look," Alex said to me, studying my own black dress and beaded necklace. "I don't suppose you find much use for that in hillbilly holler."

I wasn't about to let him bait me, not tonight. I rose and gave him a friendly kiss on the cheek, way more chaste than Anastasia's. "Good to see you, Alex, and to be back here. The closest we have in Laurel Falls is a Mexican cantina."

I didn't want that comment to sound like a put down of the honest effort of those restaurateurs. I'd always appreciated any kind of cuisine—as long as it was prepared and served with integrity. I quickly added, "Actually it's quite good. A couple of migrant workers opened it so they could enjoy their own food, for a change. But this," I waved my arm at the luxurious Moorish décor, "I needed a treat like this. Thank you, especially today."

"Bad news?"

Before I could answer, the sommelier arrived with a bottle of Dellaques De Riscal Rioja 1979. He spoke cordially to Alex, opened the wine, and poured some in his glass.

"Wonderful, Emilio. Excellent choice."

"Madam chose it."

I shrugged. "I took the liberty. It's a wine we used to like."

"Good memory. That had to be more than a year ago," Alex said to cover his forgetfulness.

"I remember things for a long time."

The sommelier scurried away, knowing when to skip the chitchat and move on. We clinked glasses and sipped the velvety wine. "Yes, bad news, or make that sad news. But I'm better now," I said, though I felt my chin quiver. I cleared my throat and added, "Nigel confirmed the forgery, and I don't know what to do."

Alex looked startled. "That means she was murdered?"

"I told you."

"I know, I'm sorry. I thought you were ..."

"I know what you thought," I interrupted. "Now tell me something I don't know. What can I do with this information?"

"Talk to that sheriff. He'll have to do something now. Turn it over, get it out of your hands. You can let it go now."

"I don't know. I wish if this had to happen it had been on Forest Service land. Gregg O'Donnell would be a lot easier to approach than Brower. I'm not sure he'll even believe me. He's a lazy son of a bitch who won't want to open up what he considers an easy closed case."

We sat in silence, leafing through the thick menu, elegantly bound in dark Spanish leather. We both looked up at the same time, silently acknowledging the vast distance that had grown between us. I felt pummeled by the events of the past weeks, today's report from Nigel, the months of separation. But I didn't want to ruin our special meal. God, how long had it been since I'd dined with white linen and fine wine?

"Let's forget that for now. I can't do anything tonight, and I'll know what to do by the time I get home again."

Our waiter, Felipe, dressed impeccably in a black tuxedo, arrived just as the tension broke. The waiters were all trained in Europe, and I was sure they learned how to read their customers' moods and body language.

I nodded at Alex, letting him know he could order for me. He spoke fluent Spanish, which always got us the best service and usually something special—an amuse bouche or extra dessert. Josu spoke excellent English, but many of the waiters weren't as comfortable with the language.

We started with a ragout of exotic mushrooms and prosciutto di Parma with melon. My entrée was the lamb steak with roasted garlic cream, accompanied by butter beans and dandelion greens, Alex's the grilled New England rockfish with salsa verde. As had been our habit, halfway through our main course, we switched plates. Alex taught me that trick—much classier than dripping samples across the white linen to the other's plate.

Over dinner, we talked about safe things, mostly politics. What else in that town? Fortunately, we mostly agreed on the topic, unlike a lot of couples I'd known there. And the evening worked its magic. By the time I polished off the last bit of our shared flan and my glass of port, I felt as though nothing untoward would happen again in my life. But eventually, reality won out.

"Do you think you could help me, somehow?" I asked. Alex had investigated—and embarrassed—more than a few politicians and business leaders inside the Beltway. And since he was working freelance, I figured he could make time to help me, if he wanted to.

"And I thought you were going to comment on this exquisite dinner."

"I'm sorry. Yes, thank you for all of this. You know I love it here." I paused just long enough to be polite. "But I can't get this off my mind. I *found* that girl."

He nodded, as though he understood. But then he said, "I'm pretty busy. Some papers and magazines are willing to give me another chance."

"That validates how good you can be," I said, honestly glad his talents weren't going to waste. "But I think you owe me."

He frowned and sipped more port. Finally, he broke the silence. "I'll do what I can, Della. I did a story about rural crime last year—in-depth, with a national focus. You may not realize how many bad guys are doing business in your Mayberry."

"I want to make you a copy of the notes," I said, ignoring his comment and searching through my purse. "And I brought along a drawing of the tattoo I saw on that guy's arm in the woods. I don't know why, but I remember it vividly. Adrenaline, I think. That afternoon, it raced through me."

"I'll check LexisNexis and see what else I can find for you. Not much to go on, but I've started with less before. We can make copies at my home."

"You mean the one that used to be mine, too?" I asked. I felt foolish before the last word was out of my mouth. I was more on edge tonight than I'd anticipated, even after all the wine. But being back in D.C., and in one of my favorite haunts, brought up a lot of old issues. "Never mind me," I added, waving my hand as though I could clear the air. "I'd like to see it again."

"You won't recognize it. I finished the restoration we started."

We'd bought a Victorian townhouse ten years ago, when prices in Georgetown were lower. I loved the high ceilings and spacious rooms with strong natural light throughout. Alex had completed some of the work himself, and he brought in a crew to finish. I felt nervous walking up to the house, but once inside, I recovered quickly. To be honest, it had been borderline dumpy when I lived there, and I wondered why Alex hadn't had the work done then. Of course, I could have shared that responsibility, but we were both busy with work. Always work.

We went upstairs to his office and made copies of the tattoo and the two notes. While they were slowly spitting out, Alex started kissing my neck. That used to work, but that evening, all I could think of was finding him in the next room with his editor. I told him that, and the effect was like watching a flower wilt in the heat, or some such thing.

"Okay, but why not stay here—in the guest room?" he asked, dejected.

"I think that might hurt worse than leaving." I suddenly felt so damned sad. He nodded and called a cab.

"What are you doing tomorrow? Didn't you say your train doesn't leave till six o'clock?"

"I'm going to take trip down memory lane. I plan to catch my favorite bus, the 42, and go down to the Mall. The National Gallery has a Matisse exhibit I want to see."

"I don't suppose you want any company?"

"Another time. I really have enjoyed my visit, our evening together."

The next day at the National Gallery of Art, I explored the galleries like a pilgrim touring Lourdes. The Matisse exhibit was everything I'd hoped, and I spent time in the permanent collection, as well. I treated myself to a late lunch in the museum's Garden Café, where I buzzed with yet-to-be-understood excitement. That happened to me every time I visited the museum, as though the creative energy from the artwork radiated throughout the marble and limestone building, whispering encouragement and inspiration to anyone who'd listen. Sitting there, breathing it in, I could feel my brain getting sharper and clearer. Of course, nature inspired me too, but something about the museum—manmade and replicable—spoke to me in a different way. I paid my bill and emptied the dregs of the teapot into my cup. As I sipped the bitter brew, I knew what I needed to do. I took one more look around the grand building and left for Union Station.

Chapter 22: Abit

Della seemed different when she got back. It was kinda hard to describe, but it was like she was both relaxed and hepped up. I didn't see her drive in—her train had some weird schedule that got her in at two o'clock in the morning. And then she still had to drive more than an hour to get home. That would either wear you out or make you crazy with the coffee fidgets, which was probably why she seemed out of sorts. By the time I got down to my chair, the lights were already on in the store, in spite of her late night. I started tapping so she'd know I was there, and sure enough, she came out.

"Howdy, Mister. I missed you."

I still wudn't used to anyone missing me. "You too," was all I could think to say. She smiled at me.

"Well, I wish we could sit around and drink coffee, but I've got to get things organized in the store today."

"Did Billie leave things a mess?"

"No," she said, laughing. She always saw right through me. "But there are some things I need to take care of. We'll have a good talk later."

About five o'clock that afternoon, she had a big powwow with Cleva, which kinda pissed me off. It didn't feel good getting mad at people I liked, but she'd promised to have a talk with *me*. Before long, though, I felt bad, because she invited me in to join her and Cleva.

They trusted me with the fact that the so-called suicide note was a forgery. I couldn't even tell Mama, which was fine by me. She'd probably have pooh-poohed it, anyways, especially if *I* told her. And the fact that the guy Della met with was a forger. I can hear Mama saying, "Imagine trusting the word of a criminal!" I thought he sounded cool.

Then we got down to business and talked about Lucy. It got kind of confusing—Cleva calling me Vester and Della calling me Mister, but ending up saying Abit half the time. You know, I didn't mind that name so much anymore. I didn't think about how it came about; it was just my name—that nobody else had!

Anyways, nobody had reported a missing daughter or girlfriend or sister to any of the cops in the area, and our stinkin' sheriff didn't give two flips about who she was. All he cared about was a quick closed file and off for a few beers at the Whippoorwill.

I told Della and Cleva what I thought—that Brower wouldn't budge, and maybe we should put a notice in some of the local papers to see if we could stir up some tips. I'd probably been watching too much TV (no *probably* about it), because when I offered them five dollars toward the ads, they both went quiet and gave me a funny look. I reckoned it was a stupid idea.

Chapter 23: Della

"Honey, what's wrong?" Cleva said, after she caught me wiping my eyes with my shop apron.

"Oh, Cleva, that boy just gets to me sometimes. He's so beautifully human. I see so much potential, but it's going to waste."

"Well, I know what you mean, but you've been a big help to him. He used to be so much more withdrawn." She patted my back and added, "What's brought this on?"

"Oh, I'm just tired, I guess. I got in so late last night. Hell, this morning. But it kills me the way people diminish him—and yet he won't let them win. I don't know if he even realizes how much spirit he's got. He just keeps at it, learning and growing, and that's a beautiful thing to see in anyone, but especially him."

"I've taught a lot of kids over the years, and I've got a good feeling about that boy. Look at that idea he came up with. He's a thinker."

"I know. That's what got to me. Imagine him offering five dollars when his savings account can't have much more in it. Yet."

"What's that mean—yet?"

"Well, it's getting to the point that I need more help in the store, and I may even revive the rolling store." That made Cleva's face light up. A lot of folks missed the old school bus that used to roam the backwoods, selling canned goods and fresh produce. Gradually, though, as they increasingly owned their own cars and could come to town whenever they needed, it became a financial liability. But I had plans.

It was almost six o'clock, so I asked Cleva to join me for a glass of wine. We opened a cold, crisp pinot gris and tucked into a couple of new cheeses. That plus a fresh ciabatta and some of her sour pickles, and we were both happier than we'd been all day.

Chapter 24: Della

"I can't do that," Gregg said. I'd given him a call to check in; we hadn't spoken since he'd brought me flowers. "I can't be just friends with you, not the way you want."

"But we've been friends that way for a year now," I said, stunned by his sharp tone and over-the-top anger. I was truly sorry to have to tell him I didn't want any romantic entanglements, but after his reaction, I was relieved I had. Just to end the conversation with a modicum of civility, I added, "You know, I wouldn't have gotten through The Day without you."

"I'm glad I could help, but let's just leave it at that. Besides, I'm seeing someone."

"Oh. Well. Good. I hope that works out for you, Gregg." Silence. Dammit, this wasn't what I'd expected.

"Me, too. And take care, Della. I'll see you around. And I'll still shop at the store, now and again."

Well, great. *That and fifty cents would buy me a cup of coffee*, I thought, feeling the same pain of rejection he must have felt earlier.

The next morning, I got up with what felt like a hangover, even though I'd had only one glass of wine with Cleva. That call with Gregg lingered like an unwelcomed guest, and I hadn't slept well. My upcoming—and dreaded—trip to Brower's office didn't help either.

When I got there, Brower was on the phone. Lonnie said it was something to do with county business. I stifled a laugh when he used air quotes on "county business."

"I'll just wait, if you don't think he'll be too much longer," I said, easing into the ladderback chairs in the small office.

"Hard to say with the sheriff," Lonnie said, making a face that told me more than he felt comfortable saying out loud. Lonnie had hoped for the sheriff's position himself. He'd spent a decade or more as deputy and expected to move up when Sheriff Cunningham died from a heart attack while changing a flat tire a couple of years ago.

"I wish I had more to offer you, but the coffee is old and worse than usual. How about a glass of cool spring water?"

"Thanks, Lonnie. How's your mother doing?"

"Just fine, though this hot spell's made it too hot to bake."

I chuckled. "I wasn't hinting. Honest."

We sat silently for a good while, which meant we could hear the heated conversation rumbling behind Brower's closed door. Lonnie kept his head down, working on a report while I picked at my nails. Bad habits die hard. I practically had to sit on my hands to stop the obsession. I looked around for something to distract me, and a photo of President Ronald Reagan did the trick. I fanaticized about moving it inside one of the jail cells and watching Brower fume when he discovered it there. But I chose instead to sit on my hands.

The ladderback chairs were remarkably comfortable, handmade by Bobby Mason, whose family had been crafting furniture since Daniel Boone lived nearby. They took the time to carve the back of the chairs to conform to the human back, instead of making their slats from flat wood. Good thing these chairs were already in the office when Brower took over. With his rigid posture—and thinking—he'd never have appreciated such thoughtful detail and would have ordered standard-issue metal chairs.

Lonnie was stuck with a small desk chair, his girth spilling over the seat and straining the springs. He couldn't have been more different from Brower, and I thought about how uncomfortable it must be for them to work together in such a small office. I'd seen that happen so many times—life bringing people together with an opposite to make them both whole. Worth it in the long run, but hell to pay getting there.

The door banged open and Brower dropped a couple of pounds of reports on Lonnie's desk. His face was flushed, and I wondered what that phone call had been about. Brower glared at me. "What do you want?"

"I want to show you something."

"Okay, show me."

I fumbled for the file in my backpack. *Goddammit, you are one lousy elected official*, I thought to myself. *Don't you show respect to anyone?* I flashed on Kitt and hoped she'd just given him the boot.

"I know you're busy. I won't take long," I said, holding out the notes. "It's about the two notes written by the dead woman, Lucy—her so-called suicide note and the thank-you note to Cleva Hall. The handwriting doesn't match. I had an expert in Washington check it for me, and he assures me the same person didn't write both notes."

"Oh, great. Thank you, Nancy Drew. And here are some things I'd like you to PAY ATTENTION TO," he shouted. Using his fingers to tick off his edicts, he continued, "First, what do you mean *so-called* suicide note? It was deemed a suicide by people way more knowledgeable than you. The tox screen showed hemlock, for Christ's sake. She meant business. And we found a book on wild edibles—and not-so-edible plants like, oh, let's me see, HEMLOCK, in her pack. Two, who authorized you to go running back to D.C., that hellhole of *so-called* experts who anyone can pay off for whatever they want? Three, we don't need you playing detective around here. Stick to your cheeses and cookies, okay? And finally, and I do mean *finally*, THE CASE IS CLOSED. That's it. Fini. Complete. Finished. Done."

"Please," I added before he could shout again, "just take a look at the notes."

"I've already seen them," he said, grabbing the notes but not looking at them. "So who's your expert? Somebody at the FBI?" Brower used the notes to brush a speck of dust from Lonnie's clean desk.

"An expert I know who works with the Treasury Department."

"I said, *who*?"

"Someone I worked with when I lived there. An expert on forgery."

"Good. Now we're getting somewhere. And what are his qualifications?"

"As I said, he's working for the Treasury Department, and he's worked with other agencies." Brower just stared at me, and out of nervousness, I added, "He was a very successful forger, but now he's been hired by various agencies to help them spot forgeries."

"Oh, great," he said again. "A criminal. And was he ever caught?"

I didn't answer.

"Well, was he?"

"Yes."

"Okay, so you want me to reopen a case based on the word of a convicted felon—who is so great at his job that he gets caught!"

"Just look at these notes. Please."

Brower looked down at the two notes he was holding. "I'm looking, and they appear to be written by the same hand."

"Look at the R's and the upswing at the beginning and end of the words," I explained, just as Nigel had for me.

"I'm looking, and as I just said, they were written by the same hand. How many times do I have to say it before you to get it? Hell, she was crazy with something—fear, depression, whatever—when she wrote that second note. She wasn't exactly striving for an A in penmanship."

"You don't care, do you? You just want this case off your desk. You're not even listening."

"I'm listening, all right, and I'm hearing bullshit." He leaned on Lonnie's desk, stretching his face up until it was uncomfortably close to mine. "Why. Do. You. Care. So. Much?"

I stepped back from him and said, "How. Can. You. *Not?*"

Brower flinched, but just for a moment. As I quickly packed up my things, grabbing the notes and hurrying toward the door, he growled at Lonnie, "And how the hell did she get a copy of that suicide note?" I caught a glimpse of Lonnie shrugging. As I closed the door, I heard Brower mumble, "Probably that reporter."

Chapter 25: Abit

I got a real job! I'd just said to myself that if I didn't get off of that blamed chair and get to go somewhere or do something, I'd go crazy. A little later, Della stuck her head out the door and asked me what I was doing on Wednesdays. Like she didn't know. I musta made a face, because she laughed. Then she told me she needed help fixin' up the Rollin' Store.

Man! I loved the Rollin' Store. When I was a kid, I used to climb in before it headed out and play in that tiny version of Daddy's store, more my size. And to be honest, I'd steal a candy bar or two. Daddy was never very good at running the store, so the driver didn't get in trouble when the stock was lower than the take. Besides, if someone didn't have quite enough to pay, Daddy was nice enough to let it slide, now and again.

I hated it when he parked that big bus behind the main store and let the air out of the tires. It'd been there a couple of year now, which was sad because it'd been helping people out for a long time. Daddy inherited the bus from the man who'd sold him the store. Before that, the Rollin' Store'd been in an open-bed truck, though I don't remember that one, just heard folks talk about it. Anyways, Della wanted it to help people again. As long as it broke even, she said, we were doing the community a good turn.

So me and Duane Dockery started cleaning it, and Jake—the mechanic, not the dog—worked over the engine and brought over four new tires. That reporter from the *Mountain Weekly,* Tony somebody, even stopped by and ran a story in the newspaper.

Della hired Duane to drive, which was nice since we got along good. And maybe with another job (people had to work two and three part-time jobs, just to get by), he wouldn't worry about money so much, which might make him nicer to Mary Lou. Oncet we got the bus fixed up and started rollin', we'd both have a regular job every Wednesday. Coming round midweek made sense since the farmers and folks who lived way back in the hollers usually went to town on Saturdays, so if they ran out of supplies midweek, they'd be happy to see the Rollin' Store coming down their road.

I let out a hoot when Mama said I could, which meant I had a steady job that paid me twenty-five dollars for just riding round and seeing folks (and a little time on Tuesdays to get ready). Add that to my extra money to help Della with Jake and supplies, and I needed a savings account. Mama took me to town, and we opened it together, both our names on it. That felt fine. I didn't think she'd ever clean me out and leave town. Just thinking about that made me laugh.

Funny how things worked out. After the article ran about the Rollin' Store, more people started stopping at Coburn's, too. It was getting busy enough that Della needed me more for stocking, and she could hire Billie some so she didn't keep pissing people off with those Sorry signs.

After dinner (Mama invited Duane to join us, which was fun, for a change), Duane and I were out back working on the bus when Della drove in from the sheriff's. She came round to see what we were up to, and, boy, did she look wrung out. Usually she had all kinds of energy. Oh sure, I'd seen her hopping mad and sometimes really sad, but at the moment, she seemed give out.

I asked about picking up supplies later, like she'd mentioned that morning, but she said not today. I wudn't mad at her, just disappointed. I'd been enjoying those breaks from the same old, same old. Then I heard her slamming round the store for a while, and I guessed that was better than being wrung out. I could hear her on the phone with someone, probably that Alex guy. He was a million miles away, for God's sake. I was right there.

Jake was upstairs whining, too. I was about to offer to take him for a walk out back, when she came outside. "Let's go, Abit," posting another Sorry sign on her door. "You were right—we need supplies. And I can't stand it here right now. I know it will piss, uh, make some folks mad, but we need those supplies. We should be back in thirty minutes."

I didn't want to tell her that thirty minutes might as well be three hours for folks stopping by. If they'd drove all the way over for something, they didn't want to wait. But Wednesdays were slow. They'd always been slow, as long as I'd been keeping watch (which was another reason the Rollin' Store on that day was a good idea).

I thought it was funny the way she tried not to use swear words round me—like I didn't hear all that stuff, especially if I were sitting at the store when she'd locked up early and some motorcycle guy rode up for his Pabst and Slim Jims. But I liked it when she changed them, 'cause I knew she was trying to do right by me. Daddy or Mama acted all high and mighty and got all fussy about me hearing a bad word, but that just made me *want* to use swear words.

We rode along, me riding shotgun, Jake in the middle, Della driving. I started thinking that I could really help out someday if she'd teach me to drive. Daddy wouldn't teach me—said I weren't smart enough. But the way I saw it, if Willie Westfield and Eustace Smith could drive (with a half-empty twelve-pack on the front seat and not a lick of sense between 'em), I knew I could learn to drive, too. I asked my Cousin Ned to get ahold of one of them driving rule books for me, and I hoped he'd bring it on Sunday when he came for dinner.

Della and I talked mostly about the store and the supplies we needed. I was dying to ask about Lucy and what Brower'd said, but I could tell she was trying to leave that behind, for one day, anyways. I wanted to ask her about Alex, too, but I reckoned that was none of my business. Maybe I didn't have book smarts, but I knew a thing or two.

After I loaded up the supplies, I wudn't looking forward to just turning round and heading home, but I knew Della had the store to worry about.

"How about an ice cream, Mister?"

Well, that was the best idea she'd had in a while. We stopped at the drugstore where they'd added an ice cream counter to make a little money offa tourists. Over the years, I'd heard folks talking bad about tourists and newcomers, but if they brought mint chocolate chip ice cream with them, they was fine by me. Della had a vanilla cone dipped in chocolate. Jake got to lick the bottom of both our cones and eat the crunchy bits. We sat out front of the shop and took our time. So much for the thirty-minute trip!

Seems Della wasn't dying to get back to the store either, 'cause as we headed home, she said, "We're out of honey. Let's stop at Elbert Totherow's on the way." I'd've agreed to stopping by Sheriff Brower's just to stay out. And I liked Elbert's daughter Annie, who might have been home from school at this hour. She was always pretty nice to me, not stuck up like some of the girls. And he had a little black feist that I figured Jake would like to play with.

We'd just pulled into his driveway when Elbert popped out the door and waved at us. He looked huge standing on his porch, at least three or four inches taller than me. And that porch! It went all the way round his house, and there weren't one square foot that didn't have something piled on it.

"Come on in," Elbert said with a voice that could compete against a bullhorn. "I know it looks like we're moving, but we're not. We're here to stay."

Della was chuckling when she looked at me and said, "He says that every time."

As we came up his front steps and walked past stacks of stuff, I noticed a lantern and an old metal canister Daddy'd taken to the dump just that week. I was surprised anything was left in the dump after folks combed through it, regular-like.

Ends up, Annie wudn't home from school—she'd stayed late for band practice, Elbert said—but Jake played with Muppet, the feist, and Della got a couple of cases of honey, which I loaded into the back of the truck. I hoped we wouldn't stay long—it was so damned hot inside their house. Elbert's mama, who had to be close to a hundred, sat right next to the woodstove, which was belching out heat like it were December! I know old folks get cold a lot easier, but I was sweating like a pig. Elbert asked us to stay awhile, and Della, being the nice person she was, said yes.

We made small talk what felt like forever. Before I thought I'd explode from the heat, I excused myself to use the bathroom, just to get away from the stove. As I walked down the hallway, I passed Annie's room, pink and girlie, in a nice way. I smelled something like her perfume or shampoo, and thought about how much I'd've liked to see her again.

When I got back, thank heavens Della had stood up. She told them she hated to leave, but we had to get back to the store. It still took a while, because they started gathering up jars of put-up blackberries and dilly beans and such.

Back in the truck, I rolled the windows all the way down and turned the fan as high as it would go. I wanted to hang out the window like Jake did sometimes, but I had on a new shirt, so I sat tight. Whew! That shirt was going to need a good washing.

As we were driving back to the store, I shouted: "Turn right here!" Della jumped and the truck kind of swerved, but she got it under control and did what I asked. We headed down Cane Creek Road a ways, and then Della pulled over across from the schoolyard. "How'd you know?" I asked. She just smiled and cut the engine.

I could see into the school, where the little kids had their classes, with bright pictures of dogs and suns and such on the walls. I looked hard for Annie practicing with the band. I'd hoped they were marching round the field, but I couldn't see nothin' other than the kids playing softball. I remembered some good times. Of course, some not-so-good ones, too, like mean old Bobby McKeever. And another really bad one. "When I went here, one day lightning struck the school," I said, my voice breaking a little.

"Were you hurt?" Della asked.

"I wudn't. Lilly Cunningham was. She sat next to me, and she got a funny look on her face. I leaned over to check on her, and when I held her wrist I ..." Dammit. I started to blubber. That happened five year ago, but it never got any easier to tell.

"What happened, Abit?" Della patted my back and looked so sad I really started bawling. When I got it out of my system, I told her.

"I reached over to touch her arm, and my fingers and thumb touched each other. Through her wrist. Weren't nothin' there keeping my fingers apart, just a little skin and guts." I blew my nose on the tissues Della pulled from her purse.

"Oh, honey. What a terrible thing for anyone to experience, but especially a kid."

"I was almost eleven," I said.

She gave me a hug. We sat there together for a while, then she asked, "You ready?" I nodded, though I could've sat there all day.

When I was out of the truck, Della handed me a five-dollar bill and said more was comin'. I still couldn't believe I had my own money! I used to overhear Daddy say I'd never get a job, but I'd showed him.

A few year ago, I was trying to think how to make some money, and I asked Daddy if we could sell some of them old signs he'd stashed back of the house. He had a lot of junk back there, and some good stuff mixed in. I knew I could set them out front during tourist season and sell 'em fast. I told him we could put the money in a kitty for the family, and we could all do something fun with it.

"And what kind of fun would that be?" he grunted behind his newspaper.

"I dunno. Go to a show at the Hen Theater or out to dinner oncet in a while. I've never been to that place overlooking the falls."

"You can see the falls anytime you want for free."

"I just thought we could do something together, like a real family."

Daddy lowered the paper and looked at me funny. "We'll think about it."

We never did sell them signs, but oncet I had my job helping Della, I didn't think so much about them. I'd growed tall and strong, and Della needed my help and was happy to pay for it, which helped me out. That's what I meant about acting like a family.

Chapter 26: Della

The sound of flying gravel and a slammed car door brought me to the front window. The bell on the door clanged as Cleva ran in, nearly colliding with me.

"Honey, you need to get over to Blanche's. She's got the girl's clothes. Maybe you could find something." Cleva placed her hand on her chest as she stopped to catch her breath.

"Let's sit over there, Cleva. I'm not with you yet." We sat behind the counter, near the register.

"Okay, I had to go into the laundromat early this morning to wash that big rug of mine. The one in the living room? Anyway, Blanche Scoggins came over to me while it was in the dryer, making an awful kerthump every time it went around. You know how picky she is about her machines. She's like a librarian who gets all the books nice and tidy and doesn't want anyone to check them out. So she was all out of whack because of the noise and said to me, 'You're making as much racket as that dead girl did.' She is so coarse, I can't stand her— but I couldn't stand the rug one more minute. It was so dirty that …"

"What about Lucy, Cleva? I honestly don't see how I can do anything else to help. Brower shouts down everything I bring to him. I've done all I can."

"Oh, don't stop now, please. At least take a look at her things before you give up."

I nodded as Cleva continued. "Blanche showed me a bundle wrapped in brown paper—the girl's clothes and such. I guess Lucy had a blanket that made the machine get out of balance and made that racket like mine was doing. Blanche said it was getting late, so she told Lucy to run on, she'd finish up. But Blanche told me that it was really because she didn't want 'that tramp' in her establishment. Did they ever give any reason to call her that? Tramp?"

"No, that's just Blanche. Go on."

"That was the day Lucy died, so she never picked up her laundry. Can you believe Blanche was mad about that too? She said she was out $3 on the dryer. That woman is so harsh."

"Why didn't she tell Brower she had those things?"

"I asked the same thing. She said because he was a lying SOB and because she didn't want the cops to come in and bust up her place looking for clues. She's been watching some crazy preacher on TV who has all these conspiracy theories. I'm going to have to drive to Blowing Rock next time I need to wash that thing. Or maybe I'll be a good American and throw it out and get a new one. Whatever, I'm not going back in there."

"Would she let me have those clothes? The case is closed, so I don't see how I would be obstructing Brower's case."

"I knew you'd want to have a look, so I asked her that. She said if you paid her twenty dollars for the dryer and for several days of storage—can you believe her?—she'd be happy to be shed of them."

Fortunately the laundromat was open late; I'd been taking off way too much time from the store. At six o'clock I closed up and drove to the Wash 'n' Swear—that's what someone dubbed Blanche's Wash 'n' Wear laundromat. Probably the same comedian who named the *Mountain Weakly*.

Blanche was up on a ladder installing a new sign when I walked in. I studied some of the other signs she'd tacked up over the years. Their degree of discoloration gave the chronology of her evolving frustrations. One of the earlier ones: "Keep Children Under Control" had "This Means YOU!" taped under it. Next to that: "No change for anything bigger than $10." She'd crossed through $10 and written $20—likely right after she raised the cost of each load. Other signs included "No Tie Dye," "No Sitting on Machines," "No Drying w/o Washing," "No Clothes Left Unattended." How long could it be before she tacked up the sign: "No Dirty Clothes"?

I cleared my throat, as much out of nervousness as trying to get her attention. Blanche turned and said, "Oh it's you. Give me a hand, would you?"

I walked to the ladder and could see the new sign: "No Clothes Kept Past One Week." Oh hell, were Lucy's clothes already gone?

"How can I help?" I asked.

"Just make sure this ladder don't tip, so I don't break my fool neck!" When she finished with the thumbtacks, she dusted off her hands and asked, "Okay, what do you want?"

"Cleva Hall mentioned you found clothes from the dead woman." I looked at the new sign and asked, "Do you still have them?"

"Wait one minute. I didn't *find* them. They've been here taking up valuable space for almost two months now."

More like five weeks, I thought. But I couldn't help but smile. Blanche was so ornery, she could be amusing—in small doses and if you were in the right mood. "I can imagine how annoying things can get here," I said.

Blanche looked me over for any signs of sarcasm but seemed content with what she found. "Yep, I've still got 'em. They're over there," she said, pointing to a corner near the dryer vents.

"May I take them off your hands?"

"If you pay for the dryer and the storage fee you can. Cleva thought you'd be willing to pay for them. She's a good apple, you know?"

I nodded, trying to hide my surprise at the first kind words I'd ever heard Blanche utter. "She sure is." *And she thinks you're bat-shit crazy*, I thought. "And I appreciate this. I hope to find out more about her, Lucy, that is. Brower has closed the case; he's content with Jane Doe."

"He's a sorry son of a bitch," Blanche said. "That man is useless. I had some kids in here one night, acting all weird, and I called him. You would've thought I was picking on some choirboys, just because his nephew was one of them. Those boys were up to no good, but he didn't care. Told me to get a life and be more careful when I called next time. Well, I haven't called since, including about these clothes." She crossed her arms and punctuated her statement with an exaggerated nod of her head.

"What were the boys doing?" I couldn't douse my curiosity, even though I knew I was in for more ranting.

"They were waiting on some wash—school tracksuits or something like that—and making a lot of racket. I told them to read that sign." She pointed at "No Horseplay." "That's when they started galloping around, whinnying like a bunch of fools. I was furious."

When weren't you? I thought, stifling a laugh. By the time I'd packed the clothes into the truck, my ears were ringing. It was a wonder anyone came here, but lots of people didn't have their own washers and dryers, and it was the only laundromat for miles.

I was closing the truck door when I heard, "Hold on there, missy. Aren't you forgetting something?"

I couldn't think which sign I'd violated. I'd paid up and wasn't partaking in any horseplay, at least not at the moment. "I left the money on the counter, Blanche."

She shook her head. "You didn't pay for the extra day of storage. That's three more dollar for today. You're a businesswoman; you know you've got to run a tight ship."

Chapter 27: Abit

My forehead hurt like the devil. I got a bump on it from banging into that dang front window up at the house. I was sitting on the couch after dinner, and I saw a car come cruising by—driving real slow-like. Something about the way it was creeping past the store didn't feel right. Some kind of sedan I ain't seen before. It might've even been like Alex's car. I tried to catch another look at it, and that's when I banged my head into the window. For all of that, I didn't get a good look.

Maybe I was just trying to make somethin' happen, because everything seemed to have stopped. There'd been no progress with the murder, and I needed Duane to work with me on the Rollin' Store, but he had another job he had to do for a few days. Besides, the bus needed an inspection permit before it could head out. None of the regular guys who sat with me, whittling and telling lies, was coming round, neither. They was busy with calving and gardening and such as that. So I kept rubbing my blamed forehead, the way you worry something that hurts, and wishing Della would ask me to help out somehow.

The other evenin', I saw her come home with a brown package. The next morning, she came out of the store all of a sudden with something in her hand and asked me to watch the store for a second and holler at her if someone drove up. She ran up the steps and was gone a while (no one came), and when she came back, she was carrying an old pair of jeans with stains on the knees. No way they was hers—I reckoned they were the ones she got from the laundromat looney.

I was there when Cleva came flying in to tell her about the clothes at the laundromat. I sure was glad Della didn't ask me to help her visit that place. When our washer gave out, Mama made me haul our clothes down there for a couple of weeks, along with every bedspread and rug we owned. She figured as long as we were going, we should wash everything that was too big for her regular washer. Well, that crazy woman took a dislike to me the minute I walked in. She told me not to do so many things, I just about froze. Mama told me not to pay her no mind.

I had to hand it to her—she did a smart job of folding people's raggedy old clothes, and I recognized the package Della carried in as one of hers. But I felt sad, thinking about people pawing through some dead girl's underwears for clues.

Chapter 28: Della

The store was slowing down after the initial rush on gossip and news, so I'd been able to catch up on chores and do the stocking myself. I knew Abit wanted to get back inside, but I honestly didn't need him. Inside the store, that is. While I sat at the register, I called Alex and brought him up to date about Blanche Scoggins and Lucy's laundry. I called Cleva, too, and told her what I'd found. Basically nothing.

But as I hung up, I dropped the receiver before it was set in the cradle. When I bent over to pick it up, I felt something poke me through the little watch pocket on my jeans. My earrings, the ones I'd meant to put on that morning, were sticking into me with their sharp wires. That reminded me I hadn't checked that pocket on Lucy's jeans. I'd gone over her clothes a half dozen times, but overlooked that.

I asked Abit to hold down the fort and ran up the stairs. Jake was close behind, thinking we were playing a game. Inside, I grabbed Lucy's jeans and dug deep in that little pocket. I felt something. A piece of paper? It was washed and dried in there, stuck actually, so I got some tweezers and slowly pulled it out.

I went back down the steps, Jake flying ahead of me. "Abit, how far is ESTEND, NC?" I asked, waving the piece of paper and a AAA map of North Carolina. "I can't find it on this map."

"I never heard of such a place, but maybe Daddy has. We could go ask him."

I saw the look on his face, eager to help, but not so much that he wanted to deal with his father. "No, I'll just call Cleva."

"Can I see?" Abit asked. He looked at the map's index, then ran his finger over the map. "I don't see nothin' by that name."

"I know, it's not on the map. I saw it here," I said, holding out a washed-out receipt.

Abit took the paper and studied it. "This looks like what Mama gets from the bank. But it's been through the washer."

"I found it in this little pocket," I said, pointing to my own jeans. "I think it's a bank receipt. From ESTEND."

"That's WESTEND. I can just about make out where the W used to be, before it were washed. And that's about an hour from here. My aunt and uncle and a couple of cousins live over there. I've never been, but they've been here before." He was busting with pride at solving the mystery.

"I should go and find out if they have any missing persons in Westend. I'd call, but I can't imagine they'd give out any information on the phone. It's doubtful they'll talk to me in person, but more likely than calling." I took back the receipt and headed toward the steps.

"Hey! Not fair!" Abit shouted, coming down hard with his chair and stomping his foot. That got my attention. "I solved that town for you, and I want to go, too."

"You're right, Mister. How about a road trip? Besides, we need some supplies." I managed not to smile at how surprised he looked, unaccustomed to getting his own way.

Chapter 29: Abit

Jake ran down the steps and gave me a big kiss. Like we hadn't just seen each other. I didn't want to like him at first. Well, it was really that I was *afraid* to like him. Daddy had a pack of beagles he used to hunt with: Missy, Sissy, Prissy, and Fuzzy (the only boy dog). I grew up with them dogs (and named them), and when they got old and died, I just about died right along with them. I swore I wouldn't get close to another dog, because you'd look in those big brown eyes and just knowed the pain that was waitin' down the road.

But after I thought about it, I decided it were a sin to do that. I didn't use that word very often, unlike the folks at Mama's church. They thought everything that was different was a sin. One day I told Mama I wudn't going no more because those people despised anything that was different, and I was different, so I wadn't hanging out with people like that. She looked sad, but nodded. I couldn't believe it, her giving in that easy. No telling what she'd heard people say about me behind her back—or about her, too. She gave birth to me, after all. She got enough comfort from the church to keep going, but I was glad she'd eased up on me.

I only used that word when I needed the strongest word I could think of. Not like you were going to hell or nothin', just that what I was talking about was real serious. Like about it being a sin to avoid love because

A LIFE FOR A LIFE

of the pain that surely laid ahead. Besides, I tried not to look too far into the future, because that's when I got myself in a terrible state. I tried to live one day at a time. That's what my Uncle Abe, Ned's dad, always said after one of his binges, when he was all sorry about how he'd acted.

So I figured Jake and me were friends, and I just wanted to enjoy the time we had together. When I rubbed him behind the ears and scratched down either side of his spine, his back legs went kinda limp. I wished I knew how good that felt.

"Hey, I hate to break up this little love fest," Della said to me and Jake, "but we need to get rolling. You ready? What did your father say?"

Earlier, Della had told Daddy that she'd pay me to ride along and help her whenever she needed supplies, depending on how far we had to go and how much I had to haul. He seemed surprised that anyone would pay me good money, but he'd agreed. He even said that as long as I was working on the clock, I didn't have to get his permission every time. This trip was a little longer, so I asked him, just to be on the safe side. "He told me not to get into any trouble."

"We'll try not to," Della said, raising her eyebrow the way she did when she was joking. She put up the Sorry sign again, but said she'd been able to catch Billie, and she'd come over and open back up in a little while. We piled into the truck like always—me shotgun, Jake in the middle, Della behind the wheel. She handed me a map with our route marked in yellow. "Okay, co-pilot, watch for any turns. And do you want to stop and see your cousins while we're there?"

"Uh, not really. I wudn't planning on it."

"Abit, there's no D in *was not*."

"Okay, whatever. I hate to say it, but my cousins are more than a little strange. Ned, he's the nice one, but he's from Mama's side of the family; these cousins are Daddy's."

She seemed to get it. And when I thought about it, I hadn't seen any of her relatives visitin', either.

We drove what felt like forever on that windy old road, but pretty soon I spotted the sign "Westend – A Peak Place to Live – population 4,895." The town had a pretty little square with grass and flowers and such, plus a few shops round it. We found a small police department just off the square.

Inside, a man wearing a badge looked up from his desk when we came in. I was waiting for him to snarl at us like Brower would've, but he kinda smiled and asked if he could help. The sign on his desk said he was Ralph McGurk. And I thought Vester was a stupid name! At least it didn't sound like something Jake said after his dinner.

"Well, I hope you can. I was wondering if you'd had anyone reported missing in the past month. Someone by the name of Lucy," Della told him.

"And you are …?"

"Oh, I'm sorry, I'm Della Kincaid and this is V.J. Bradshaw." You could have knocked me over with a feather! Where in the world did she come up with *that* name? "We're from Laurel Falls, where I found a dead woman." She paused when his eyebrows shot up. "Oh dear, that's some introduction, isn't it? Let me start at the beginning."

Oncet she'd told him the whole story, she asked if Brower had sent him anything about that. He explained that the state had sent out a notice, but he hadn't paid much attention, since no one was missing. Or at least no one had reported anyone missing.

"This is a small community. We know each other pretty well, and word gets around." He looked at me and asked, "Any relation to the Bradshaws here, son?" I didn't want to lie, but I didn't want to get into a family reunion either. I nodded, and he seemed to be a good people reader. He just nodded back. Must've known them the way I did.

"Well, we found this in her laundry—it was tucked inside that small watch pocket, but it was washed and dried. She died before she could retrieve her laundry."

"Yep, it looks as though she did get some cash from our local bank. Did Brower see this?"

"He's turned a blind eye to everything we've shown him. He prefers his case closed as a suicide."

"To be honest, ma'am, based on what you've told me, it does appear to be a suicide. I can't blame him for that, though the notes …" He paused, like he was thinking of something. "I honestly can't think of anyone who might know this girl. I'm sorry. One idea, though. If you've driven all this way, why not spend a few bucks on an ad in the local newspaper? You might find someone who lives farther out or who didn't realize a family member was missing. Folks go on camping trips or the like and aren't missed right away."

Della thanked him for everything, and we said our goodbyes. Oncet outside the office, she looked right and left, like she was looking for that newspaper office. "Are you hungry?" she asked.

"Always."

She laughed. "Me, too." We found a great diner where I got a big barbecue sandwich and fries and coleslaw. I needed a couple of Coca-Colas to wash it all down—that vinegary sauce caught in the back of my throat, but I loved it. Della got a bowl of Brunswick stew, which smelled pretty good. Daddy'd told me they made that with squirrel meat, but that musta been back when he was a kid. I didn't mention that to Della, though, just in case. Jake woulda loved it, but he had to settle for some of my fries. Her bowl was clean.

"Now let's go place that ad—the one you'd already thought of," she said, patting my back.

We found the newspaper office behind the drugstore. It cost just over twelve dollar to place an ad that would run for a couple of weeks. I even helped write it. And I gave Della a five-dollar bill, which she wouldn't accept. I kept at her, and she finally took it.

The ad started with thick black letters asking, "Do You Know Lucy?" The rest of it said, "If you know a woman, aged 20+, long dark hair, who went camping in Laurel Falls in April, please call." Della added her name and phone number.

Sure made me sad, thinking about somebody reading that and starting to worry real bad. Like their day was going along just fine: a cup of coffee, an easy chair, reading the paper, and then, wham! Life would never be the same. Della musta been thinkin' the same thing because she treated me to some ice cream at the drugstore counter. Butter pecan helped get me back on track.

On the way home, we were both pretty quiet. I spent some time thinking about V.J. After trying it out in my head for a while, I said, "I like it."

"You like what?"

"V.J."

"Oh, good. I think it's kind of dapper." I must've looked funny because she added, "I mean, cool." I'm pretty sure that's the first time that word had ever been used about me.

Closer to home, Della veered off at the Cash 'n' Carry, where we picked up some goods. I was happy 'cause that meant I'd get to unload them and hang out inside the store a while longer.

"This has been the best day of my life," I told Della, as I was heading up to the house. At first, she looked kinda happy, then a little sad, for some reason.

Chapter 30: Della

"Is this the person looking for Lucy?" a woman asked.

Almost a week after our trip to Westend, I picked up the phone around mid-morning. I thought Cleva was calling back after having to hang up to deal with a repairman. "Hey, Cleva. What time … uh, yes, this is Della Kincaid."

"She's my sister." Long pause before the caller continued, "She came here for a visit, then left to head down your way. Is she all right?"

Over the years, I'd been in the middle of a lot of bad news, but this was the hardest I'd faced. My throat closed up, and I couldn't speak. I swallowed a time or two and finally found my voice. "No."

We talked a while longer, and I filled her in on what I knew. When she said she wanted to come to Laurel Falls, I mentioned that Lucy's body was in Asheville. I had my wits enough by then to leave out the words *in the morgue.*

"I can go there after," she said. "I want to meet you. *You found her.* And cared enough to come here, to try to locate her family." I gave her directions to the store and hung up. Just as the phone hit the cradle, I realized I didn't know her name or when she was coming.

When a stranger walked into the store later that afternoon, we knew each other immediately. Lucy's image had been branded on my brain, so I had no trouble identifying a sister who shared her long dark hair and creamy complexion. And large brown eyes, though hers were rimmed in red.

"Della?"

"Hello—and as soon as I hung up, I realized I hadn't asked your name."

"Isabella—but I go by Izzy. Izzy Martinez, though that's my married name. Before, I was Sanchez. Lucy's last name."

"Please, have a seat by the fire." Our warm May had turned into "blackberry winter," that surprise cold-snap (though it happened every year) that came just as the blackberries were beginning to bloom. We settled in, coffee in hand, fresh banana bread refused with a sorrowful shake of her head. Neither one of us knew where to begin, so we sat in silence.

Finally, Izzy said, "Lucia was a lovely person. Our mother died a few years ago, so that left us alone to deal with our dad, Miguel Sanchez. She cared for him long after he'd given up caring for himself."

"Did she ever live in Westend?"

"No, no. My husband and I moved from Atlanta to a community about thirty minutes this side of Westend. We're trying to make a go of it with a small farm and some other things. I'm a jeweler, he's an artist," she said, sipping her coffee. "Lucia—though she preferred Lucy—stayed in Atlanta to be near our father. I begged her to come live here, surrounded by nature instead of all that filth she put up with."

I didn't want to intrude on her recollections, so I just poured myself more coffee. She put her hand over her cup and continued. "Lucia had a nice enough apartment for herself, but she kept going down to that dump where our father lived. He'd been in a mental institution on and off for years, but when funds were cut for those facilities, he was planted in one of those oatmeal factories that made people sign over their Social Security checks to the proprietor to pay for a bed and meals. No care, just food, water, and a roof."

"Why did you call it an oatmeal factory?"

"Because they served the cheapest, worst food— mostly oatmeal. A disgrace, but those facilities were his only option, at the time. He was a large man—at least the last time I saw him—six feet tall, and no way could we control him, especially when he was drunk or on goodness knows what. I couldn't take it any longer, but Lucia wanted to be able to visit him regularly. Like I said, she was a lovely person."

The tears flowed while she talked, at times turning to sobs. I didn't know if she wanted comfort from a stranger, but when I tentatively reached out, she grabbed my hand and hugged so hard I spilled my coffee on my jeans. She didn't notice, and thank heavens it was cold by then, so I didn't even flinch. After a while, she wiped her face with the backs of her hands and blew her nose. "When he died a few months ago, I asked her to come for a visit. If I hadn't invited her—no, if I hadn't *begged* her to come—she'd still be alive." She blew her nose again and didn't speak for some time.

As a reporter, I'd heard that refrain so many times—*if only I hadn't ....* But I knew my consolations wouldn't help. Only time would. I sat with her for a while and then asked, "How long was her visit with you?"

"Almost a month. We had a good time together, too. I'm at least grateful for that. She got bored after a while, though, and started looking for things to do. Not much going on, and that's how she got involved with that hateful Green Treatise. My husband, Javier, went one time to their meetup, and he took Lucia with him—but only the one time. He came home telling me how weird the members were—all tattooed up, grassed up, messed up.

"Lucia, though—she came home wired. Something really got to her about the group. But what did she know about their issues, living in a studio apartment in Atlanta? She went back a couple more times, borrowing my husband's truck. The last time, she came home and told us she had to come down here. We drove her down to a campground, and that's the last I saw her."

"What's your take on the Green Treatise? Any idea why she got hooked?"

"None. The whole way down today, I kept trying to figure out why she kept going to those crazy meetings. You can imagine what they're like. Lots of guys with motorcycles, bandanas, weed, and a grudge against the world. Not her type of guy at all. As for their philosophy, Javier said they just spewed a lot of hate about the wilderness being taken over by the government. What we see as land protection, they saw as theft. But again, not the kind of folks Lucia would want to hang out with—unless her experience with the government turning its back on our father turned her head."

We talked a while longer, then Izzy said she'd like to shop a little in the store before dealing with Lucy's identification. "Chorizo!" she called over her shoulder, a wan smile briefly easing her grief. "And marcona almonds! I miss some of these foods living on the farm, but not enough to move away." When she came to the register, I refused payment, which caused a good-natured standoff, for a while. It seemed like the least I could do.

"But you're doing so much to find out what happened to Lucia. That's so much more than the sheriff you described. Please let me pay."

I told her I just couldn't—this time—but I hoped she'd come back, and I'd let her pay then. She nodded and picked up her bag of groceries. I walked her to her car and gave her directions to the sheriff's office.

It was suppertime, and Abit was home, tucking into a meal that was undoubtedly a lot better than the one I was about to make. I was relieved that I didn't have to explain who Izzy was—though I wondered if much got past that big window in the front of their house. I thought I saw the curtains twitch as Izzy drove off. I walked back to the store to get Jake, wondering how—or if—that damned Green Treatise figured into her sister's death.

Chapter 31: Della

"I couldn't sleep."

"So you wanted to make sure I couldn't either?" Alex asked.

"No, I wanted to get your help." To be honest, I didn't mind waking him so I'd have someone to talk to. I'd been wide awake most of the night, worrying about Lucy and Izzy and that damned militia. I wanted to know everything about them, and I'd either have to wait until Sunday to head down to Asheville to scroll through the library's microfiche—or I could get Mr. LexisNexis to do it for me.

I didn't have a fax machine, and his report would be too confidential for the one at the drugstore. In the night, I'd remembered that the only lawyer in town, Marjorie McCrumb, owed me a favor. She was the customer who'd begged me to carry those baked goods from Asheville. I had to do a lot of haggling to get them to deliver once a week, and when I succeeded, she told me if I ever needed a favor, to give her a call. Then she added, "Besides legal representation, that is. You're on the clock with that." So all those scones she'd been stuffing her face with seemed worth a fax or two. I gave Alex her number and planned to alert her once I got off the phone—and the sun came up.

"I'll see what I can find," he said. I could hear the coffee grinder in the background. "So you want me to look up this militia in Timbuktu, right? I'm sure that homegrown group of idiots won't even make a blip on the screen. Same goes for Lucia and Miguel Sanchez."

"Hey, don't take out your anger with me on them. Though I'm sure you're right about those guys. Like the ones who came to the funeral and looked so out of place in the church? I can't imagine this militia is more than a bad-boy club in the woods."

I heard his coffee machine start to gurgle, and he mumbled something and hung up. I didn't dare go back to sleep since the store opened in a couple of hours. I made some coffee, sat in my Barcalounger, and read the arts section of last Sunday's paper. Next thing I knew, a horn was honking downstairs—and Jake was barking upstairs. I'd drifted off to sleep, and when I checked my watch, it was just after eight o'clock. I ran a comb through my hair, kissed Jake, and promised I'd be back to fix his breakfast.

The rest of the day, I felt jangled. I actually nodded off at the register around eleven o'clock, but the phone woke me. All I heard was whistling on the other end.

"Who is this?" I asked.

"Me."

Groggy from my short nap, I asked again, "Who?"

"Come on, Della, it's me. Alex. Did I wake you?" He seemed amused, enjoying tit for tat.

"What was that sound you made?"

"I was trying to do that whistle people do when they've found something important. I should have wet my whistle before trying."

"Next time. So what's up?" I patted Jake, who'd been sleeping at my feet.

"Too hot to tell you over the phone. You need to get up here so I can tell you in person."

"Not going to happen. I've got a store to run. And that's a six-hour drive I don't want to make. I'll just wait till Sunday and go to Asheville and do some research of my own." I heard a click. "Hello? Hello?" He'd hung up.

Chapter 32: Abit

Earlier that morning, Della came running round the corner and stuck her key in the front door. She looked like she'd tangled with a bobcat—until she smiled at me and looked as good as ever. Not sure Roger Turpin agreed. He'd been honking since eight o'clock. Roger gave me the creeps with his bandana over his head like a pirate and all them tattoos. I mean, tattoos looked kinda cool, but on him, they were scary.

As they went inside the store, Della nodded while Roger grumbled something; in a few minutes, he was back out the door with a brown sack. Good riddance. Before long, Della came out with a cup of coffee for me—just the way I like it with cream and two sugars. I didn't even try to hide it from Mama anymore. I was nearabout 16 year old, after all. If they wanted to worry about me acting like a man in other ways, well, then I was old enough to drink coffee.

"Roger sure was in a rush this morning," Della said, sitting down on the bench next to Wilkie Cartwright, who was whittling the prettiest little lamb out of holly wood (and never seemed to drink coffee, or she'd've brought him some, too). I didn't say anything about Roger because he was there at opening time. Della musta read my mind, because she chuckled and said, "Okay, it *was* opening time, but he raced in in such a bad mood.

And bought a six-pack. At eight o'clock in the morning?"

"You know what they say—from mother's milk to Coca-Cola to beer, that's how men round here growed up," I said. Wilkie sort of grunted, which was about all he ever did.

"If they ever do grow up," Della added.

That kinda stung. I hated being lumped in with guys like Roger and his pals. But I wasn't about to complain to my new boss. Besides, I liked to think she didn't mean me.

I'd started worrying about when the Rollin' Store was finally gonna to start rollin'. I got my answer when Duane drove up in his pickup and parked round back.

"What's up for today, Duane?" I asked as I walked toward the bus.

"Painting. That school bus is bigger than it looks. And it needs a good cleaning inside. You up for that?" When I nodded, he took out a coin and flipped it. "Heads or tails?"

"What for?"

"Whose gonna paint and whose gonna clean. I know neither one of us wants to clean, so …"

"Tails!"

He looked at the coin. "Shit. You win. The brush and paint are in my truck bed. Run a damp towel over the bus first, though. We scrubbed it good yesterday, but we need to get off anything that fell overnight. Good thing the sun came out for a while."

That was how we spent the better part of the day, working close by but not getting in each other's way. I told Mama not to count on me for dinner, since I'd be working all day with Duane. Della brought us sandwiches from stuff in the store, and I wasn't sure what everything was—no yellow mustard and meat between white bread like Mama made sometimes for supper—but it sure tasted good. Duane washed his down with a beer; I had a Coca-Cola. We started laughing when we were eating and looking at each other—we figured we both looked a sight with paint and dirt and cobwebs all over us.

Chapter 33: Della

Alex hadn't called back after hanging up on me. I tried calling him, but I kept getting his answering machine. That was so like him, and I was mad at myself for falling for his bullshit again. I trusted him to help out, but I could see that wasn't going to happen. I'd have to spend my Sunday down in Asheville finding out what I could on my own.

Things had never been easy with Alex. With enough distance, I finally could see how my hang-ups tweaked his hang-ups, and vice-versa. Since my parents' crazy relationship had been scarred by drunken fights, I tried a different tack: give in and give up to keep the peace. But that wasn't love, just reactive thinking and conditioning. After he won his Pulitzer, things got worse. He started staying out late, holding court in restaurants and bars, as though he'd found the Holy Grail. And then he lost it. It wasn't so much plagiarism as sloppy work habits, but the P-word in a newsroom carried a stink too nasty to ignore. He lost his prestigious role at the *Post*, and joined my ranks as a freelancer.

Both of us working at home proved disastrous. He started staying out even more, and later I learned, in a most uncomfortable way, that he was sharing more than his keen mind with a bevy of infatuated women. That was when I moved out and into a condo not far from my office.

At closing time, Jake and I trudged up the steps, both dog tired. (I wasn't sure why he was dragging; he'd slept all day.) When I opened my apartment door, the answering machine was blinking. Cleva had left a message, inviting us over for dinner. Good timing. Even with a store full of food, I couldn't for the life of me figure out what to fix for dinner. Jake heard Cleva's voice and started running around, then standing by the door. What a dog.

We enjoyed our evening together, talking about men, spring flowers, and dogs. (Jake put on quite on a show with one of his oversized Milk Bones.) The wisteria framing her front porch intoxicated us more than the sherry we sipped. When I returned home around eleven o'clock, I slept deeply in a starch-induced fog from her amazing macaroni and cheese, topped with thin, cheese-filled pinwheels of biscuit dough.

On Saturday, I worked in the store during the morning, and then got ready to go to Asheville. I'd changed my plans and decided to go then rather than Sunday. I couldn't spend my only day off inside a cavernous building, no matter how much I loved libraries. Billie agreed to keep the store for half a day, and she was already inside, waiting on a couple of customers.

I gave Jake a good run in the back and checked with Abit about supervising another one at the end of the day, since I'd be late getting back. He and Duane were putting the final coat of paint on the rolling store, so they just waved and told me to have fun. Yeah, right.

Jake and I went back upstairs, and I came down again with a cooler for the truck. (I never knew where I'd find something I wanted to sample for the store.) As I secured it in the bed of the truck, I heard a distinctive rattle behind me. The car pulled up next to me, the driver's window rolled down. "What in the world are you doing here?" I asked through the open window.

"Well, you wouldn't come to D.C., so I thought I'd take another trip south," Alex said, looking penitent enough for me to offer a small smile.

"That's pretty fast research, fella. You didn't cut any corners did you?" I regretted my comment the minute I saw his face. "I'm sorry—I just meant we'd talked only a couple of days ago."

"I told you I'd already done the research. I worked on it earlier this week for you."

"You could've faxed the information, you know," I said, as we headed up the steps. Jake could hear us coming and was wildly scratching at the door.

"And have Checkpoint Charlie and everyone in the county know what I found?"

"I'd hardly call Marjorie McCrumb Checkpoint Charlie," I said, but I dropped it after that. He'd never met her, and it wasn't worth arguing about. Besides, I was glad he'd brought it. I didn't have to drive to Asheville, after all.

From the landing at my apartment door, Alex shouted hello down to Abit and Duane in the backyard, waving at them like the pope at the Vatican. They both responded as though he were, indeed, some visiting dignitary. When we went inside, it was Jake's turn to fawn. Once all the pomp and circumstance of his arrival calmed down, I sighed and said, "Okay, show me what you found."

"Coffee first, please." I poured him his usual—black, easy to remember—and put out some croissants and cheese and Cleva's apple chutney on the dining table. Alex tucked into his late lunch, and I cleared my own lunch dishes and chatted while he finished. Just when I was about to sit back down, we heard a knock on my apartment door. Jake was barking like crazy, so I grabbed him by his collar and shouted through the door, "Who is it?"

"Hello, Della? It's me, Kitt."

I opened the door, and before I could say anything, Alex stood up, brushing crumbs from his cashmere pullover. "Oh, hello, I'm Alex Covington," sticking out his hand. I wondered if she'd give him her special handshake.

"Oh, sorry, I didn't mean to interrupt," she said, overlooking me and smiling at Alex, as she gave him a plain Miss Manner's handshake.

"Oh, you weren't interrupting," he said.

"I'm Kitt Scanlon. Very nice to meet you." *I bet*, I thought. *Ms. Long-blonde-hair-and-black-leather-boots meet Mr. Wavy-hair-graying-at-the-temples-and-Gucci-loafers.*

"What's up, Kitt?" I asked, breaking up their banter.

"Well, I'm going to have to cancel our wine and cheese tonight. Something important has come up."

Oh, and I'm not important, I thought, but then I realized I'd forgotten our arrangements for tonight, which I would've missed if I'd gone to Asheville. "Well, another time," I said magnanimously. "They both improve with age, unlike us humans."

She looked confused. "Wine and cheese?" I explained.

"Oh, right. Well, I'll let you two get back to your, uh, time together." She glanced at Alex and added, "Bye-bye. Hope we meet again."

"Same here," he said with a stupid grin on his face.

Everyone was smiling and nodding as I closed the door. "Well, ta-ta for now. I hope we meet again," I mimicked once I'd locked the door.

"Hey, I didn't realize you had green eyes."

"They're not green with envy; they're brown from bullshit."

"I didn't know you cared." Alex smiled, his face so irritatingly smug I almost forgot I was a pacifist.

"I don't," was the best I could muster. To cover my pathetic comeback, I opened the door again, and started swinging it back and forth. "The pheromones are a bit thick in here. Now where were we?" Alex was laughing at me, and pretty soon, I had to laugh at me, too. I closed the door and sat next to him, eager to hear his news.

Chapter 34: Della

Alex handed me the report he'd pulled together from a variety of news stories and government documents. As I read, I noticed a few names that looked familiar. Roger Turpin, the guy who started my day off wrong earlier in the week, and his buddy Wayne Burnett. They'd been at the funeral, and they were both in the Green Treatise.

"What's their raison d'etre? I mean, do they have a cause besides drinking and wreaking havoc in the woods?" I asked.

"The answer is in my report, but I'll give you the Cliff Notes version. They hate everything government—or at least they hate the government when it stops them from doing what they want to do. I doubt they mind it when they collect unemployment or granny gets her Social Security and Medicare—or when their kids get to go to public school and are eligible for Medicaid or food stamps for the family. Or even paved roads and fire engines, and ..."

Alex was on his soapbox, which I didn't blame him for. I agreed—but I didn't want to hear it all over again. "Anything more serious than ignorance?" I interrupted.

"This particular militia doesn't seem to have the organized guerilla training camps some of their brethren have—yet. So far, they're using local firing ranges and a place in the wilderness where they congregate."

"Did you find anything about a club tattoo?"

"Della, this isn't a bad-boy's club, as you called it earlier. You need to grasp how crazy and dangerous these guys can be. But no, I couldn't find any Green Treatise tattoo. I wouldn't be surprised if the tattoos are just something a few of them did together, probably after too many Pabst Blue Ribbons. But you need to think about them like the dangerous sons of bitches they are."

I thought about what Izzy had shared about Lucy and couldn't imagine why she was attracted to that group or why she went back after the first visit. I told Alex about her sudden interest.

"Well, maybe she was into rugged men. Stranger reasons for doing things."

I shook my head. That just didn't fit. And Izzy felt certain that the group didn't include the kind of men Lucy would hang out with. But obviously something grabbed her attention.

Alex broke into my musings. "Let's attend their next meeting. Tonight."

"Let's? Just like that? We all pile in the Merc for a good time at the Green Treatise hootenanny?" He just looked at me, self-satisfied, as though my questions weren't worthy of an answer. I said, "I'm not going with the likes of you. We'd stand out like, well, a Mercedes in Laurel Falls."

"Okay, get that friend of yours—Cleeta or Clinga—what's her name? Cleva. Get her to go with you. I'll stay in the car as backup. So you two women aren't alone in the wilderness."

I wanted to make a smart retort, but he was right. If Cleva and I decided to go, I didn't want to venture out alone and jeopardize the life of an almost septuagenarian. And Jake was definitely staying home. He'd be useless, barking and giving us away—or wagging and carrying on with all the men. And women, I suppose. I felt a frisson of both excitement and fear ripple through me.

Cleva whispered names as the members of the Green Treatise streamed in, clucking her disapproval as she identified her nephew among them. Alex had plotted exactly when and where the Green Treatise met, including a map with coordinates. I didn't know how Alex found all his sources—it took a lot more than plugging into LexisNexis—but then that's how he'd won his awards. I wished he were with us and not back in the truck (which we'd decided to take instead of his car), tucked behind a thicket of tall rhododendrons.

Cleva and I found a good hiding spot on the ridge above their gathering place. I couldn't get comfortable, and neither, apparently, could my stomach. Around six o'clock, just as I closed the store, Cleva showed up with a picnic supper: fried chicken, potato salad, and pecan pie. We'd had a warm, sunny day, so we sat around the picnic table on the side of the store, under the gentle shade of two willow trees that some patient soul planted a couple of decades ago. The food tasted great at the time, but as I watched the evening unfold, I started to feel seriously sick.

Next came Roger Turpin, pulling up in his pickup with Wayne Burnett riding shotgun. They scrambled to get some boxes out of the back of the truck. About twenty men and four women were milling around a crackling campfire, the spew of pop tops syncopated with chirrups of crickets. I had to admit I was surprised to see women who had spoken kindly to me at the store, thanking me for ordering their favorite bread or buying from local farmers. At first, I thought their presence at the gathering represented loyalty to their men, but that didn't seem to be the case. They picked up rifles and automatic weapons and pointed them with deftness that spoke of practice. One woman aimed a rifle near where we sat, though in the dim light, I knew she couldn't see us. She was just admiring the precision of the gun's sight.

"Good Lord," Cleva said softly, patting my hand. "That's Dexter and Geneva Skinner. And Butch Soderquist and Erlene Patterson. What's this world coming to?"

My stomach grumbled again when Madras Man got out of a brownish pickup, its original color competing with rust and Bondo. He carried a boom box, which he set on a flat tree stump near the center of a circle of folding chairs and logs positioned around the fire. With a touch of a button, music blared. Waylon Jennings sang "Mamas, Don't Let Your Babies Grow Up to be Cowboys" and The Highwaymen harmonized on

"Desperados Waiting for a Train." Cleva had gone quiet—eating a biscuit she'd tucked into her pocket like a squirrel, nervously gnawing at its edges. "I don't know that fella," she whispered.

"That's the guy who was running away from Lucy's body." He didn't have on his Madras shirt, and I couldn't see his tattoos, even though he'd partially rolled up the sleeves of his plaid flannel shirt (standard issue for wilderness men). But I'd never forget his face.

Another car came speeding down the road, spewing gravel in its wake. A woman got out. "Ain't that the girl from the new art gallery?" Cleva asked, reverting to her mountain roots as she watched the strange scene below.

"What the hell? What in the world is Kitt Scanlon doing here?"

They turned off the boom box, and Turpin ordered everyone to take their seats. The meeting was about to begin. We weren't close enough to catch everything, but sometimes they shouted loud enough for us to hear: "Goddam gov'ment," "Open OUR roads," or "Don't tread on US!" All their fists shot in the air to punctuate their hate-filled slogans.

"This gives me the flibbertigibbets!" Cleva said.

I hugged her and whispered, "I moved here to get away from so much vitriol. I didn't know I'd be in the midst of it again, on an even scarier level. I don't know how much more of this I can take." My stomach grumbled its agreement.

They turned on the boom box again and played a canned speech by Grissom Wells, a militia bigshot, I assumed. The volume was way up, so we could hear, and his speech scared the bejesus out of us both. He was basically granting listeners myriad justifications for their baser desires. We looked at each other and mouthed the words, *Let's get out of here.*

As we made our way back to the truck as quietly as possible, a man approached us, and we both jumped. It was just Alex, but the fright he gave me was all my stomach could take. I threw up dangerously close to his new Fabiano hiking boots.

"Oh, honey, I hope something I made for supper didn't make you sick," Cleva said, handing me some tissues from her bag.

I wiped my mouth and moved away from the mess. "No, Cleva, it was all that hate I couldn't stomach. And the fact that we're spending such a beautiful evening immersed in it."

Alex shepherded us back to the truck, where he ran the heater on high to ease our chills—at least the ones on the outside. We rode home in silence. When we pulled up next to Cleva's car, we said our goodbyes and promised to talk more in a day or two.

I slept poorly, unable to shake off the Green Treatise experience. I'd covered a Ku Klux Klan rally back in the seventies, and the Green Treatise triggered flashbacks. Witnessing evil emanate from under a sheet—or a canopy of trees—could keep a narcoleptic awake. And something we'd seen didn't quite fit. I lay there with an uneasy feeling, straining to figure out what was bothering me. I finally gave up.

When I did sleep, I had a long, involved dream with a lot of fighting. It seemed like World War I, with people shooting at each other from trenches. I was glad when I awoke around four o'clock. My mouth was parched, so went to the kitchen for a glass of water. I found Alex awake and reading, Jake sacked out next to him. I hadn't even noticed Jake had abandoned me. I told myself that was because I was thrashing about and had nothing to do with his wanting to be with Alex. We talked for a while, and I loved on Jake. They eased my mind enough that when I headed back to bed, I finally slept peacefully.

I had to admit I appreciated having Alex around, sharing ideas and getting to take advantage of his sharp mind. And maybe more than that. Though he'd spent his nights on the couch, I felt closer to him than that last year we shared in the same house. On Sunday, we'd put his designer hiking boots to real use on some of the trails surrounding the falls. I enjoyed watching him get excited about spotting a thicket of flame azalea or a belted kingfisher diving for its dinner.

But by Monday morning, he was ready to get back to the city. We had a quick breakfast and headed downstairs. Abit was already in his chair. I said good morning and opened the front door. Alex sat on one of the benches.

"Great to see you again, V.J.," Alex said, sticking out his hand to shake. Abit looked pissed off at first, but his good nature won out. He smiled and shook Alex's hand. They chatted a while, though I was certain Abit was more than ready for Alex to leave so things would go back to normal. If only they had.

Chapter 35: Abit

I was glad when Alex finally left. He was nicer than I'd thought, but still, they'd been awfully busy, and Della hadn't been round to talk to. She came out and sat with me later that day, telling me all about the militia stuff Alex'd discovered. Man, I knew I didn't like those guys, but they sounded worse than I'd imagined. I got it that they despised all the rules about what they could and couldn't do on the land where they'd growed up, but, to me, it was like any place with more than one person in it. You needed some rules or else nobody knew which end was up.

While she and Alex had been traipsing round together, Duane and I finished up the Rollin' Store. Duane painted the inside and then helped me put the final coat on the outside. It was light blue, a real pretty color that would make folks notice as we rolled down country roads. Duane musta had artists in his family tree, because he added some flowers on vines on the sides of the bus. Della clapped her hands together when she saw it.

We had to flip another coin, that time about the name—we knew people would trust us more if it said Coburn's Rollin' Store, but dammit, it was Della's store. So Duane painted Coburn's Country Store and then painted "Della's" above it. (Nobody much knew her last name, anyways.) Best of both worlds, he called it. She agreed.

Daddy had disconnected the STOP sign that stuck out from the bus when it stopped and the doors opened. Duane thought it would be a good idea to reconnect it. I did too, especially after I painted over the top of the T and made it an H, so it read SHOP. Della yelped when she saw it, like them Beagle pups used to do.

Duane fixed up the shelves in the bus for fruits and vegetables, paper towels, toilet paper, Band-Aids, matches, stuff like that. And Della bought us a big cooler for the cold stuff—milk, butter, eggs, bacon, ham, and such. We planned to hit the ice factory first thing. Lots of folks had their own milk or eggs, or bought from neighbors, but others, especially them hippies who started making their homes back in the woods, still needed to buy theirs.

Just as we were finishing up, Della added a big box of things that weren't selling—both fresh and in cans—and let me decide who to give 'em to, just to be neighborly. And to help them love the store again, like we already did. Some folks still held it against Daddy for stopping the Rollin' Store, but he couldn't help it. They didn't buy enough to keep it rollin'. People were peculiar that way. They didn't always get it that what they did led to what somebody else did.

I was beside myself when Duane pulled the bus out of the driveway, me riding shotgun. It felt like I was on the trip of a lifetime. We'd be on the road till two o'clock—the longest I'd been away from our patch in three year.

Della came out and waved at us like we was heroes or something. Mama and Daddy even stepped outside to see us off. I rolled down my window and let the air blow my hair. Man, it felt good. Duane was chuckling at me, and he looked pretty darned happy. I couldn't help but hope that would last, and it'd keep his fists from forming back at home.

And what a day we had. Folks came out, even if they didn't need nothin'. One feller said, "I ain't saw you lately," like he'd somehow missed us, instead of the bus being parked for two year. Everyone took a tour of the inside and young'uns were climbing all over the bus. One mama shouted at her kid to take care and not scratch the beautiful flowers on the side. I was proud they'd noticed Duane's handiwork. And I felt like Santa Claus giving out the old groceries—you'd've thought they were bags of money the way people looked at them and smiled.

Chapter 36: Della

"Hello. Hello? Anyone there?" Dead air.

I didn't think much about a call like that. Lots of folks around there just hung up if the person answering didn't sound like the one they wanted. Efficient, if not particularly neighborly.

That evening, I wished I hadn't been so pigheaded about not getting cable. I turned and twisted the foil-draped rabbit ears, hoping something would make a difference. It didn't. The steep mountains guaranteed varying degrees of television snow. But I couldn't justify the cost of cable, given I was still working hard to make the store turn a profit.

I wasn't one of those anti-television fanatics who made everyone feel guilty for seeking a little entertainment. Television had a lot of potential for sharing ideas and creativity. Okay, that potential hadn't panned out—yet. But so what? At that moment, I was seeking only a nice, vacuous blur. I hated to admit it, but I was feeling lonely.

Jake had just curled up next to me on the couch when the phone rang again. And again. A hang-up each time. By the fourth call, I started to feel uneasy. I'd had my share of menacing phone calls over my career, and these felt similarly creepy.

"Hello," I said. Dead air again. "Come on, pal. Either say something or quit calling."

"Get out of our lives, bitch."

"Who is this?" was all I could think to ask.

"None of your goddam business."

"Well, then how can I get out of your lives?"

"Move. Go away. Stop what you're doing, if you know what's good for you. Go back where you came from," he spat out before hanging up. At least I think it was a man. Sounded like something—a tobacco-stained red bandana popped into my mind—covered the receiver.

I couldn't imagine the caller was referring to Duane and Abit's successful first day with the rolling store. Even Brower's father with his SuperMart wouldn't care about that. And I'd lived in Laurel Falls too long to have the unwelcome wagon calling. Sure, early on, I experienced some animosity from those who resented a newcomer taking over "their" store, but that edge had worn off. At least I thought it had.

I checked the locks on the doors and sat next to Jake. "Keep me safe, okay, Jakey Boy?" He looked me in the eyes, licked my face, and curled up again in the nest he'd made on the couch. I gave up on the TV and decided to turn in, as well.

As I lay in bed, I wondered what the caller hoped to accomplish. Was I going to stop looking into Lucy's death just because some jerk cursed and threatened me? Move away? The amateur nature of the demands eased my fears. Just crazy thinking, I told myself.

But night demons began dismantling my newfound confidence, reminding me of the time I was cornered in the Dupont Circle Metro station by an irate interviewee. When he grabbed me, a Vietnam vet nearby literally picked the guy up and carried him to the tracks. I learned later that the vet had held him over the third rail until I could escape the station. On other occasions, I'd had to defend myself with mace or self-defense techniques.

Turned out, these memories actually had a fortifying effect on me. A few phone calls, I told myself, weren't going to stop me. Finally, I drifted off to sleep, and the phone remained mercifully quiet.

Until the next night. And the next. I tried to imagine who was making these calls. I called Alex.

"It's bound to be one of those yahoos from the Green Treatise. Maybe someone spotted you, or was aware of your inquiries," he said. "Get that idiot sheriff involved; he speaks their language."

"That sounds worse than receiving the calls. Besides, he'll just deride my concerns."

"Okay, hon. You're probably right. I just don't know what you see in that place. It's time to come on home."

"I *am* home, Alex. Besides, you make D.C. sound like Disneyland. I had plenty of troubles there, too." I didn't remind him that many of them were *inside our home.*

"Okay, but what did you expect? That they'd welcome your inquiries into their testosterone treatise?

Or that the murderer wouldn't mind your solving this case?"

"I underestimated how fast news spreads here. I worked under the radar in D.C., but here there's no such thing." It had finally struck me what I'd gotten myself into. I felt like locking the store and running away.

"Hey, I know you. You couldn't *not* help someone, or her family. You *had* to do this. Just be careful. These folks may be more dangerous than the Armani-suited snakes in D.C."

"Well, at least there are less of them here."

"Fewer."

"Oh, shut up. I'm not in the mood for your wordsmithing. Do you ever take a break from AP Style?"

"Not hardly, to quote Abit."

"Leave him out of it."

"Okay, we're getting on each other nerves. Gotta go."

"Me, too." When we said goodbye, we both sounded sad.

Chapter 37: Della

The following Tuesday, I was working in the back of the store when the bell over the door jingled. I came out front but couldn't see anyone. As I headed over to check the cash register, a deep voice made me jump. Tattoo Man was standing behind a tall display in the canned goods aisle. He was still clean-shaven, but his hair had grown out since the funeral.

"Have you been calling me and threatening me?" I barked at him, surprising myself as much as him. He winced and waved his hand in that universal motion meaning "no way."

"No ma'am. I'm not here about that." Did he even know what I was talking about? I couldn't tell. He looked over his shoulder and asked if we could go in the back.

"What for? I like it right here, out front."

"Yeah, but I don't." I tried to outwait him, but he won. As we settled into folding chairs in the back, I asked him what he wanted.

"Look, I didn't kill that girl," he said in a hushed tone, as though he was afraid of being overheard. Or that my store was bugged. Conspiracy theories did that to people. He looked over his shoulder and asked, "That retard outside? He seen me come in. Will he talk like everybody else in this town?"

"Start over, pal. Abit is my friend, and he's no retard. I'm more concerned about *his* safety than yours."

"Yeah, yeah, that didn't come out right. I'm just scared, you know?"

"Yeah, I do know—those phone calls are giving me the creeps. Is that why you're here? Getting me to stop looking into this mess?"

"No!" he said, pounding on the table. "Just the opposite. I was set up for that murder, and I didn't do it. I barely knew that girl. I'd seen her at a few of the GT meetings, but she didn't do no harm, that I saw, anyways."

"Okay, back up. You *don't* want me to stop looking into this?"

"Right. Word is out that you aren't letting this thing go the way Brower is. Fine with me. I want you to find whoever did it, because it weren't me, and I don't like the idea of this hanging over my head. Sure they say it's a suicide, but the statue of limitations don't wear out for murders. That means somehow, sooner or later, someone could try to pin this shit on me."

"Statute," I said, ever the wordsmith.

"Huh?"

Never mind. "What shit are you talking about?"

"Her death. Why else would someone call me and tell me I was needed out at that clearing. I thought the call was some GT prank, you know? Like some kind of initiation rite or test. Grissom, our leader, is always asking folks to prove their allegiance. I was told to go meet with some gov'ment guys who were trying to 'broker a deal.' They said dress nice, so I pulled my hair back and found that shirt in the back of my closet. I showed up, and there's that girl. I touched her to see if she was dead, and she was cold. And looked a mess and ..."

I motioned for him to move on. I remembered all too well what she looked like. He stood and started pacing. "So my prints are probably on something—if that lazy-ass sheriff had bothered to look into it. I was glad he didn't. Well, at first. But now I figure I want the shit who did this to get caught. That would clear me—and my conscience."

"So you've got a conscience?"

He nodded, as though my question deserved a legitimate answer. Maybe he *was* telling the truth. "This GT crap is out of control," he said. "I don't want no part in it anymore. I think that's why I was sent out there. They don't like it that I'm questioning Mr. High-and-Mighty Grissom Wells. And they don't want no one to leave and spill the beans. I wished I'd never heard of the GT; I wouldn't be in this mess." He ran his hand through his hair and shook his head. "I know I'm ramblin' here— I just mean I feel kinda contaminated by the whole thing. I can't get her face out of my mind, and it's killin' me."

"Would you like some coffee, uh, what *is* your name?"

"Bruce. Bruce Canning. And no thanks, ma'am, my nerves are already shot. You don't happen to have a spare PBR?"

As I pulled a can of beer from the cooler, I could see Abit sitting in his chair, whittling on the head of a walking stick. How was I going to explain this to him? I got myself some coffee. "Here you go, Bruce. Now why did you come here today?"

He took the beer, popped it open, and drank half the can in three long gulps. "I guess I came in to clear the air. I know you musta thought I did it. I saw you at the funeral, and I've been hearing about your snoop... 'er, looking into this. I figured maybe I could help. Man, I've got to get some sleep. I thought maybe helping you would help me."

I sipped my coffee, which wasn't very fresh but gave me something to hold on to. I was starting to believe him, but he still made me nervous. "Do you have any idea who called you?" He shook his head. "Okay, then, tell me what this Green Treatise is all about—just the Cliff Notes version." He gave me another blank look. "A brief description," I added.

"It all started about the road closure into the wilderness. These guys like to hunt, and that wilderness has been ours for our whole lives and on back into our granddaddies' lives and beyond. It's a slap in the face—not only can't we hunt in there no more, but we have to pay taxes to maintain it. That pisses a bunch of us off. But it's not worth all the bullshit and hate stuff going on. I mean, they built this road through my granddaddy's land, you know? He hated it at first, but then he was happy to have an easy road into town. Some things are worth fighting for, but other things just create a shit storm and make life a bitch."

"Okay, so if you didn't do it, it's likely whoever called you must have—or is working with whoever did. What did the voice sound like? Man? Woman?"

"I couldn't tell—like someone had a rag over the phone and was talking funny. It sounded ..."

The phone interrupted Bruce, and a few beats later, the bell above the door started jingling. I ran to the front of the store, grabbed the phone, and asked the caller to wait a minute. I looked up and saw Kitt storming in.

"Gregg's been arrested for the murder of that girl," she blurted out.

It took me several seconds to take that in. My brain just couldn't make sense of it. Then I realized someone was shouting, "Hello, hello?" on the phone. That was Cassie, Gregg's assistant, calling to tell me the same news, though I had trouble making out what she said because Kitt was still talking. "Cassie, let me call you back. I need to talk with someone first."

"He couldn't have done it," Kitt was saying. "What in the world would be his motive?"

"Okay, slow down, Kitt. I know this is a blow, but fill me in on why he was arrested—and who arrested him."

"Brower. He said he heard from Cassie, when she found some suspicious writing in his office."

"That doesn't sound like Cassie."

"Oh, sure it does. She's such a goodie-goodie. Oh God, this community. Why did I ever decide to come here?"

Yeah, some days I shared that feeling, but this wasn't about us. I shooed her out the door, telling her I needed some firsthand information. I headed back to the storeroom.

"Well, you're off the hook, Bruce. Gregg O'Donnell has been arrested for Lucy's murder." His face was a picture of bewilderment, but I didn't have the answers. "Look, I don't know more than that." I paused, suddenly worried he might have been behind this. Quite a coincidence that he showed up playing Mr. Innocent just when Gregg was arrested. "Wait a minute. Did you plant that shit in Gregg's office?"

"What? I have no idea what you're talking about. And I wouldn't step foot in a gov'ment office. That ain't the kind of action you take in GT, if I still cared about that."

"Well, maybe. Anyway, you'd better get out of here. You can use the back door. And keep your ear to the ground. You'll hear all about it soon enough, I'm sure."

He grabbed his coat, opened the backdoor, and disappeared into the meadow behind the store. I went back to the front of the store and decided to close up so I could see Gregg before it got too late in the day. Then I remembered my promised call to Cassie. I couldn't figure out why she was calling me about this mess, except maybe because I'd been the only one looking into the murder. And I was Gregg's friend, even if he didn't feel that way about me. I thought about calling her back, but I didn't have time. She'd just have to deal with her actions on her own until I knew more.

When I stepped outside, Abit was standing near the door Kitt had left open. "Hey there, Mister. Big news, eh?"

"I haven't heard nothin'—just seen all the commotion."

"Gregg's been arrested for Lucy's murder," I said. "I don't know any more than that, but I plan to find out."

Chapter 38: Della

Cleva pulled up as Abit and I were talking. She'd already heard the news, of course, and didn't want to go to the jail alone. I knew she was fond of Gregg, and her maternal nature was stirred by his troubles. We took my truck. When we walked into the sheriff's office, Brower was alone. Too bad, because Lonnie usually helped mitigate his orneriness. I braced for a caustic greeting.

"Hey, Missy, I owe you an apology." I must have looked shocked, because he quickly added, "I know, I know. I didn't believe this was more than a simple suicide, but the evidence is black and white now. Lonnie's out checking Gregg's truck for fingerprints, as we speak. And the SBI is sending someone over to help us out."

I was disgusted by his "simple suicide" comment, but I kept quiet. And who was he kidding that the State Bureau of Investigation was *helping him*? They'd be *taking over* the investigation. But I needed to stay in his good graces so he'd allow us to talk with Gregg. "That's good, glad you're getting some help," I said. He studied me, trying to detect any sarcasm, but seemed content there wasn't any (at least not that he noticed). "Can we see Gregg—just for a few minutes?"

Brower looked at his watch. "It's past visiting hours."

"Oh, come on, Sheriff. You don't even have visiting hours. When was the last time this jail was actually used for what it's intended for?" I asked. "We just want five minutes to check with Gregg. He did right by me when I was alone in the woods, and I just wanted to see if there's anything I can do for him."

"Yeah, well, he wasn't even supposed to be on that call. That was in *my* territory."

"No one's questioning your authority now. I just want to see if he needs anything."

"He needs a good lawyer, that's what he needs. So unless you've recently added Juris Doctorate after your name, I ..."

"Come on, big guy, help us out here." Both Brower and I turned around to see Cleva standing with her hands on her hips. She had the voice and presence of authority—just like my memories of a school principal. From the look on Brower's face, he must have had the same reaction. "Let us see Gregg for five minutes. Then we're gone," she added.

Brower unlocked the door to the jail area, and motioned for us to enter. He locked the door behind us, scrunched his face up to the small reinforced-glass window, and mouthed, "FIVE MINUTES!"

Gregg looked rough, though he seemed relieved to see us. "I honestly don't know what's going on," he said. "They came down to Asheville and hauled me out of a Forest Service meeting like a common criminal, in front of my friends and colleagues. Then Brower rough handled me and practically threw me in this cell. This is ridiculous. It's a total misunderstanding."

"What about the note?" I asked straight away. We needed to jump right in; Brower wouldn't give a second over five minutes.

"What note? Like I said, I don't know what this is all about—other than Brower enjoying some tit for tat."

"Well, you can thank that little miss holier-than-thou Cassie for all this …" Cleva said. She didn't hold much faith in the Church of God, and neither did I, but I needed to stop her before she got on a soapbox.

"Gregg, we have only five, no, make that four minutes," I said. "What can we do for you? Do you need anything from your home? A lawyer? I plan to talk to Cassie and get the full story for you first thing in the morning."

"I need my dopp kit and a change of clothes. There's a key in the wasp trap behind the house." *Not a likely place for burglars to poke around*, I thought before he added, "Della, please come see me tomorrow after you've talked to Cassie. All I know is she turned me in because of some note—that I didn't write, dammit. That's so crazy. If it weren't for her high-standing in the church, I'd think *she* wrote that note. As for the lawyer, let's hold off on that. Like I said, this is just a big misunderstanding."

Brower was unlocking the door to the cells. I needed to comply so he'd let me visit again tomorrow. As he'd pointed out, without the JD after my name, I had no official right to see Gregg. "Okay, will do. Try not to worry. We'll get this all straightened out." I squeezed his outstretched hand and Cleva reached through the bars to pat his back.

"Okay, girls, time you broke out of jail," Brower said, chuckling. We waved to Gregg and fled that hell hole.

Chapter 39: Abit

Wild. Totally wild. I'd never seen the store like this. Cars coming and going, Della running round, putting up her Sorry sign and leaving me and Wilkie to take the flak. But she wasn't gone long. She and Cleva drove up just as Wilkie was leaving for a doctor's appointment. I figured they'd go inside, and I'd have to sit out there by myself and get the news later. But they came back out, each with a coffee mug, and Della offering a Coca-Cola to me. She knew I didn't much care for coffee this late in the day.

Seemed that silly woman, Cassie, Gregg's assistant, found something inside a book that scared her. Della said it was some kind of copy of Lucy's suicide note—like he'd been practicing making it or something. Anyway, when Cassie saw that, she called Brower because she said it was her Christian duty.

Man, I'd heard that kind of thinking my whole life. She went to our church, well, the church Mama still went to, and that's what folks said when they wanted to justify doing somethin' mean. I'd heard that her and Gregg didn't get along all that great because of her Bible thumping, and I guessed that had come back to bite him in the ass. I mean, even if Della came out of the store with a smokin' gun and blood all over her, I'd still wait to hear her side of the story. But no, little Miss Christian had to go running to the sheriff. Never mind that Gregg was one of the nicest guys around. I hoped she'd get fired oncet Gregg got cleared.

While we was outside talking, a few customers drove up, so Della had to go inside. That's when Cleva asked how I was doin'. She went on to say that she wondered if I thought I might go back to school. Her question surprised me—and made me choke up a little, grabbing my throat so I couldn't speak for a minute. She was surprised, too, and started fussing over me, saying, "Oh, Vester, I'm so sorry I upset you."

I really liked her and didn't want her to feel bad, so I got myself together and told her I'd love to go to school, and if she could find a way to help make that happen, I'd be obliged to her for the rest of my life. I don't know what made me say that. It just slipped out. By then, I think she was kinda choked up, too.

Chapter 40: Della

"I don't understand why you went straight to Brower." I was standing in front of Cassie's desk at the Forest Service office. She just sat there with her tissues and trembling chin, determined not to be cheated out of her pity party.

"I was afraid to ask Gregg about it because it seemed like he was some kind of monster. Make that *is* some kind of monster. How else did those so-called suicide notes get inside that computer book? He probably thought no one would look there. Listen, Della. I was scared, scared through and through."

I couldn't think of a good argument for her, other than the fact that we both knew Gregg. But I had to admit that a strange series of seemingly unrelated events had conspired to land Gregg in jail. She went on to explain that an electrical outage started it (a common irritant around there). That interrupted her work on a flyer for her boyfriend's band while Gregg was away at a Forest Service meeting in Asheville. I recalled that the band had a ridiculous name—The Naked Outlaws—especially since they weren't naked when they performed (though who knew what happened during rehearsals), and they weren't outlaws, unless being a Christian rock band was considered a crime against music.

The outage crashed her computer, which refused to reboot once the power was restored. She said she called someone she thought could help, but that person was at a loss, too. They figured her only bet was the computer manual, which led her to Gregg's office. While she flipped through the pages, the notes fell out. As she told it, her hands started shaking when she opened one, read it, and screamed for help.

"I couldn't believe it. They were exactly like the note everybody's been seeing around town, word for word, but one had some cross-throughs, as though he'd been practicing. And the second one was the same—only perfect. Like he'd got it right. In that poor girl's handwriting."

"Why would Gregg leave something incriminating like that lying around?" I asked. "Especially if anyone could go snooping around and find it."

Cassie stomped her foot. "I wasn't snooping. I was honestly trying to work on something, and one thing led to another."

"Honestly working on your boyfriend's flyer, you mean."

Cassie gave me the most unchristian look. "Well, if it weren't for the power outage, I would have been doing my regular work."

That didn't make sense since her work on the poster was interrupted by the power outage, but I could tell Cassie wasn't going to offer anything useful. "Something stinks, Cassie."

"Hey, whose side are you on?"

"To be honest, Gregg's."

"Listen to me. That note was in Gregg's office. Hidden in a book he figured no one would ever look in because he hadn't in the two years since we got computerized. I rest my case."

"Well, good for you. You're the only one who can rest. You've stirred up a hornet's nest and put someone in jail who I seriously doubt was stupid enough to leave incriminating evidence lying around his office. Who else has access to his office?"

"That's just it. No one. Except me, and I sure didn't kill that girl."

"I know you didn't, Cassie. But someone must have planted that evidence. Who cleans your offices?"

"I do," she said, with an angry tone I couldn't blame her for. Just hire the little lady to do everything.

"Well, I'm sure Brower won't care about the unlikely details of this, but I sure do." I may have stomped my foot, too, before I slammed the door and left Cassie sniveling.

I headed over to the jail and caught Brower in another relatively good mood. I guessed he was basking in the thrill of having caught a dangerous outlaw. He let me in to see Gregg without so much as a smirk. "What's with him?" I asked Gregg, once Brower had locked me in the jail area.

"I think he's enjoying his new status—capturing a bad guy." Gregg looked pale, a two-day growth and tangled hair making him look like a stranger.

The evidence against him was piling up. When Lonnie checked Gregg's truck for fingerprints, he found Lucy's underpants under the passenger seat. Gregg insisted they must have been planted, which seemed obvious to me, too. I told Brower (who did have a smirk on his face that time) that since she hadn't had sex recently when she was murdered, they were irrelevant. Brower counter-argued that the underwear was likely left behind at an earlier date and showed that Gregg knew her quite well. And who better than a forest ranger to know the perils of hemlock, he added. They saw it as a crime of passion when Lucy spurned Gregg's attention.

At first, I wondered how they knew the underwear was hers, but then I recalled the laundry she'd left at Blanche's—which I'd turned over to Brower. Everything had the initials LS on the elastic, including the pair in Gregg's truck.

And Lucy's fingerprints were in his truck; those couldn't have been planted.

"Oh for God's sake, I gave that girl a ride," Gregg told me, his arms thrust out as though he were pleading for his life. "She was walking to the campsite, which was over a mile away, but not far from my office, where I was headed. Big damn deal. Arrest me for breaking Forest Service Code 666, but I didn't harm that girl."

"Anyone with any sense knows you're no killer, Gregg."

He sat back down and held his head in his hands. He sat like that for a long time, then finally looked up. "Hey, listen, Della. I'm really sorry about being so harsh on the phone a while ago. It kinda stung that you'd turned me down, but I know you're a good friend. If the offer still holds, I accept—and not just because I'm in this mess."

"You bet, Gregg. I appreciate that. So who has access to your office beside Cassie?"

"Anyone who can pick a lock," he said, "and I'm sure there's no shortage of folks around here who could do that. But why me? Why pin this on me?"

"Have you gotten into it with anyone about the wilderness area?"

"You mean those Green Treatise idiots? Yeah, we've gone toe to toe a time or two."

"Anyone else?"

"Oh, hell, there's always someone who's trying to steal or poach or burn something down." He dragged his fingers through his hair, looking ready to break.

"We'll figure something out, Gregg. I promise." As I stood to leave, I couldn't resist asking, "Is your relationship still going well?"

He grimaced. "It lasted about as long as our phone call." I slipped out the door to avoid embarrassing him any further.

When I got home, I started my search the same way I did the last time—contacting Nigel. I mailed him copies of the traced notes and the details surrounding them. (At least Cassie had done something right—she'd made copies of the notes before Brower got his hands on them.) As I dropped the envelope in the out-of-town slot at the post office, I wondered when or if he could help me again.

Chapter 41: Della

"At first I thought Gregg couldn't have done it. But then I remembered how mad he got when I broke it off."

Kitt came back the next day, right at closing time. I had a special shit list of people who did that. She was pacing around the store, ringing her hands, picking up cans and putting them down in the wrong place.

"I didn't know you knew Gregg that well," I said.

"We went out a few times, but it didn't go anywhere. I thought he was a good catch, but then something seemed off. And like I told our dumbass sheriff, he got so mad when I told him I didn't want to go out anymore that he scared me." She punctuated that by slamming a can of beans down in the soup section.

At first, I didn't take her opinion of Gregg very seriously. I knew this guy, right? But then I recalled how unlike himself he sounded when I basically told him the same thing. Maybe we didn't know him that well, after all.

Kitt interrupted my thoughts. "You know, everyone's been wondering why you're so concerned about this girl. I mean, none of us knew her."

"I just care, like any red-blooded human being ought to. And I'm a nosy reporter."

"What have you found out?"

"I have my sources." I'd used that line a time or two in my career. "Which, now that we're talking about this whole mess, maybe you could tell me why you were at a recent Green Treatise meeting." She reeled around and almost knocked over my display of homemade jams and relishes.

"What are you talking about?" Lame. She was stalling.

"The Green Treatise meeting a couple of weeks ago."

"Were you there?"

I ignored her question. "You just don't seem like a good candidate for the Green Treatise."

"You'd be surprised. I'm not crazy about all the taxes and permits and red tape I've had to endure just to open a little gallery in the middle of nowhere. But I guess you'd say I get their frustration, and I was trying to serve as a go between of sorts—a level head to help them *not* make big, stupid mistakes."

"Well, they sure need that. How well do you know them?"

"Not that well. I met a few of the guys at the Whippoorwill." She was referring to a cinderblock dive just up the road. The interior was always dark, day or night, probably so you didn't notice you were standing in a puddle of what you hoped was spilled beer. "I don't like the tension they bring to this otherwise—at least sometimes—peaceful town," she continued. "Before the gallery, I was involved in this kind of work. I was a social worker. I guess it's in my blood—I like to help make peace." Her gallery did have that kind of New Agey peace-and-love look, in spite of the edgy art.

"Well, thanks, Kitt, for stopping by. It's closing time, and I want to get over to the jail to see Gregg again."

"Lucky you. Brower and Gregg—two of my least favorite men, at the moment." She headed out the door, and nearly tripped over Abit, who was leaning against the door. Cleva was sitting on a bench, clutching her purse in that way older woman seemed to do. I wondered at what age we started doing that.

We didn't learn anything new from Gregg that evening. He was so in the dark, we actually brought him news. I was glad we could lend a little moral support, but that was about all we could do in five minutes. Brower was being a stickler.

Standing outside the jail, Cleva and I decided to go out to dinner. We didn't have a lot of choices in town, so we ended up at Adam's Rib. I wasn't in the mood for the special—baby-back ribs, home fries and beans—and apparently Cleva wasn't either. We both ordered salads, though Iceberg lettuce and wan hothouse tomatoes weren't enough to call dinner. We added one order of barbecued chicken.

"Honey, that man looks devastated. I hope he doesn't have to spend much time in that jail. Brower must be loving this. He's always been sorta jealous of Gregg."

"Jealous? Or just on a power trip?"

"Both, probably. But I think he might be jealous of the way folks naturally enjoy Gregg but not him. People like that are sad—like a kid watching others play but not knowing how to join. They jump in and next thing you know, they've started a fight."

"Well, I don't care about Brower's sad upbringing. Like Freud said, sometimes an asshole is just an asshole."

She chuckled. "Even I know that's not quite how he put it, but I get your point. Let's drop that and talk about you. You seem kind of jumpy."

"Sure, aren't you? The injustice that Gregg, of all people, would be wrestled out of a meeting and thrown in jail?"

"I don't mean that. Yep, I'm pissed off about what's happened to Gregg, but I've never seen you so alive. So, so—as the kids say, in a groove."

I stopped mid-bite and put my drumstick down. I wiped barbecue sauce from my face, more for time to think than good manners. She was right. I was getting to work again at what I'd spent my whole adult life doing: interviewing people, digging deeply into a story, and even sometimes righting injustices. Being a journalist had been exciting, especially in D.C., where the culprits I dealt with were often players in the biggest show in the world.

"I guess you're right," I said. "This is what I used to do, and it made life interesting."

"Past tense?"

"Oh, let's not go there."

"Okay, but there's something else. I mean, you seemed kind of jangled. Obsessed even."

Dammit, Cleva could see through a blackout curtain. I'd recently realized that my dogged search was fueled, in part, by a memory—and a load of guilt—from a tragedy a year earlier. "Well, there is something else," I said.

After a long silence, Cleva said, "And?"

"Someone killed herself, in front of me. She'd been depressed for a while, and I'd been a pretty loyal neighbor and friend. I didn't abandon her when she got in dark moods. I stuck around, including some harrowing evenings listening to her rant. But it wasn't all bad—we'd had some fun times, too. Then one night she had me over for dinner and started telling me what a shit I was. I should have known it was the depression talking, but I decided to try some tough love. I told her she needed to get more help. She'd refused drugs, and for a while, that made sense. I mentioned that she might want to try a prescription, just short term to help her out while she worked on her issues. I added that she couldn't go on the way she was living. She ran from the living room into her kitchen, dumped the spaghetti sauce and pasta and boiling water onto the floor, grabbed a kitchen knife, and shouted, 'You're right. I can't go on like this.' The slashes she made were the serious kind, right down both arms. I called 911, but she bled out before they arrived."

Everything tumbled out so fast, all Cleva could muster was, "Oh, I see." She sipped her iced tea, gathering her thoughts. Finally, she said, "Honey, that makes sense, what you said about redeeming the past. The way I see it, life's built on our past, though we can't stay mired in it. We've got to move on. But you couldn't *not* have seen that scene in your head. I'm sorry you've had that happen—twice."

"Thanks, Cleva." I looked around for the waiter; I needed something stronger than tea. After he brought me a beer, I took a drink and went on. "As long as I'm spilling my guts, I want you to know that my interesting life is *not* past tense. Yes, I've had an exciting life, maybe too exciting. I was ready for a change, which is why I moved here. Then along comes something big again, and I'll admit, it does feel good to be in that groove again. But you know, the store keeps me on my toes, too—ordering and maintaining inventory is a juggling act. And customer service is a new challenge for me." I tried to chuckle, but it caught in my throat. I drank more beer and continued. "Fortunately, the real jerks in town don't come in, not even for beer. I think they're pissed that I won't sell tobacco, which in North Carolina is worse than burning the flag. But I love folks like you and Abit and Myrtle and Roy and …"

Cleva interrupted. "You sound like you're trying to convince yourself."

"You're good, Cleva, but this time you're not one-hundred percent right. Sometimes I do have to give myself a pep talk, but right now, sitting here with you, eating terrific North Carolina barbecue, even the Iceberg lettuce tastes good."

"Good to hear. I'm feeling mighty fine about your sitting here, too. Now, what kind of pie should we order?"

Chapter 42: Abit

Duane and me and the Rollin' Store were on the road by seven-thirty. Over a couple of weeks, we'd gotten our act together—refilling the paper bag bins when we got back from a run, restocking inventory Tuesday evening, and such as that. That cut down on time we needed Wednesday mornings before we rolled out. I felt useful for the first time in my life.

Otherwise, everything else exciting had slowed to a crawl. Nobody was running into the store with the latest news or sitting outside the store with me, hoping to pick up on some gossip about Gregg.

Speaking of Gregg, he was out on bail. Della explained that a lot of accused murderers weren't allowed out, but Gregg weren't likely to skip town and didn't have no record. The Forest Service got him a lawyer from Asheville, Alfred Bonner, and he got the judge to agree to bail. No one who really knew Gregg for a minute thought he'd killed that girl, except maybe Brower. Oh, and them militia guys. I heard Roger Turbin talking about how they was glad it were a gov'ment man in jail. (That was how they said it—gov'ment. Even I knowed better than that, and I only finished fifth grade.)

Della wouldn't let it rest, though. Even Cleva told her to slow down. I'd been thinking Cleva enjoyed the chase as good as Della (not that *enjoyed* were the right way to put it). But Della said it was in her blood—like a bloodhound—ever since she spent so much time writing stories. And every time she was about to give up, something would happen. Like the call she got from Lucy's sister, asking if Gregg were the killer. That put her right back on the track of the killer. The way I saw it, she liked the truth and went after it. Maybe that's why she liked me. I'd almost always told the truth. I reckoned I weren't smart enough to tell believable lies.

Chapter 43: Della

After Gregg was arrested, the calls stopped. To some, that pointed another finger at Gregg, but I still didn't believe it. More likely the guilty party felt the heat was off.

I kept trying to help Gregg, but he just walked around in a daze, unable to fathom how his life had turned into such a nightmare. I invited him over for dinner so we could talk about a plan of attack. He arrived looking rumpled, as though he'd slept in his clothes. Maybe he had, or maybe I was so accustomed to seeing him in his crisp uniform, the faded flannel shirt and jeans looked odd on him. We each had a beer, and when Gregg asked for another one, I handed it to him and said, "I want you to help me find out what really happened."

"That would look bad," he said, taking a long pull. I didn't follow his logic, and told him so. "Dammit, Della, I can't go around the county quizzing people and acting like a law officer. Besides, everyone is looking at me like I'm some mad rapist and murderer. I appreciate what you're doing, Della. I really do. But if you want to be effective, you don't want *me* along." He rubbed his face; the three-day growth probably itched like crazy.

"Okay, so maybe you don't go up to the door, but you could go along. Keep me safe." I was trying every angle I could think of.

"You'll be safer *without* me. All those Green Treatise idiots have poisoned everyone against me." Before I'd found Lucy's body in that cove, what felt like years ago, I'd never heard Gregg swear beyond the occasional hell or damn. His nerves were shot. I decided to let my idea drop.

We managed to enjoy the rest of the evening, talking about his extended family and my store. I even successfully grilled steaks outside—with perfect char marks and juicy pink interiors. I didn't know much about grilling meats, but Gregg advised, and we polished them off.

Of course, word got out that I was "entertaining" Gregg, as though I had to be more than just a friend helping another friend. (I didn't understand why most people limited their circle of friends to those they'd never go to bed with.) Anyway, we shared a chaste evening, with Gregg leaving about eleven o'clock.

The next day, after I'd closed the store, I stopped to chat with Abit. Given my busy schedule lately, we hadn't had much time to talk. We caught up on how well the rolling store was doing, and I thanked him for being such a good employee. He gave me that crooked smile again. When he shared some ideas he had for managing the inventory based on what people bought, I realized he had the makings of an entrepreneur. He saw trends I hadn't seen, and, even with more time on my hands, likely wouldn't have noticed. We talked for a while longer, and then I remembered I needed to run by the hardware before it closed.

"I'll take care of Jake for you—no charge!" Abit said.

"Thanks, Mister. I won't be gone long."

When I drove back, I parked the truck and I headed upstairs, so ready for my day off tomorrow. I imagined a quiet evening with a long soak in my claw-foot tub, but when I unlocked the door, Jake didn't greet me.

Chapter 44: Abit

"Jake! Jake! Come on, boy, time for dinner." I called and called but he was gone. We were out back playing, and then he ran to the front of the store. I thought Della was home, and he'd heard her truck. By the time I got there, though, I couldn't see him, just a cloud of dust from a car or truck driving fast.

We'd had a good Saturday. I say *we* because I'd been helping Della and spending more time in the store. Well, mostly the storeroom, but still. People were coming in and saying thanks for the Rollin' Store, and they were buying more things from Coburn's, so it was working out real good, all round.

When Della closed up, she went off to do an errand, and I took Jake out for a good romp. He'd gotten used to me, and seemed to look forward to a different kind of play than Della could give him. I liked to roll round with him in the back and throw his toy—especially his knotted rope we played tug of war with. I threw it toward the meadow in the back, but he ran round front. And then he was gone.

Mama had supper on the table by the time I got up to the house. I wanted to spend more time trying to find Jake, but I knew better than to keep Mama waiting. All I could do was hope he'd turn up before Della came back. I didn't tell Mama or Daddy about Jake. Daddy might've popped me one upside the head, though he was doing less of that these days. He was even taking an interest in my job. It didn't take long to tell him what I did all day, but still, that felt good. And my passbook was up to $246. The way I saw it, it was a savings account in case the family needed anything or ran short one month. And maybe, someday, it would be my ticket out of town. I didn't even have to spend money on sodas anymore. "On the house," Della said, though she was always trying to get me to switch to healthier drinks I wasn't crazy about.

During dessert, I kinda picked at Mama's coconut cream pie, my favorite. "What's the matter with you, son?" Mama asked.

That's when we heard Della calling "Jake, Jake, Jake!" and running round the store. She sounded so sad, calling his name, I nearabout started crying. I asked to be excused and didn't wait for permission.

"I'm so sorry, Della. I was just throwing his rope, and then he was gone," I said, after I'd run down the steps and caught up with her. I told her about the dust in the driveway and how I'd heard some kind of vehicle. "How can I help?"

She sat down on the bench and said, "I don't think we're doing any good here. He's gone. Tomorrow, if he hasn't come back, you can help me put up signs."

I didn't sleep much that night. I was worried sick. I replayed and replayed what happened, until I wasn't sure of anything. The following morning, Sunday, the store was closed, but I headed out to my chair and tapped it against the store. At first that didn't work, but after a while, she came down with coffee for the both of us.

"I'll help with those signs, though I don't write so good—but I can put them on posts and poles for you."

"That won't be necessary. I got a call last night."

"I thought they'd stopped."

"*Those* calls have. But I guess I stirred things up when I kept trying to help Gregg. To me, this new call really proves he didn't do it. I know Brower won't agree—and especially not now that the state is more involved."

"What did the caller say?"

"More of the usual threats. Though this time he said they'd kill Jake if I did any more investigating—or snooping, as the caller said." She paused, then kinda shouted, "This is such bullshit. We don't have a sheriff worth the cost of that cheap badge he wears. None of this should be happening." She stopped, her anger spent, for now. In a quiet voice, she added, "And I miss Jake!"

We sat together without saying a word. Eventually, she pulled out some Kleenex and headed back upstairs. I sat there till it turned dark, hoping I'd see that golden fur crest the hill behind the store.

Chapter 45: Della

No sign of Jake after three days. I couldn't think of anything else to do for Gregg, so I was passively complying with the caller's demand that I stop "snooping." When the phone rang, I was expecting a return call from a supplier, so I was surprised to hear that now-familiar voice congratulate me on staying quiet. He told me Jake was in good spirits. I doubted that. I said something stupid about returning my dog, that kidnapping was a crime. I doubted that cruelty to animals was a crime in North Carolina, but that was all I could think to say. I hung up.

The phone rang again, and I'd had all I could stand. "Listen here, you son of a bitch, bring back my dog or, or …" I stopped, sensing an uncomfortable silence on the other end of the line.

"Um, did I call at a bad time, dear?"

"Nigel?"

"Yes. I was just calling to see how you were doing. Sounds as though things could be better."

Just hearing the voice of a dear friend made me burst into tears. He let me sob, then sniffle, then blow my nose. "I've been better. But I really appreciate your call, Nigel. I've been thinking of you, and I should have let you know how things have progressed. Or maybe I should say devolved. And thank you for looking at the latest notes."

I rambled on about the sheriff not believing Nigel's earlier findings (I heard him tsk) and the unfolding situation with Gregg. And Jake. "I know you don't know Jake, but he's a lovely golden brown dog, and now he's been kidnapped or whatever you call it when a dog is involved. I miss him and fear for his life."

"What kind of Wild West are you living in down there?"

"Oh, usually it's really quite nice. A lot nicer than those outlaws in D.C."

"Well, you've got me there. Yes, I can imagine. But when things go wrong down there, it sounds like the O.K. Corral."

Under different circumstance, I would've laughed. I was often amused by how fascinated and knowledgeable Brits, and maybe folks from other countries, were about our frontier history. Nigel once told me he admired our bravado, but he'd rest easier when it was tamed by a touch of civilization.

"What are you going to do, dear?" he asked.

"There's not much I can do. They told me if I keep investigating, they'll kill Jake. And I believe they would."

"Well, surely they don't know about this phone call, so let's talk a bit about those traced forgeries you sent me. Of course, I haven't seen the originals, but no self-respecting forger—not one of the quality you showed me earlier—uses tracing paper. That forged suicide note definitely was *not* traced. I suppose one could argue that he was just practicing for the real forgery, but in my experience, that doesn't happen. You've either got the touch or not. It would be like Monet tracing his water lilies. Never!"

The idea of Gregg as a forger in the making was ludicrous, but as Nigel and I talked, I remembered my earlier concerns. I didn't know the first thing about Gregg. *Maybe he has a second life,* I thought.

Nigel and I talked a bit longer, before he ended the call with, "Sorry about your little dog. Let me know when he comes home safely. And come see us up here. We'll treat you to a break from those, uh, bandits!"

I felt even lonelier when I hung up. I picked up the receiver again and dialed Alex. By some miracle, he answered before the machine picked up. "Jake was stolen," was all I could get out before breaking down again.

"Oh, for God's sake. Tell me all about it." He waited while I got it together and told him what I knew. "Jesus, I don't know why you live there. Seriously, why do you stay?"

"We've been through this before, Alex. Remember the guy who stalked me in D.C.? Or that article I wrote—the way after it was published I had to change my phone number? This is just life anywhere these days. Man's inhumanity to man—and dog."

"Okay. Okay. What can I do to help?"

"I can't think of anything more to do for Jake. I've got folks looking for him, and that's about all we can do.

I'm lying low until he gets home. I don't want to jeopardize his safety."

"Well, don't forget about yours!"

"I won't. Oh, wait," I said. "There *is* a way you can help. Could you look into Gregg's past? I don't know anything about his life before he moved here, and hell, he could be another one of those guys who has all the neighbors scratching their heads, saying what a nice boy he was."

"Really? That park ranger I met?"

"Forest service."

"Whatever. Hard to imagine."

"I know. I'm grasping here, but who knows? Before I stick my neck out any further, I'd like to know more about him."

"Farther."

"No, further. It's an idiom, not a real neck that can be measured." Alex was silent. He hated being wrong. I knew I was right because I used to joke, once I got my sense of humor back, that the best thing I took away from our marriage was Alex teaching me the difference between further and farther. "Besides," I said, changing the subject, "aren't you the one always questioning why I'm working on this case? Maybe this will get me to stop."

He agreed, and we talked about the store and Abit. I think he could sense I didn't want to get off the phone, unlike my usual distaste for long conversations. He told me about his latest *paying* gigs (emphasis his), one in particular that involved research into the National Film Archive in Culpeper, Virginia, a charming town that was rapidly becoming a posh bedroom community for D.C.

"Why don't you come up? We could stay in one of the B&Bs there."

"How could you suggest that with Jake missing?"

"Hey, throw me a bone, er, I mean, help me out here. I'm just trying to cheer you up. Once you find him—and I have a good feeling he'll get loose or someone *will* find him—you could come for a visit. Get away for a while and let things settle down."

I thanked him and told him I'd think about it. A trip to Culpeper did sound nice. And the Southern Crescent train even stopped there. Or I could drive and bring Jake along. If we had time, I could take him into the city and show him Lafayette Park, Rock Creek Park, and all my old haunts, including the house I used to live in. I was feeling excited about the trip, but then remembered I had to find Jake first.

Chapter 46: Abit

"Stop the truck," I shouted.

It was raining pretty hard as the Rollin' Store headed through the Beaverdam community. Duane was grinding the gears, working hard to get us through some bad ruts. We'd just left our stop near the Ledford's place when I saw something in my rearview mirror—a blur moving round behind us.

"I cain't stop it here. We're in the mud."

"STOP IT!"

"What's the matter with you, Abit? Cain't you hear me?"

"There's something in the road!" Duane went a few more feet and found solid ground. He put the brakes on, and I was out before he fully stopped.

"What the hell, are you …"

I ran back the way we'd just come, and that's when I knew for sure what I'd seen. A little skinny with a nasty old rope tied round his neck, but that was Jake, all right, coming about one hundred miles per hour straight at me. He jumped into my arms, and I'd never felt anything so good in my life. He licked my face all over, and if he hadn't been so covered in mud, I might have done the same back at him. I carried him to the bus, and Duane's face lit up. We walked back to the Ledford's to ask if we could use their phone to tell Della we'd found Jake. Mrs.

Ledford welcomed us in and even gave us some coffee. Duane said Della was beside herself with happiness.

On the way back, Duane and I talked about how Jake'd probably chewed through the rope when he heard the bus's gears grinding. Dogs are smart like that—they knowed things we didn't. He sure stank from being wet and all, but he stank good. I was able to get most of the mud off him—but Mama was going to kill me when she saw how much was still on my overalls, which were my best since I was working with the public. But I didn't care. We pulled up and Duane just laid on the horn, toot-tooting it. Della came running out the door, and I held up Jake to the windshield best I could since he was wiggling like a baby pig, and she came running alongside the bus as Duane drove toward the back where he parked it. What a reunion!

"Oh, Jake, honey, where have you been?" Tears were streaming down her face, and truth be told, me and Duane had wet faces, too. We all huddled together and patted Jake. Duane had to get on home, so Della and I sat together for a while, just loving the way Jake felt.

Chapter 47: Della

That night, Jake and I walked around our property well after dark. I'd bathed him, fed him an extra helping of his dinner, and threw his favorite chew toy. We were venturing out together for the first time in a week. I knew I couldn't be overly protective, but I sure wanted to keep him close.

While he was sniffing something mysterious in the meadow, I looked up at the sky sparkling with stars I'd never seen before, city lights having stolen their luster my whole life. I felt a jolt run through me, a reminder that the power of nature was always available, though most of the time I was too worried or self-absorbed to notice. A visceral sense of gratitude and creativity took hold of me.

In D.C., I'd experienced something similar whenever I looked at the Jefferson Memorial or the U.S. Capitol. Glorious, imposing buildings. Or the astounding cherry blossoms along the Tidal Basin, when spring wasn't too cold or wet for them to thrive. The inspiration they offered kept the mean old bastards in that city from blinding me to all we could be as a nation and as individuals.

Standing there, I felt my heart beat fast as I thought about how much I really did love my new life. I could see funky old Coburn's in the moonlight, and I was struck by how my humble store drew on every skill I'd acquired over my lifetime. I felt a sense of purpose like never before. And there was Jake—running free. Home again. Happy.

The next day, though, I returned to my usual troubles. Besides Gregg and what to do next, I woke up in the night worried about where Abit had found Jake. I was so relieved that he was safely home, I'd forgotten to ask. And I wondered when Alex was going to get back to me about Gregg.

Two of those questions were answered later that afternoon, while Abit helped me put up supplies in the storeroom and stock the shelves out front. The phone rang when I was in the bathroom, so I shouted at Abit to answer it.

"Really? You want *me* to answer the phone?" he asked. I could hear how incredulous he was.

I cracked the door and shouted, "Yes, please. I'll be out in a minute." (I'd learned that a small store offered little to no privacy.) "And hurry up—the phone's about to go to the machine." I heard a voice so serious I thought, for a moment, that someone else had come into the store and grabbed the phone. Then his voice became more animated. He even laughed. Who in the world was he talking to?

When I came out front, Abit mouthed, "Alex." He was really enjoying himself, and I didn't want to break in. I was glad he no longer seemed suspicious of Alex. He recounted how he'd found Jake and then said, "We don't know exactly. It wasn't that far from the Ledford's, but we know *they* hadn't taken him and tied him up."

Then he said, "Here's Della," holding the phone out but suddenly grabbing it back. "Er, when are you coming down here again? You promised me a ride in the Merc." I chuckled at him and took the phone.

"Hi there. What's up?"

"Great news about ol' Jakey Boy."

"Yeah, we're all pretty happy about it. Thanks to Abit," I said, looking over at him in the canned goods. He was beaming and started juggling three small cans of creamed corn (a favorite here—especially since the empty can made a dandy receptacle for tobacco juices). *When did he learn to do that?* I wondered.

"I did that research on Gregg you asked for."

"And?"

"Well, he must have lied on his Forest Service application, because after some digging, I found some youthful indiscretions."

"How youthful? Were they sealed?"

"Yeah, teenage shit, I'd imagine. So maybe he didn't have to lie. I shouldn't have made him sound like Kipland Philip Kinkel."

"Who?"

"Oh, some sick teenager in Oregon who went on a killing spree. You know how it is with journalists—we know way too much trivia."

"So nothing serious in his background, at least not beyond his teenage years? What did he do before the Forest Service?"

"He was involved in banking, of all things. Which could speak to his skill in forgery, if he kept up his delinquent ways, that is."

"Oh, that's a stretch. But I'd never pictured Gregg as a banker."

"Which is probably why he's not one any longer. You don't seem like a bookkeeper, either." He was referring to my first job, right out of college, when that was all I could get, even with a journalism degree.

"Anything else?"

"He was married for about five years in the '60s; they didn't have any children and divorced in 1968. One thing—she did get a restraining order against him. I couldn't find any violations of that, though, so I don't know if he just lost his shit when she left him."

That worried me, given what Kitt said and my own experience with his ill-tempered rejection. I didn't want to talk about that with Alex, so I asked, "When did he leave banking?"

"About the same time as his divorce. That's when he worked with runaway kids. Not sure how he qualified for that, but so many kids were in trouble then, he probably fell into it. I couldn't find anything much after that and before the Forest Service. He's been a model employee there—quickly rising to ranger in your Podunk town."

"He doesn't work in a town. He oversees half a million acres—or at least his district."

"Okay, he's ranger of the year. Whatever. That's my report. I still think you need to be careful around him. Looks can be deceiving."

I thought to myself, *you'd better believe it* as I pictured Alex taking off his wedding ring so someone could run her fingers through his wavy hair with good conscience. "Thanks, Alex. I really appreciate your research. But I haven't heard any reason to stop believing he's the good guy we all think he is."

"Not 'all.' If he's been framed, someone in that wilderness you call home doesn't like him."

"Or someone needs a patsy, and it has little to do with who."

"Whom."

I felt like hanging up. He was right that time, but so what? Nobody used "whom" in conversation. "Okay, I guess that's it," was all I said.

Abit's head popped up like a whack a mole. He dramatically mouthed "When?" I knew what he meant, but I shook my head.

As though he could read Abit's lips, Alex added, "I thought I might drive down again. At least Abit would be glad to see me."

I didn't know how I felt about another visit from Alex, but the look on Abit's face encouraged a welcome-mat response. "Sure, come on down. But you've got to give Abit a ride this time—maybe a long drive up the Blue Ridge Parkway to that restaurant I like." I gave Abit a thumbs-up and said goodbye to Alex. We went back to work.

Chapter 48: Abit

When Alex drove up, I walked over to say hi. I was getting to like the guy. We had a good talk about his Merc and other car things before he headed in to see Della. I had some stocking to do, so I followed.

I interrupted their big hug, but they didn't seem to mind. They even invited me to tag along on that dinner he'd promised Della—up on the Blue Ridge Parkway. Assuming Daddy agreed. Turned out he did, though he didn't seem crazy about the idea. But who cared, as long as he didn't say no. He gave me a twenty dollar bill and told me to bring him the change. I offered to use my own money, but he said to keep that safe.

We all piled in the Merc and drove up to a fancy place called the Inn at Jonas Mountain. Della sat in the back the whole way so I could really see where we was goin'. I don't know when anybody's thought about me like that.

They talked back and forth from front to back, and they seemed to be getting along real good. They even included me and asked me what I thought. We talked about Gregg and Lucy, mostly bringing Alex up to date. But then we made a pact that when we got to the restaurant, we wouldn't talk about murder! I don't know why they weren't still married—but I told myself to let sleepin' dogs lie. I sure didn't want her leaving us to go live with him.

I ordered a hamburger because Mama never made anything like that, and it was the cheapest thing on the menu. Della said she'd get her usual—rainbow trout. It looked good, especially after they took the head off. Alex ordered a steak. I sorta wished I'd got that, but I was happy with mine. They asked me if it were okay for them to order wine, and I laughed. I could tell they was thinking Mama might even have spies up here. But they was just making sure she didn't get the wrong idea, which was nice. We finished off our dinners by splitting pieces of German chocolate cake and straw- berry cheesecake. I couldn't believe they didn't mind eating after me.

And I couldn't believe I nodded off on the way back! It'd gotten dark by then, and all that good food made me sleepy. They woke me a few minutes before we were home, so I wouldn't be too groggy to get up all them steps. I couldn't remember when I'd had so much fun. And Alex picked up the tab. Daddy kinda grabbed the twenty dollar bill I handed back to him. But he wasn't being mean; he was relieved.

Chapter 49: Della

"I can see why you find this place so beguiling," Alex said, catching his breath. We'd gone on another hike around Laurel Falls, this time taking a trail that gave us an even better view of the falls. We were both a little out of breath by the time we reached the lookout. Too much store time for me. For Alex, who worked out most days, climbing steep trails used different muscles than his urban hikes on a NordicTrack.

"I love the way nature makes me feel," I said. "Especially this spring. The rains have brought out so many flowers and smells."

Alex just nodded; I could tell he didn't want to disturb the peacefulness with chatter. We stood for a while, drinking in the beauty, until a loose dog, two noisy teenagers, and a couple of alleged parents took over the lookout. Jake didn't bother the poufy dog and followed us as we hiked farther into the woods.

We walked together in silence, enjoying the birds and the rhythmic sound of our boots on the pine needles. Out of the blue, he said, "I do miss you."

I waited a beat before saying, "By now, I even miss you."

"Ouch."

"And I worry about you," I said. "How have things been, you know, since the debacle?"

"Not bad, really. I honestly didn't mean to plagiarize, and I have a new system in place that helps keep that from happening. Anything I type or handwrite from sources gets highlighted in yellow. That way I can't accidentally lift anything, thinking it's my own. I've still got plenty of naysayers, but I'm building a freelance business, and they trust me." He paused. "Any chance you're trusting me again, too?"

"Yep, just like they do—with research and writing."

Alex planned to stay around a few more days, though I wasn't sure why—he couldn't do any research here, for me or his clients. But he hadn't taken time off in a while, at least not good time off. He'd had plenty of downtime after he was fired, but that was different from a relaxing stay in the mountains.

The next morning, just as the percolator made its last gurgle, I heard a horn honk out front. I thought it was some impatient customer or someone who couldn't walk and needed help. I looked out the kitchen windows in time to see Abit climbing into Alex's car, looking like kid on a field trip. I thought Alex was still in the bathroom, but he must have gotten up and out early.

Alex saw me standing in the window and walked over to the bottom of the stairs. I opened the door and stepped onto the landing. "We're off on a men-only drive!" he said. "Abit wants to see Mystery Hill—he says balls roll uphill there, and now I want to see it, too. We should be back by lunch. I'll bring a surprise."

Just before one o'clock, I heard Alex's car rattling its way home. I couldn't imagine they hadn't eaten yet—dinner was usually served next door no later than noon, so Mildred would be furious that Abit was late.

"I thought you'd've eaten already," I said, as they came through the front door. Alex, true to his word, carried several bags and Abit had a couple, as well.

"Ah, you of little faith. We come bearing fine foods from Blowing Rock's best home-cooking diner."

"We ate some in the car," Abit added, "but there's plenty left. Alex thinks we should all have a picnic. Including Daddy and Mama!" Abit was smiling like a bandit who'd gotten away with the big haul, but I was pretty sure Mildred would be ready to spit—her dinner all for naught.

Turned out, Alex had called her from the road, so she wouldn't have to cook, for once. Abit went up to get his parents, and they came down the steps together, Vester looking like he was dragging Mildred to the picnic, and Mildred like she was dragging Vester. But we had a surprisingly good time together, sitting around the picnic table next to the store. We all tucked into fried catfish, coleslaw, green beans, hush puppies, and an assortment of home-baked pies. Jake was busy hoovering scraps and bits that weren't always accidentally dropped.

I had to hand it to Alex. The ultimate Yankee stranger had started to make inroads with those two, something I hadn't been able to do in over a year. I knew some of that involved the store purchase and Abit's devotion, but still, Alex was doing me a favor—life would be a little more civil at Coburn's Country Store.

The next morning, Alex mentioned something about Abit asking a favor of him, and he wanted to oblige. They'd be gone most of the morning—though this time he promised to be home in time for Abit's dinner. They also planned to go out again afterwards.

"Really? Where are you going this time?" I asked. I couldn't imagine what they were up to.

"This afternoon, Abit wants to show me the route of the Rolling Store. By the way, he gave me a tour inside that bus yesterday afternoon, and I was duly impressed. He and Duane are loading up tomorrow and heading out. I suppose I should do the same."

I tried not to look disappointed. I just nodded and went back to making our breakfast. Alex showered and dressed, eating quickly before leaving for his road trip with Abit.

When I heard them pull up, just before noon, I stopped sweeping the floor and went to the window. I saw Alex get out of the car, but I didn't see Abit. Alex had picked up someone else and brought him to the store. I could say goodbye to good times if Mildred caught wind of this.

The door flew open and I heard, "Hi Della. Waddaya think?" Abit twirled like a runway model in his new clothes. No overalls and flannel shirt—khakis and an oxford-cloth sports shirt, instead. "Alex helped me pick these out—I used my own money. Come on, waddaya think?"

My throat felt tight, and I didn't trust my voice. He looked so grown up, ready for high school or even a job.

"You don't like 'em?" Abit said, his face falling.

Alex put a hand on Abit's shoulder. "She loves them, Abit. Give her a moment to take you in."

I bent over to finish my sweeping, and while nudging the last bits into the dustpan, I managed, "Abit, you look wonderful." By the time I stood up, I could add, "I didn't recognize you at first. I thought Alex had brought someone else home and your mother would skin us all alive, his leaving you in town."

"Glad I don't look the same. This is the new me," he said, twirling one more time.

Chapter 50: Abit

Mystery Hill was a blast. I felt right at home there—the gravity being out of whack, and all. That was what a typical day used to feel like for me. Then we came home and had our family picnic, and Mama and Daddy actually seemed to have fun.

The next day, Alex took me shopping, and he helped me pick out shirts that didn't look too "preppy," as he called it. Said that wouldn't fly in Timbuctoo. Not sure what he was talking about, but I think he meant I wanted to look just local enough to not stand out. He and Della said they thought I looked pretty cool, and you know, I did too.

I wished I could've hung out and talked with them, but I was almost late for dinner. Mama told me to be sure and not mess up her schedule like the day before, though I could tell she'd enjoyed herself at our picnic. Even so, when we got back home afterwards, all she said was, "That strawberry pie ain't never seen no oven." Man, we all had so much fun—her and Daddy included—I couldn't figure out why she acted like that.

I wondered what she'd say about my new clothes. I didn't think about how she might be hurt I didn't ask her to go with me. She'd been picking out my clothes for almost sixteen year. But I used my own money, and Alex was who I wanted to come along and help.

Chapter 51: Della

I couldn't sit still. I needed to get out and go somewhere to enjoy the spring weather.

Fortunately, Billie's schedule jibed with my mood; she was working the store that day. I decided a drive over to Elbert's would boost my spirits. He lived in a particularly idyllic valley, and there was something special about that household of four generations of women and girls—from his grandbaby and two daughters to his wife and mother. I thanked Billie and headed outside. Abit was in his chair, back after spending some time with Alex, doing goodness knows what. He looked at me hopefully.

"Hey, we need more honey. Want to go to Elbert's?" I asked and then added, "On the clock."

He sprang off his chair and jumped into the truck. We didn't talk much on the drive. By then, we'd grown comfortable enough in each other's presence, words weren't necessary. As soon as we hit the driveway, Elbert came out on the porch. "Come on in," he said, waving at us in the car. "I know it looks like we're moving, but we're not going nowhere. We're here to stay."

"Why does he say that every time? We know he ain't going nowhere," Abit said, annoyed.

"Anywhere. And isn't. And it's just his way of saying howdy. That and making excuses in case I might judge the looks of his front porch. I couldn't care less, but people tend to think that since I'm not from around here, I look down on your ways."

"I'm glad you're not from round here."

"Come on, now, you're the one who blamed *me* for not liking folks. What about Cleva and Duane and Mary Lou? And don't forget Wilkie and the Ledfords and Elbert. And there are others."

"Oh, yeah? Name them."

I paused for a moment. "Okay, let's not keep Elbert waiting."

Back at the store, I unpacked the honey and noticed a couple of jars in one case were cracked. I didn't think we'd broken them on the way home, but I wasn't about to haggle with Elbert over five dollars. Still, a customer had ordered a case, so I needed a full case for him and one for the store. While Billie was working, I drove back to Elbert's on my own.

We went through the same routine, as though I hadn't just been there. He apologized and wanted to give me the jars for free. I thought of all the blackberries, applesauce, and pickles I'd come home with over the past year, and I insisted on paying. While Elbert rummaged around on his porch for some newspapers— "I'm gonna wrap them jars good this time"—I killed some time picking through a pile of books on the front porch. Several tattered books lay on top, but one caught my eye: a travel guide to the North Carolina mountains. I needed another book like that, so when Elbert was finished wrapping, I asked if I could buy it.

"Oh, I'll just throw that in for your trouble. I found that at the dump the other day, and it seemed too good to leave behind. Same with them other books. Take anything you want."

"Thanks, Elbert. And thanks again for all the berries and beans and such." He just waved me off as though they were nothing. I shook my head, thinking how valuable they were to me—and how much work went into preserving them.

When I drove up to the store, Abit's chair was empty. Good for him—off with Alex again, most likely, but I wondered where since Alex's car was in the parking lot. No other cars were in the lot, so I told Billie to go on home early, before the school bus dropped off her kids.

I settled in with a cup of tea and picked up my new travel guide. Our region was filled with beautiful Arts & Craft-era hotels, cabins, and outposts, many of which I hadn't even heard of. As I leafed through the book, I scanned the notes in the margins from the previous owner. I found a café outside of Asheville I wanted to go to, maybe before Alex left again.

Speaking of the devil, he walked into the store and grabbed a cold lemonade. I set the book down with a niggling feeling, something I couldn't quite place. Alex put a five-dollar bill on the counter, and as I made change, I asked where he'd been.

"Abit wanted to show me his hubcap collection. It's really impressive. I told him if he ever wanted to sell it, I could find some folks in Virginia who'd pay top dollar."

"I hope Vester didn't hear you. He's always trying to clear that out."

"Actually, he was with us in the barn. He did perk up when I mentioned sales, but he said something about holding on to them so the value would go up even more."

"He's coming around, I think. He was almost friendly at our impromptu picnic."

"That's because we were all feeling so friendly," he said, standing behind me and putting his arms around me.

"So when are you going back to D.C.?"

"Trying to get rid of me?"

"Not really, just wondering."

"Soon," he said, "but not for a day or two more. And I want to come back next month. You didn't tell me Abit's sixteenth birthday was coming up. I can't miss that."

"Did you two cook anything up?"

"Not yet. He said his folks always had cake and ice cream, but I think we should try for something special. Either way, Abit told me his folks agreed to his inviting us this year."

"I believe you've started to win them over. I'm grateful."

"How grateful?"

"Just good friend grateful," I said, wiggling out of his arms.

Alex went up to the apartment to feed Jake and start dinner. He'd taken on a new challenge: making dinner from store ingredients that needed to be used. That seemed to spark his creativity. His chicken Marsala the other night rivaled Oscar's in D.C.

I picked up the book again and looked for the copyright page. Guidebooks went out of date so fast, I didn't want to bother with something from even just three or four years ago. I was surprised, given its appearance, that it was copyrighted last year. Of course, a trip to the county dump could do that. I noticed a dog-eared page just past the copyright page, a once-blank page that had been filled with a neat list of notes. And that's when it clicked. The notes in the margin and on that page were in Lucy's handwriting—mostly driving directions to Laurel Falls and some places she wanted to visit.

I also noticed that the book kept opening at a certain spot, and when I let it, I saw where ten or so pages had been ripped out. The last page before the tear was about Asheville, and the first page after the tear featured Jefferson and the Ashe County Courthouse. It was obvious that our region had been removed, but I was curious about exactly what was on those pages. I didn't know what that might tell me, but it seemed important to find out. Had Lucy removed them for easier handling, or had someone else removed those pages because of something in them?

On Sunday morning over breakfast—Alex made waffles topped with fresh strawberries—we talked about driving to Boone, the nearest city with a decent bookstore that would likely stock the guidebook. We cleared the dishes and headed downstairs, Jake in the lead. Abit stood up to greet Jake, avoiding the usual collision.

"Hey, Mister, whatcha up to?"

"Nothin'." He looked so glum I didn't dare look at Alex, or I'd've started laughing. I loved that boy, man, whatever, but he did pitiful so well, it was hard to keep a straight face.

"Want to go to Boone?"

"I ain't ever been there!"

"Well, stop saying ain't, and we'll take you," Alex said. "And be sure to wear some of your fine new duds."

"But first ask your mother," I added.

He ran up the steps like a boy and came back down looking ten years older.

Chapter 52: Abit

"When are we going to get there?"

Alex and Della looked back at me, both of them frowning like a hoot owl. I started laughing. "I've never said that before. Hell, I've never really been anywhere," I told them, "but I've seen that on TV shows, the way kids was always asking that on car trips." Alex gave me a thumbs up, and we was all laughing by then, so I doubted they heard me add, "If it were up to me, we could keep on driving forever."

As we rode along, I asked Alex all kinds of questions about his life in D.C. Unlike Della, he was a real talker. He told me about some of the parks and museums. And he mentioned that prize and the trouble he got into because of some mistake. I'd heard Della mention it before, and I think it musta weighed heavy on him. He told me he'd tell me about that another time, which was music to my ears. *Another time*. I didn't like him at first, but I was probably kinda jealous. I was getting to like him almost as much as Della.

"When are you going back?" I asked, hoping he'd stay a while longer.

"Ha! That's some way to put it, Abit. Let me tell you something about wordsmithing—when talking to people, try putting things positively. As in 'How long are you staying?'"

I felt a hot flush come over me. I didn't know if I was mad or embarrassed, likely both. He looked at me in the rearview mirror and musta seen it. I could feel how red my face was.

"Hey, Abit. I'm sorry. I can get pretty pompous sometimes. Just ask Della."

She turned round and smiled at me, like she knew how I felt. I pouted for a few minutes, but then I decided not to ruin such a good day over something like that. And, besides, he had a point.

"It's just that I want to stay more than I want to go back," he said after a while. "Apology accepted?"

I decided he'd meant it. I nodded. We rode along, quiet-like for a while, but then it all blew over, like we'd rolled down the windows and let out a bad smell.

We didn't talk about anything serious after that. We laughed at stuff we saw along the way, like a hand-painted sign that said "Entrance Only. Do Not Enter." And another one that read "New Image Plumbing." That made us all think of butt cracks, which really cracked us up.

They talked a lot about the beautiful scenery along the way, and I had to agree. I grew up in the mountains, but I'd never been to that area before. I really liked seeing the way the clouds dipped down into the valleys and the jagged mountain tops rippled along the edge of the sky. When we got to Boone, there were a lot of weird looking kids wandering round, but some nice tall buildings, too. Seven stories. So far, the tallest building I'd ever seen—not on TV—was two stories.

"There it is," Della shouted, pointing at a wood-sided shop with big picture windows. "Looks as though there's a parking lot in the next block."

We all piled out of the car and headed back to the store. I'd never been in one, but I imagined it would be kinda like libraries I'd seen on TV. (We didn't have one in town and our school was too small for one.) The first thing that struck me was the smell. A really nice mix of paper and leather and waxed wooden floors, like the ones in Della's store. And if I squinted at all the shelves of books, they looked like crazy quilts hanging on the walls—the way some of the books stood upright and others leaned at an angle. I felt right at home.

We each went off in our own direction. I started toward the children's section in the back, but then a book about short line railroads caught my eye. I looked through that one, and then I noticed a book on car repair. I spent all my time going from one book to another—mostly looking at the pictures but reading some, too. There was even one on the history of the Rolling Store. I took it over to show Della, who was in the local section looking at books about hiking and visiting the mountains. I couldn't imagine why she wanted that—she could've asked her customers for free.

"Would you like that book, Abit? I'd love to have it, too. If I get it, we could share it. I'd like to know more about rolling stores."

"I don't know if I could read it all that much, but I'd like to look at the pictures."

"I bet you could read more than you think. We could read it together."

Man, it was shaping up to be another great day. And it got better. We ate in a really nice restaurant, and Alex treated us. I had something called a club sandwich that was held together with little toothpicks dressed up with green curls. And fries. I loved fries, and Mama never made 'em. We all got hot fudge sundaes, too. We didn't even have to split them—Alex got us each one of our own.

On the ride home, Della showed us the books she'd bought—not just the Rolling Store book but also that one about the mountains, two novels, and a cookbook on how to grill fish.

"Alex, what did you get?" I asked.

"I've got a home full of books, Abit, so I'm trying to resist buying more. Who knows, maybe I'll move someday, and I won't be able to take all the ones I've already got." He looked funny at me, but I wasn't sure why. "But I couldn't resist this one." He nodded at Della, who handed me a book. "I got it for you," he added. "An early birthday present."

The cover had a bunch of pictures of things like stamps, coins, and such. And I could read the title: *The Collector's Guide to Everything*. It wouldn't take a genius to figure it was about collecting things, but I wasn't into stamps or coins or silver coffee pots. Even so, it was really nice of him to think of me. I saw him look at me again in the rearview mirror.

"Turn to page fifty-four."

My heart nearabout stopped. Hubcaps. Lots of pictures of hubcaps—some even from as far back as 1915. Twenty pages of all kinds of hubcaps and what to look for. I couldn't believe my eyes. I hadn't ever got a present that were so, well, me! I felt pretty choked up, so I grabbed my handkerchief and acted like I just had to sneeze.

"Good! Glad you like it, Abit," Alex said.

I asked Della about the mountain guidebook, why she didn't just ask her customers about our neck of the woods.

"That makes a lot of sense, Abit. I guess this trip was a wild goose chase since I didn't really find out anything new."

"But then we wouldn't have had this great day together," I said. Nobody said much after that. Just as well that we rode home in peace, because nothin' would be the same after that.

June 1985

Chapter 53: Abit

Mama baked my favorite cake—apple nut—for my sixteenth birthday. She made the icing by boiling brown sugar and butter and evaporated milk and poured it on the day before so it could soak down into the cake. Usually, she had to hide the leftovers from me, but that year it was pretty well picked over. I didn't mind because instead of a sorry little celebration with just the three of us, we all got together like a big family, including Della, Cousin Ned, and even Cleva. She knew Mama from way back. Actually, everybody in town knew each other, except for Alex, who came back just for my birthday!

Mama and Daddy gave me a watch, and Della slipped fifty bucks inside a funny card. Cleva handed me a card with a note about how she was gonna coach me through the driving rule book. (Cousin Ned had already gave me one, and I'd started studying on my own, but I sure needed help.) And the best surprise was driving lessons from Alex. In the Merc! He'd checked with Mama and Daddy first, and they said sure. I bet they did, so happy they wouldn't have to keep telling me no.

We didn't waste any time getting started. The next day, Alex knocked on our door, and said howdy to Mama and Daddy and thanked them for last night. He was real polite like that. Then we headed out.

"So where do you want to drive to?" Alex asked, handing me the keys.

"I've been thinking about that, and I want to go back to the Rollin' Store route, the one I showed you. I want folks to see me driving, and besides, it's out of all the traffic." He snorted for some reason; maybe he was allergic to what was bloomin' now. I got that sometimes.

Anyways, I sat behind the wheel and turned the key. The feeling was hard to describe—powerful, grownup, fun, all at the same time. As I slowly pulled out of the driveway, I noticed the curtain in our big front window moved. I did all right with the gears, and Alex didn't even seem to mind when I ground 'em a time or two. "I've done that before," was all he said.

I gave a toot-toot as we passed the Ledford' place, where Mrs. Ledford was working on some flower beds out front. I could tell she couldn't figure out who we were, but then Roy saw me and started laughing. I bet I looked a sight driving that Merc. I waved and laughed right along with him. Then Mrs. Ledford came a running, so I pulled over at a turnout and rolled down the window.

"Honey, just look at you. All growed up and driving. Ms. Kincaid said you were having your sixteenth."

It felt good to know that Della had bothered to tell anyone about my birthday. I put the car in park and jumped out and hugged her. I don't know what came over me; I just felt so damned happy. I introduced them all to Alex, though they might've met already at the store. Everyone was smiling and nodding.

"V.J. is getting his first driving lesson," Alex said, patting me on the back. They looked at each other, puzzled by that name, but then they seemed to get it. I figured Mrs. Ledford would be calling me that from then on. We said our goodbyes and got back in the car. Alex showed me about the emergency brake, which was a good idea, he said, when parked on a slope. I eased the car back onto the road, and we traveled the rest of my route, waving at more of the customers, but not stopping. I loved being behind the wheel.

Just as we rounded a bend outside of Beaverdam, I shouted, "Whoa! Hold on a minute. I've got to see this." I pulled ahead into a wide spot next to some rhododendron and cut that noisy engine. I loved that car, but it was a rattletrap. "I don't want them to hear us."

"Who?"

"I'll tell you in a minute," I whispered. I got out, real quiet-like, and crept along the bushes. I couldn't believe my eyes. Kitt, that woman who owned the art store, and Blanche Scoggins, the nasty laundromat woman, were hugging. It looked as though Kitt had been crying, and Blanche was patting her on the back. I knew that hug was about more than Kitt losing her favorite sock in the washer. They sure didn't seem like strangers to one another.

I couldn't imagine what was going on. Not that I get out much, but if they'd knowed each other, seemed to me word would've got round. I went back to the car, started it up, and got the hell out of there. I couldn't wait to tell Della about this. I explained everything to Alex on the ride back.

"Well, maybe Kitt got to know Blanche through the laundromat."

"Trust me, that wouldn't make them friends. That woman Blanche is a terror to her customers."

"Okay, maybe they met through church, or somewhere."

"Do them two look like they go to church?"

"Those two. Did you say anything to them?"

I looked at him like he was crazy. "I wasn't born yesterday."

"Yes, you were," he said. It took me a minute to get that one, and then we both had a good laugh. But that was all Alex said the rest of the way home, except when he pointed out that I was following someone too close.

When we pulled into the store's driveway, Alex told me I was a natural behind the wheel. I parked, got out of the car, and handed him the keys. I stuck out my hand and said, "Thanks for the lesson, Alex." He smiled real big and shook my hand before heading upstairs to let Jake out. I ran inside to talk with Della, who looked surprised, too, when I told her my news.

"I never heard Blanche or Kitt say—or even intimate—they knew each other," Della said.

"That's what I thought."

"Maybe Blanche befriended Kitt." We both looked at each and shook our heads.

"I just got this feeling they knew each other real well. One of those gut things you keep telling me to pay attention to."

Then Della said, "I just remembered I've got a couple of rugs that need washing."

Chapter 54: Della

Alex faced looming deadlines, and I'd let store duties languish. He drove to Asheville to work in the library and file some stories by fax, while I tackled the cheese counter and storeroom. I was surprised by how satisfying I found scraping down the cheeses. Cradling them in my hands, each cheese felt alive—pungent and ever-changing. Not to mention these frequent scrapings made them last longer.

As I worked on an aged gouda, I thought about how I was at a standstill with my efforts to exonerate Gregg. And at a loss about what to do next. At least he was out on bail, and with any luck, his attorney was worth his exorbitant hourly rate.

Alex still wasn't home when I closed the store, so I ran down to the laundromat with some rugs. By the time I got back, Abit was romping around with Jake in the back meadow, and Alex was sitting in a lawn chair watching.

"What's for dinner?" I asked, hoping he'd started something simmering on the stove.

"Reservations."

"Very funny. I don't think you can even make those here."

"Okay, omelets."

"Sounds good. I've got to go back down to the laundromat before eight o'clock when it closes, or I'll have to pay a storage fee."

Alex looked confused, but I just said, "Not worth explaining. I'm starving." Abit ran on home without any coaxing. He didn't even look sad—tomorrow was rolling store day, so he needed to be up early and out on the road.

Over dinner, Alex asked, "So what's with Kitt?"

"What about her?"

"Why was Abit all worked up about her hugging the laundromat looney?"

"I asked Blanche about that today. I didn't want to set Kitt off—not that I enjoyed talking to Blanche, but she seemed the better one to talk to. After she hemmed and hawed a while, she explained that she was Kitt's mother, and they just didn't want this gossipy town to know all about them. I let it go at that, but then in a weak moment she made some revealing comments about her laundromat and how it came in handy since they were both fed up with paying taxes and getting nothing for them."

"Ha! I told you Mayberry had more crooks than you could imagine. And laundering money at a laundromat! Priceless." He enjoyed that irony for a moment and then turned serious. "Did she say they got nothing for their taxes? Did you remind her about roads and sewers and schools and sheriffs? And volunteer fire departments and libraries and …."

"No," I interrupted, "I wanted to get out of there as fast as possible. I told her I didn't care what she and Kitt were up to."

"Wonder why she came clean, as it were?"

"She was out of options, I guess. She may write all those bossy signs, but she's kind of pathetic, and she's a terrible liar. Anyway, I didn't pursue it. It wasn't that she said anything particularly incriminating, at least not until she said she'd get me back if I told anyone. I just said, 'Tell anyone what?' and she nodded, satisfied. Believe me, I *do not* want to tangle with that woman. I know what they're doing isn't right, but folks here have a hardscrabble life. Let 'em have something extra at the end of the week."

Alex left on Saturday. Abit gave him a bear hug before he got in the car. I'd done the same earlier. We both stood there a while after his car was out of sight.

"Well, let's get back to our routine, Mister." I thought that would cheer him up, but he looked sad.

"That's okay for you, but now all I've got to do is sit here. Even Wilkie ain't here today."

"Isn't. And what about that book on hubcaps? Why not start organizing yours and cataloging them? I know your Cousin Ned helps with that, but I'm happy to help, too. Though I don't know the first thing about hubcaps—not even how to get them off in the case of a flat tire. But I do know about organizing. You could put labels on the back and put them into categories and such."

"But I cain't read what the book says about them."

"Who says? Go get it, and we'll see."

He ran up the steps to his house two steps at a time, and when he came back, we spent some time between customers going over the twenty pages on hubcaps. I got him to read lots of words, and I filled in a few for him to learn. I grabbed some yellow sticky notes, and he wrote one word and its definition per note and stuck it on that page. I enjoyed watching him get excited.

"You can bring the hubcaps down and work in the shed behind the store, if you like," I offered. "That barn of yours looks kind of snaky to me."

"Oh, it ain't bad, but I'd rather use your shed. That way I won't piss off Daddy if I don't clean up every last thing."

We both worked away at the Coburn Country Store. That evening, it almost burned down.

Chapter 55: Abit

"Fire! Daddy! Help!"

I was running round to the back of the store and shouting up at the house. I smelled the kerosene right away, because I was hiding in the bushes. I'd seen what happened.

It was about ten o'clock at night, and Della and Jake were over at Cleva's for the evenin'. The reason I was outside was Daddy and I'd had a big quarrel. Not worth goin' in to—just another night of two frustrated people getting in each other's faces. I got sick of hearing him go on, so I ran out and sat in my chair and fumed. The evening was cool, so I had on my black coat.

I guessed you couldn't see me sitting in my chair out front of the store, because the firebug, who was also dressed in black, didn't seem to notice me. Typical. Even people up to no good, people who shoulda been watching to see if anyone was round, didn't see me. Anyways, he crouched down and waddled toward the back of the store.

I slipped round the other side of the store and used a yellow bell bush for cover. When he struck a match, I shouted out, "Hey, you there!" Of course, he run off, but I was more worried about the fire than trying to catch him. I heard a car start up and head off toward town.

That's when I started shouting for Daddy. He was grumpy sometimes, but he wouldn't ignore my call for help. In fact, he knew just what to do and showed up with an ax and hollered at me to get the hose and water going. Like I didn't know to do that—I was already unrolling the hose from where we'd used it to wash the Rollin' Store. He started hacking out the burning wood, and I got water on the rest of the area round it. I think he'd probably thought *what if the store catches fire* many a night when he owned it, because it was like he'd practiced.

Mama called the volunteer fire department, and they showed up to finish the job. (Fires could look like they were out, but they wasn't.) Not long after that, Della and Jake rolled into the driveway, their nice evening ruint.

I guessed I looked a mess, my face all sooty, because the first thing outa Della's mouth was, "Abit, are you okay?" I nodded and started telling her everything I saw. She had to stop me so she could get Jake back in the truck. He was nosing round and getting in the way of the firemen.

The next day, that stupid Sheriff Brower showed up, and, of course, he didn't believe me. "Seen too many crime shows, son. I imagine Missy here left her percolator plugged in too long."

"You're full of shit, Brower, and a lousy sheriff." That's what went through my head; what I said was, well, nothin'.

Della took a breath or two, trying to tamp down her temper, before asking, "Can't you get the fire department to test for accelerant?"

"And you've been watching too many crime shows, too. We've only got a volunteer fire department, which you're lucky we have. We're not going to get a fire investigator up here for a kitchen fire. Maybe your insurance company will conduct an investigation."

"Not likely. And I'm not reporting it. Duane said he could repair it for under $500, which is lower than my deductible."

"Okay, there you are. No one harmed, nothing stolen—right? Everyone's happy."

Not me, and not Della. Only him because he didn't have to do no work. When he left, I asked Della, "Does this mean I don't have a job no more?"

She just shook her head. She didn't even correct my words. I decided to walk toward town, to see if I could see anything down where I'd heard that car start up. It'd been dry lately, so I couldn't see no tracks to speak of. I wandered round in a stand of trees near the clearing, but still, nothin'. Then I noticed where a tree had been swiped—some of the bark was scratched off and the gash looked real fresh. Just behind the tree, I found a hubcap, kinda cool looking with sixteen really short spokes. At the time, I just thought about how lucky I was—a new one for my collection. I carried it back and showed Della, but she was busy on the telephone. I reckoned it was nothin' special, so I took it to the shed behind the store where I was organizing my collection.

Chapter 56: Della

"You've pissed someone off, and it's time that lazy sheriff did something to help you," Alex said when I called him about the fire. "'Your percolator, Missy,' my ass! He's an idiot. All the more reason you need to give this shit up, Della. You're in over your head with no backup."

He was stunned when I agreed. I needed to let all the crazy detective work go. I couldn't really help Gregg anymore—that's what his lawyer was for—and I was exhausted from the turmoil. The night before, I was swearing like a card-carrying member of the Green Treatise. After I let it all out, I felt spent. Done. I wasn't a youthful reporter anymore, and I didn't want to die trying to find out why Lucy died. Or at least that was what I was telling myself. We were so close to the truth, I could feel it, but Brower figured he had his man. Even the SBI was sticking with Gregg as the culprit, weak as their evidence and motive were. Somebody needed to fight this, but I didn't see how that could be me.

"Who do you think is behind all this?" Alex asked. We were both silent for some time, thinking.

After a few minutes, I said, "Remember that article we wrote together—the one about the rich family in Chevy Chase, and how we just sensed that something was wrong? Something made our radar go off?"

"Hard to forget. Didn't you break an arm during a scuffle with those scofflaws?"

Ah, Alex. Ever the alliterist, if that's even a word. "My radar keeps buzzing around Gregg and people he came in contact with. Tattoo Man doesn't seem likely, and Cassie can't be the one. She's too caught up in her religion."

"Um, have you been paying attention to the news of the world? Religion *starts* wars."

"Okay, but she doesn't have the gumption to figure all these machinations out ahead of time. I doubt she could figure them out *after* the fact."

"I was planning to do more research on some of your town folk. I recall you said that Max the preacher man was awfully curious about the suicide note. Wasn't he from Georgia? Same place as Lucy? What's his last name?"

"Perkins. Father Max Perkins from Savannah, Georgia—not Atlanta. I honestly believe he just wanted to know what the note said to make his service more relevant." When I thought about it, though, that note didn't say enough to matter at the service. He *could* have been interested for other reasons. "Oh, surely there's no way he's involved in this."

"That's what Ted Bundy's neighbors said."

We talked a while longer. He made me promise to step back; I knew if I did, he would, too. Besides, if Brower wouldn't help, our hands were tied. Which was exactly what Brower—and the killer—wanted. But so be it—I was done.

After the fire, I was able to keep the store open, though Duane's hammering and sawing made the whole store rattle and buzz, making life pretty unpleasant for me and my customers. (They, at least, got to leave after a while.) A few things walked over the edge of the shelves from all the vibrations. Most were cans, though a couple of broken mayonnaise jars splattered an oily mess over the floor and nearby groceries.

I knew Vester and Abit were hovering around Duane in the back, giving him unwanted advice, but I wasn't about to tell them to go home. Let Duane fight his own battles. And I was grateful that they'd contained the fire. I couldn't even think about what would have happened if Vester hadn't pissed off Abit. That chair out front should be elevated to a throne!

Community hadn't figured much in my life. Sure, I had friends, but everyone was always so busy. And neighbors? Forget it. We barely said hello as we passed in the hallways or at the front door. Not to mention I had a creepy security guard who kept asking me out and following me around. Abit was the best security guard I could ever have.

When Duane broke for lunch, I enjoyed the relative quiet and pulled together a meal for myself. I was getting tired of eating things that hadn't sold, so I splurged and opened a new smoked trout, which I ate with pickled onions and French bread. When I finished, I took a couple of mugs of coffee out front. I'd seen Abit's cowlick through the plate glass window.

I handed him his mug and sat on the bench next to him. "I can't do this anymore," I told him.

"What? All the noise and hammering? Yeah, it must sound like a freight train coming through the store," he said, sipping his coffee.

"No, I mean the search for Lucy's killer. This is way out of my skill set."

"No it ain't. Isn't. We're just about there. We *can* do this."

"That's what scares me most, Abit. *We*. You could have been hurt or even killed by the arsonist—or the fire itself. I can't tell you how grateful I am that you and your father saved the store, but I'm done. I just want to do what I came here to do. Live a simpler life, sell some groceries and beer, talk with you and the customers, like now."

I thought that would please him, but instead, his face turned a deep red. "What are you talking about?" he shot back. "You were the one—I heard you say this more than oncet—that you *had* to do this. You couldn't *not* help that poor girl."

"But I can't help her. She's gone. Just like my neighbor."

Abit looked confused by my last comment, but that didn't stop him from shouting, "But we *can* find the asshole who did it. And what about Gregg?"

"He's got an attorney. Let him do his job. We can't help him anymore. And even if we could, what if you or your father or me or Jake got hurt in the process?"

"That's not what you've been teaching me. Not even close!" Abit stood up so fast the chair clattered to the ground. He stormed up the steps to his house.

I knew I was doing the right thing, and I thought he'd get over it. His folks would tell him he was out of line, youthful enthusiasm without understanding the consequences, and so on. I righted his chair and went inside.

But two days later, he still hadn't come down to sit in his chair.

When I closed up that night, I felt shattered. I told Jake that we needed a drive and a dinner of excellent food and attentive service. The word "drive" sent him into pirouettes on his hind legs. I fed him first, then we loaded into the truck and took a slow drive up the Blue Ridge Parkway. I hadn't been back to the Inn at Jonas Mountain since I went with Alex and Abit, and I was looking forward to someone else taking care of me. It was always cool enough up there to leave Jake in the truck with the windows cracked.

I grabbed my purse and a book I'd been meaning to read and headed inside the inn. On the way up, I'd already figured out my order—a reprise of broiled rainbow trout—so I didn't even open the menu when the hostess seated me in a smaller dining room, just off the main one. While I waited for my dinner, I took in the spectacular view. The sun had begun its descent behind the mountains, shooting out rays that reminded me of a proud male turkey, showing off his gorgeous fantail. The sun was definitely strutting its stuff that evening.

Off to my left, someone with long blond hair caught my eye. She was leaning over her table in an exaggerated way, either telling a secret or whispering sweet nothings. When she leaned back, I dropped my book on the floor. Kitt Scanlon. Talking to Alex Covington. The bastard was at it again.

Chapter 57: Della

I made my excuses and slipped out of the inn as quietly as possible. I didn't even remember the drive home. Somehow we made it safely. I let Jake romp around in the back meadow while I made a sign for the front door of the store. No apologies, just "Closed until further notice."

Between Alex and the fire and the crime spree in this godforsaken community, I couldn't face another day of that store. I wished it had gone ahead and burned down; if it had, I wouldn't have given a thought to resurrecting it. R.I.P. Just thinking about all those people over all those months who never smiled and rarely even spoke to me made me pour more wine into my glass.

I hadn't gotten dressed or answered my phone in five days. I could hear those coots honking their horns, and I loved it that no one was running down to kowtow to them. I kept thinking about how crazy I'd been to buy it and move there. The phone rang a few more times, but I'd disconnected the answering machine, so I didn't have to hear their inane complaints.

Later that day, I heard a knock on my apartment door. Great, some jerk invading my personal space, just so he could get some beer—or Band-Aids because he'd beaten his wife again. I got up and peeked between the curtains on the door window. Cleva. She was about the only person I'd open for.

"It's over," I told her after I shut the door.

"Well, I can see that. Your parking lot is empty."

"That's not unusual."

"Yes it is, honey—if you'd start seeing the glass half full, and I'm not referring to this," she said, walking to the kitchen and pouring my full glass of wine in the sink. "Now, what brought all this on? The fire?"

"In part." Then I told her about the Inn at Jonas Mountain.

"Well, you're divorced, aren't you?"

"Look, so-called friend, if that's what you've got to share, go share it somewhere else."

And she did.

Chapter 58: Abit

I felt as sick as I'd ever been, but nothin' was really wrong with me. Mama fluttered round, bringing me juice and soup and stuff, but I didn't eat none. She knew somethin' was wrong because I never refused her cooking.

She came in later to tell me that Della hadn't opened the store in days. Like I didn't know. I hadn't left the house in as many days, but I knew what was—or wasn't—going on down there. I could hear people honkin' and calling out. They musta been too stupid to read—Mama said Della had a sign up in the window that said the store was closed. That made my stomach ache even worse. I just laid there. I didn't even watch TV. Only thing on was those awful soaps, and I had enough troubles of my own without watching someone else's.

The next day, I thought the store must've opened again, because all these cars kept driving up. But they didn't stay long enough to buy anything, so I reckoned they just got out, read the sign, and drove off. It was going on five days now, and I was sick and tired of being in the house. I wanted to make up with Della real bad, but I wasn't about to go knocking on her upstairs door.

I thought maybe a little tapping might ease her out, so I headed down the steps. When I got halfway down, I saw Mary Lou Dockery drive off. She waved, like she was happy. What in the hell did she have to be all happy about?

As I got closer to where my chair usually sat, I couldn't see it. *Damn*, I thought, *did Della go on such a tear that she threw out my chair?* That was going too far. That was *my* chair.

But then I realized something completely different was going on. I found my chair, cleaned it off, and began tapping.

Chapter 59: Della

Dammit. I kept hearing all this racket downstairs, with cars driving up and driving off, sometimes grinding in the gravel driveway, digging for traction to get out fast. Where were they when I was open? I sat there stewing for a while and got myself so worked up, I actually called Janice Dockery, the realtor I'd bought the store through. When her answering service picked up, I hung up. But, by God, I'd try her again later.

I went back to bed; I was so tired I just wanted to sleep. Then I heard tapping. I tried to ignore it, but it tugged at me. I had to admit that I'd missed the big galoot. I felt sad thinking about how much he'd miss the store once I sold it, but maybe the new owner would keep him on. For Sale: Country Store with Live Griffon.

I'd stopped drinking after Cleva left in such a huff, and my appetite was coming back. Trouble was, I didn't have anything left to eat in the apartment. I didn't want to go downstairs, but I wasn't about to wait until dark to sneak into my own store. I washed my face, combed my hair, and put on jeans and a t-shirt. As I headed downstairs, Jake bounded past me, more than ready to get out of that apartment. When he flew around the corner, I heard Abit's chair hit the wall, hard.

Abit had Jake by the collar, and he looked up at me with a funny expression, an odd mix of fear and excitement. Then I saw why. I just stood there, not sure what to say.

The benches next to his chair were spilling over. Jars of blackberries and tomatoes and homemade vegetable soup. Small containers of jams and relishes and honey. All kinds of baked goods, including some of Mrs. Parker's cinnamon rolls. There were a couple of pots of herbs—parsley and rosemary—and one of pansies. And the closed sign I'd put on the door had an added message. Below my words, bright purple letters read: "Get well soon."

Cleva. Had Cleva written all over it.

Chapter 60: Abit

Della was back. She musta been hungry, because when I knocked on the door, she waved me inside, and I could see she was eating stuff right out of jars. I asked if she wanted me to bring in anything from outside, and she said not yet. "But could you please take down the closed sign and bring it to me?" I handed it to her, and she looked at it like it were a piece of art.

She told me about Alex and that woman Kitt, and I could tell she was really sad. When I asked her if that meant we'd never go back to the Inn at Jonas Mountain, her face fell. "I'm sorry. That was stupid," I said real quick-like. "I just had such a good time that evening."

She kinda smiled, a weak one, and added, "I did too." That was all she said for what felt like forever. Then she asked me to leave.

That had never happened before, and I didn't know whether to go back to my chair or go home. I figured the easiest thing would be to go home. But something told me to hang out for a while. Like sitting with a friend who didn't feel good, not saying anything. Just being there.

I didn't tap or nothin', though I nearabout fell off my chair when Alex drove up.

Chapter 61: Della

I was getting ready to take my gifts upstairs—a few more arrived while I was inside, not exactly hiding but sitting in the semi-dark with no lights on. Then I heard that goddam car of Alex's drive up. In a panic, I thought about locking the door and going into the backroom. But I'd just be trapped. Besides, Jake was going crazy at the sound of that car. Traitor.

The door opened, and Alex said, "Hi hon, I've found out some interesting things."

I picked up the closest object, which lucky for him was only a half-eaten baguette, and threw it at him.

"Hey, sorry I haven't called for a few days, but I've been busy." He looked closer at me and added, "Good God, what's happened to you?"

"You, you asshole."

"Whoa. Back up. What in the hell are you talking about?"

"Well, for starters, how'd you like dinner with Kitt?"

"Oh, for God's sake, that damn grapevine. Can't even bump into someone in this county without everyone gossiping about it."

"Really? That's all you can say about that?"

He looked so confused, I didn't know what to say next. But he did.

"She told me who killed Lucy. I'm not sure how, yet, but we're going to solve this mess, once and for all."

Chapter 62: Abit

Man, I couldn't believe Alex had the nerve to show up, but I was glad to see him. I was hoping he could talk some sense into Della. And I was bustin' to show him the hubcap I found down the road after the fire, but I wasn't about to stick my head in that store now, not even if you paid me. Besides, I was real clear where my loyalties laid.

I heard Della in there, her voice loud—not yelling, but plenty mad. Nothin' was smashing or anything like that, so I guessed they were talking things out. When Alex came out, he looked fine, maybe a little wore out, but nothin' bad. I decided I'd tell him then about the hubcap. After I did, he told me that was important and to hang on to it.

"Oh, and thanks, pal, for saving the store."

"Well, it were me and Daddy."

"Was."

"Yep, it was me and Daddy."

"I'll thank him too, but for now, I'm thanking you." At first I thought he was doing one of those picky things he does about saying things just right, but then he smiled, and we shook hands. It wasn't until he turned to get things out of his car that he noticed all the stuff on the benches. He looked confused.

"Did somebody die?"

"Not hardly. More like somebody came back to life."

Chapter 63: Della

"Well, you've certainly been blazing up and down the highways," I said to Alex, as I dried my hair with a towel. I'd taken my first shower in five days and was starting to feel human again.

I'd decided to believe his story. It was too convoluted to be fabricated. Alex explained that he'd found out some details he wanted to share in person—though I think this place was growing on him—and to offer moral support after the fire. He couldn't get out of D.C. until early afternoon, so on the way down, he stopped at the Inn at Jonas Mountain because he was starving. And about to fall asleep at the wheel. At the bar, where he'd ordered a cup of coffee while he waited for a table, Kitt Scanlon sidled up next to him. She told him she was waiting on a table, too, so why didn't they sit together?

"Okay, sounds plausible," I said. "And even you aren't that good of an actor—or that much of a cad—that you could've put on such a show of innocence when you arrived today." I picked up the hairdryer and turned it on. Then turned it off almost immediately. "Wait a minute," I said. "That happened *five* days ago—when I went to dinner at the inn, trying to cheer myself up. Sure didn't work out that way."

"Well, I'm sorry about that, but I wish you'd come over and spoken to us."

"Yeah, right. But what did you and Kitt do for the next four days?"

"I don't know what Kitt did, because I got called back to D.C." Something Kitt had shared triggered a new avenue to pursue, so he called his assistant, Devlin, to ask him to start researching it. But Devlin interrupted to tell Alex his best client—the publisher of a prestigious D.C.-based political magazine—had an emergency that he needed to deal with. Too important to dismiss, he said, so Alex turned around and headed back up Interstate 81 to D.C. It took him three days to resolve, after which he drove back down.

"What a mess. I can't believe you made that drive three times in five days."

"Yeah," he said, "but you've got to admit it was worth it."

It was. We'd put all his files in a couple of storage boxes, and as soon as I got dressed, we planned to take them to Brower's office. While I finished up (I had some catching up to do with my personal grooming), Alex anxiously paced around the apartment.

"Let's get going," he said. "I want to get that sheriff off his fat ass. He won't be able to sweep this under the rug."

"Ah, nothing like a good cliché from a Pulitzer winner!" I shouted from the bedroom.

"Yeah, and a stitch in time, saves nine, so hurry up. I can't wait to see Brower's face, which by the way, is a face only a mother could love. But if he has any smarts, he'll realize he's going to look great, even though he can't see the forest for the trees. Which, come to think of it, makes me madder than a wet hen."

"Oh, stop it," I said, laughing at his wordplay. I grabbed my purse and keys. "I don't care who gets the credit. I just want it over."

I felt wiped out when we got back from Brower's, so I lay down for a few minutes. By the time I woke up, I was starving. My appetite had come back with a vengeance. I'd promised Abit that we'd take him to dinner—just to Geri Cantwell's (I hadn't been back since The Day), but by the look on his face, you'd have thought it were La Taberna. He'd already eaten supper with his family, but he was happy to eat again.

It was my turn to hurry Alex along, but he insisted he needed a drink first. After making himself a gin and tonic, we sat together and talked about what we'd just done. Lonnie had made a low whistle when he read one report, and Brower bowled us both over by admitting it was good investigative work. I was glad it was out of my hands now, though I wasn't completely out of the action. I still had a role to play in the plan Brower had agreed to.

"We'd better get Abit and go to dinner, Alex." As we went downstairs, Jake ran ahead. Abit managed to avoid his greeting, trying to keep his new togs clean.

"Did Mildred say it was okay?" I asked. He rolled his eyes, letting me know he wouldn't be standing there in his khakis with wet hair, neatly combed, if she hadn't. He piled in the back with Jake, and I sat behind the wheel.

"Hey, why do you get to drive the Merc, Della?"

"Handsome here needed a drink after our talk with Lonnie."

"What kind?"

"Gin and tonic," Alex told him. "With lime."

"Sounds good."

"Well, when you're twenty-one, I'll make you one," Alex said, then quickly added, "But don't tell your folks I said that."

"I'll hold you to that," Abit said, not sounding at all like the boy I'd met last year.

Chapter 64: Abit

This time there were only three black and whites in the driveway. And I wasn't getting up from a nap. Honestly, even if I had been, I wouldn't't've had any trouble believing my eyes, not after the spring we'd had.

I wondered why Mama asked me after dinner to help her with the garden out back. She just wanted me well away from my chair in the front of the store. Something big was happening, and while I was curious, for oncet I was happy not being in the middle of it all.

Chapter 65: Della

I flinched when the bell over the front door jangled. The customer was smiling, ready to say hello, until I held up the hubcap and asked, "Look familiar?"

"Yes. It looks like a hubcap." So smug, I wanted to slap her.

"Kitt, you drive a BMW, and not many folks around here do. This hubcap was found nearby, right after the fire."

"I'm not the only person driving through here with a car like that. And I take good care of my car. I don't have any missing hubcaps."

"But I saw your car with a missing hubcap when you were out at your mother's place in Beaverdam. I was riding on the rolling store when we spotted it. And you were there with your mother."

Her face froze. But just for a second. She was that good. "What's going on? I thought you wanted to have another one of our little wine and cheese parties." When I didn't say anything, she added, "Look I don't know what kind of game you're playing at. I thought you were kinda cool, but I guess I misjudged you."

"No, I misjudged *you*. I never imagined you could be behind at least two of those so-called oatmeal factories in Atlanta and taking—hell, stealing—money from men like Roberto Sanchez. Now does *that* sound familiar? You know, Lucy's father? Just like you misjudged that you could get away with murdering Lucy. Why did she have to die? Because she recognized you at the Green Treatise gatherings, and she knew what you'd done to her father? Was she going to tell Brower about your creative financing? You may not have directly killed her father, and who knows how many others, with your lousy oatmeal, but you stole their government checks and any remnants of their pride. And somehow you figured out how to keep drawing on their accounts. But not anymore—sister."

Kitt glared at me. I stood my ground. "You've cheated and killed for the money that paid for that stupid gallery full of crap art nobody cares about. Just because someone has an urge to paint or sculpt doesn't mean it will look any better than that mush you fed those poor sods."

"They were a lot safer in my houses than on the streets."

"Safer from what? They were malnourished, corralled liked chattel, and you were draining them dry. That's not safe."

"I gave them a roof over their heads and cooked for them," Kitt said.

"I can't quite see you slaving over a hot stove, stirring Quaker oats into a gluey glob, though I bet you looked cute in your apron."

"You're crazy. So full of shit. I'm getting out of here." When she turned to leave, Brower and Lonnie stepped out of the backroom.

"Stay right there, Ms. Scanlon or Scott or Scoggins, whoever you are. We've got more questions for you," Brower said, finally sounding like a sheriff. She picked up a jar of Cleva's bread-and-butter pickles and threw it at him, hitting him just above his right eye. She threw another one at Lonnie, but missed, then jerked open the door and sent the jingle bells flying. Outside, she faced two SBI officers, their guns drawn, without a pickle jar in sight.

Chapter 66: Abit

We were all sitting round the woodstove inside the store—me and Cleva, Alex and Della. I was just taking a break from some stocking, and Alex was drinking coffee, explaining how he'd found out all that stuff on Kitt.

"That evening at the Inn at Jonas Mountain, she said something that gave her away. She told me, and I don't think she realized her slip, that something I'd said reminded her of all the old people she worked with in Atlanta. That's when everything just clicked for me. I knew she'd done it, but we had to prove it. I started my search with Kitt Scanlon. Nothing except for a North Dakota business license dated last year," Alex told us, rocking in his chair as though he were born to it. "So then I decided to play with the idea that she might be related to Blanche Scoggins, after you'd discovered their connection, Abit. Nothing for Kitt Scoggins, but hey, Kitt's usually a nickname."

"Like Kit Carson was really Christopher Houston Carson," Della said. A frown from Alex had her adding real quick-like, "Sorry, Sherlock, proceed."

"So I tried Kathleen Scoggins, and I found some folks in Montana and Tennessee who didn't match our Kitt. But then Katherine Scoggins, and bingo! The proud bouncing baby of Blanche and Dick Scoggins in Asheville, N.C., December 29, 1956."

"I guess that's why I saw them hugging," I said.

"Yeah, but it gets even more interesting," Alex said. "When I searched further on Katherine Scoggins, I found a reference to a Katherine Scott in Atlanta, Georgia—which is where Kitt Scanlon told me that night at the inn that she'd moved from, not Raleigh. Not sure why that came up in my search, but that's LexisNexis for you. Sometimes I think it has artificial intelligence. Anyway, she was featured in an article about working with the homeless. Doing good works to help them manage their meager finances, mostly through Social Security. The woman in the picture was a dead ringer for Scanlon/Scoggins/Scott—and she was posing with a woebegone man named Roberto Sanchez."

"That's Lucy's last name. Were they related?" I asked.

"Lucy's father. Who, as we now know, Kitt Scoggins/Scanlon/Scott stole from and abused, overtly and covertly, causing his death. I doubt they can pin his murder on her, but there are enough other charges to keep her locked away for years."

He went on to explain that she'd set up what Lucy's sister had called oatmeal factories, houses offering down-and-out folks a bed and hot meal—mostly oatmeal. Ugh! I get the shivers just thinking about that.

According to Alex, Kitt was stealing from old folks while living in Atlanta, and later from up here. She used the gallery and her mama's laundry to run the money through. She kept taking trips back to Atlanta, so she could connect with what she called "her artists," but Alex said she was connecting with the two *con artists*—guys running her operation down there. They'd been arrested in Georgia.

Nobody knows exactly how she got Lucy out in the woods. Kitt wasn't talking. She may have just switched the poisoned syringe in her case—or she might have taken a walk with her, pretending to want to talk things out but really getting her far away from help. And the detectives found enough evidence in the back of her art store to nail her, including a wax kit for making key impressions.

That was when Della said something about how Kitt was using a belt and suspenders. I finally figured out she meant that Kitt faked the suicide note and, just in case that didn't work, framed the guy Della called Tattoo Man. When Della's investigation heated up and Tattoo Man didn't take the fall, Kitt faked a romance with Gregg to help her set him up. While they were dating, she made a wax copy of his office key so she could get inside his office and plant those traced notes. Whew! That was some conniving. And we figured she'd learned her forging skills while faking signatures on all them government checks. She was really good at being bad.

"Thing is," Alex said, "she says she hated paying taxes to the government, but that's exactly how she got so much money out of those poor sods—thanks to their government checks. And even though I can't prove it, I believe her association with the Green Treatise was a lot more involved than that peace-making crap she told you, Della."

"Wonder what *they* think of all this?" Della asked. "I bet they've disowned her. Or maybe they admire her ripping off the gov'ment. And poor ol' Gregg. She just used him to deflect suspicion from her and frame him— a gov'ment man." She said it like them. I wanted to laugh, but it weren't the time or place.

Earlier, we'd all seen Brower walking round with a black eye. He'd had to get stitches where those pickles of Cleva's hit him. I swear Cleva was getting a kick out of that, nice as she was. Then I asked what happened to that tattletale Cassie.

"She's at work—with Gregg," Della said, while Alex poured each of us a fresh cup of coffee. Della looked up at him and added, "I told you he was a nice guy—he didn't even fire her. I wished I'd thought to ask her who she called when the computer wouldn't reboot. Turns out it was none other than Kitt. She'd told Cassie she was a computer whizz and to call her if she ever had any trouble. While Gregg was out of town, Kitt threw the circuit breaker at Gregg's office and went home to wait for the call. Damn, that woman is a setup artist. It just didn't pay off the way she wanted."

"So will Blanche Scoggins go to the slammer, too?" Cleva asked, opening some of her now-famous pickles. No one else seemed to want any. I'd eat just about anything, but even I didn't think pickles and coffee were a good combination. Cleva munched away, kinda nervous-like as she listened to all these bad things Kitt did.

"We're not sure," Della said. "She really didn't know what Kitt was up to, though she freely confessed to helping her hide her income. But she swears she didn't know it was from sick old people. She just thought they were saving money on taxes. And she's been helping the authorities, so they'll likely go easy on her."

"So did Kitt make all those calls and steal Jake?" I asked.

"Either she did or she was behind them," Della said. "And we believe she was the person you saw setting the store on fire, though again, we can't prove those things. But your finding her hubcap clinched it for us."

That felt good, but we all knew it was her and Alex who did the hard stuff. "Why did you add that part about seeing her car when you were in the Rollin' Store? You ain't even taken a ride yet."

"Haven't. I know, I just said that to get Kitt riled, and to let her know we knew Blanche was her mother. But I plan to join you and Duane, from time to time, now that things are getting back to normal. Whatever that means."

"I think she might have killed you next," I said.

She patted me on the back and smiled. "I doubt that, Mister. Too many people were starting to pay attention. And she was counting on Gregg taking the rap."

We all sat quiet-like, and then the strangest thing happened: Della started laughing. Alex and Cleva and I just looked at each other and didn't have a clue about what was going on. She carried on so that we started laughing too, for no good reason. Finally, she caught her breath. "Gosh, that's the first good laugh I've had in months."

"Well, are you going to let us in on it?" Cleva asked, wiping her eyes.

"I just pictured Blanche up on her ladder, adding a new sign to her wall: 'No Money Laundering!'"

Chapter 67: Della

"I feel like such an idiot."

Alex and Abit had left for another driving lesson. Cleva and I were enjoying the relative quiet and a glass of Champagne.

"Why's that, honey?"

"I'm such a bad judge of character. I never saw through Kitt."

"Well, maybe that's just as well. You're not meant to go around judging all the time. It wears a body down being too vigilant. Just pay attention and do what you can. That's what you did, and it all worked out. At least for us, not poor ol' Lucy. Besides, you don't want to be so cynical that you suspect or dislike everyone, do you?"

I shook my head. I was tired of trying to outthink the world. I was feeling better every day—and grateful that I hadn't had my recurring dream in over a week. I thanked Cleva again for sending out an SOS to all my customers.

"Well, you needed to see that you *do* belong to a community."

After that, things started to settle down. We'd had a media frenzy for more than a week, with reporters from the *Atlanta Constitution, Charlotte Observer*, and other news services in town, filling up neighboring hotels, cabins, and restaurants. I even ran into an old freelance buddy of mine, who was covering the story for the AP.

Brower was taking all the credit, and I was glad—that meant I could get on with my life. The only interview I granted was to Tony Benedict, who wrote a dandy series on the crime, from our local perspective, for the *Mountain Weekly*. He did such a good job, I heard he was on his way to Charlotte for a job with the *Observer*. I was happy for him—always glad to see a fellow member of the Fourth Estate excel.

Brower, on the other hand, had granted every interview he could talk his way into. He seemed to appreciate my bowing out, letting him have all the glory. I saw him buying a stack of newspapers in the drugstore, and he did that guy thing of holding up the paper and nodding at me. Man-speak for thank you.

And I'd sent my condolences to Izzy. When she got my note, she called, and we talked for a while. She'd heard from Brower earlier, asking if Lucy had ever mentioned Gregg to her. Of course, Lucy hadn't even met Gregg until she came to Laurel Falls. To his credit, Brower did have the courtesy to follow up once Kitt was arrested. Izzy was wrestling with the idea that her father was likely murdered as well—or at least grossly neglected, all for his meager income. When she thanked me for getting to the bottom of her family's story, I assured her I'd had lots of help. I invited her to come down again and meet Abit, who played such a big role. I didn't mention Alex, but he deserved a lot of credit, too. And even Brower, hard as it was to admit. She said she would—and she'd call first to make sure I had plenty of chorizo in stock.

Alex had been back in D.C. for a while. He seemed moody, unsettled even, since we wrapped up our caper. I wasn't sure why, since he had plenty of projects to work on, though he'd wisely chosen not to write about Kitt and her life of crime.

Later that afternoon, the phone rang. "Remember when I did that story a few years ago when the movie *Gandhi* came out?" Alex said, without as much as a hello. "The one about how much was fact and how much was Hollywood? I was always struck by the part in the movie when Nahari killed a child from a Muslim sect after the Muslims killed his Hindu son."

He paused for such a long time, I finally asked, "Okay, and where are you going with this?"

"Gandhi told him, just a minute, I have it transcribed from the movie." I heard papers shuffling, and then he said, "Gandhi told him, 'I know a way out of Hell. Find a child, a child whose mother and father have been killed and raise him as your own. Only be sure that he is a Muslim and that you raise him as one.' That's what I need to do."

"Raise a Muslim?"

"Dammit, Della, you're being intentionally obtuse. Please, I'm trying to figure something out. It's been rumbling around in my head, and I need to get it straight."

Once he told me the rest of his idea, I couldn't wait for him to come back down here.

Three days later, I was dreading our visit next door, even though Alex and I had what I considered great news to share with Vester and Mildred. I had a niggling feeling it wouldn't go well. When we knocked on their door, we could see through the screen door that they were just finishing supper. Vester opened the door, welcoming us in his own way.

Mildred offered peach pie and coffee, which were impossible to refuse, even though my stomach was churning. She waved away the fuss we made over her delicious baking. "They're just last year's peaches I'd put up." Just.

After we chatted a while and finished our pie, I cleared my throat and said, "We've got something we wanted to share with you. Abit, I didn't want to tell you about this before we talked with your folks." He looked scared, and I saw a marked change in Vester's expression. I looked at Alex.

"Well," Alex said, clearing his throat. "It will come as no surprise that Della and I think the world of your boy." Abit shot him a look that made Alex stumble. "I mean your young man, er, your son." Abit nodded, though he still looked worried.

"Well, I have an editor friend in D.C. whose son went to a school in Boone. A great school that's affiliated with the university that's for kids, er, young folks who need a little help with their schooling. It's a remarkable program. Anyway, I told him about Abit and how much potential he has, and this editor, well, he owed me a favor. So he talked with the board members—he serves on the board. Cleva Hall also knows some of those board members from her school principal days, so she wrote letters and made phone calls. The board …"

Alex paused. The tension in the room thrummed, and he was struggling for the right words. "… is offering a two-year scholarship for Abit. I know it's a long drive, so Abit, with your permission, of course, could stay in one of the dorms there—supervised housing—and I want to pay for that. I made a big mistake a few years ago, and I have longed for a fresh start. I want to give that fresh start to Abit, which could help me heal, too, and do something worthwhile for your family at the same time. We could drive up there and I could show …"

"Thank you, but we don't take no charity," Vester interrupted, spitting his words out like a bad taste.

No one said a word. A long, painful silence hung in the room, until Mildred finally spoke. "This ain't no charity, Vester."

"The hell it ain't. We can take care of our own. These bigshots think they can come down here and show us the way. If that ain't charity, I don't know what is." He untucked his napkin, threw it on the table, and stood up, his chair scraping on the linoleum floor.

Mildred stood too, looking him in the eye, her voice stronger than I'd ever heard. "It may be charity, but it's

Christian charity, and that's not the same thing as what you're talkin' about."

"Christian?" Vester said, sneering. "I bet that man ain't seen the inside of a church since, since …"

"Since you did?"

"Woman, whose side are you on?"

"Vester Junior's. And you don't have to go to church to love people and do the right thing." She turned to Alex and said, "We accept. With open hearts—and broken hearts that we cain't do it for him ourselves."

Vester glared at her, then sat back down and sighed like a dying man. No one budged. Except for Abit. He jumped up, tears streaking his face, and threw his arms around his mother. Then he awkwardly hugged me and Alex, trying to get his arms around us both at the same time. Mildred dabbed at her eyes with her napkin.

Vester looked horrified when Abit headed toward him, and, without a thought about whether the man deserved it or wanted it, hugged his father as hard as Vester's rigid body would allow. Abit wouldn't let go. Slowly, Vester reached around his son's back, and Mildred moved to stand by her family. We slipped away, down the steps toward home.

Chapter 68: Abit

I barely slept last night. I felt both excited and scared about the idea of school. I'd always wanted to get away, but once I got the chance, all I could think about was what if I couldn't learn—even at that special school? And I hated to think about leaving Mama, especially with only Daddy for company.

I tossed and turned and then woke up from a dream where I was wandering round a building, opening all these doors, but no one was inside. The building wasn't spooky. It felt good being there, but those empty rooms felt all wrong. I lay there, kinda sweaty from being all twisted up inside, and thought about that for some time. Then an idea just popped into my head: those empty rooms were waiting for *me*.

The next morning, no one said a word at breakfast. I gobbled down some eggs and bacon and a couple of biscuits, and asked to be excused. I expected Daddy to say no, but he just sat there, looking sadder than ever. Mama nodded.

I took the steps too fast and almost landed on my butt, but I steadied myself and ran to the store. It was only seven-thirty, so I was the first one there. I took my seat and watched the stairway. I could hardly wait to see Alex and Della.

When Della came down, she smiled but looked sad. "Sorry if we caused you any trouble, Mister."

"Trouble? Are you kidding me? I can't believe my good luck meeting you. And Daddy's always a big grump. I can deal with him. You didn't do nothin' to upset me or even Mama. We're both grateful."

"Anything."

"You didn't do anything to upset us. Mama didn't say much at breakfast because of Daddy, but last night she told me she was proud of me. *Proud of me!*"

I followed her into the store and started helping out, putting stuff on the shelves. Della said she could get it, that it wasn't my regular workday, but I told her today was on the house! She smiled and poured us each some coffee, which we took a few minutes to drink, sitting round the wood stove. I told her how happy I was that I had such a big savings account—thanks to her.

"You earned every penny, Mister," she said. I'd noticed she hadn't been ruffling my hair lately. I'd overheard Alex telling her I was getting too old for that, and as much as he was right—it *had* started to annoy me—I kinda missed it, too.

We worked together all morning, and I caught myself whistling from time to time. Alex came down later, all shaved and fresh looking. He was off to Boone to check on a few things for me. I wanted to go along, but I knew better than to ask Daddy today. Alex seemed to think the same thing, though we didn't talk about it.

He stopped long enough to tell me he was planning on writing a book about the school, and he wanted to follow my progress over the next two years. Man, that *really* scared me. He knew it, too, because he patted me on the shoulder and told me I'd do just fine. He said he'd start with how it all came about—how earlier that spring someone had lost her life, while later on, someone had found his. I told him that sounded good, though I hoped I could be a worthy character in his book. He told me that he wasn't worried, so I guessed I shouldn't be either.

He got back about closing time. We were all standing round in the store while he shared a bunch of stuff about the school and other things, like my dorm room and meals. He warned me that the school cooks couldn't hold a candle to Mama's cooking, but even so, he'd found the food pretty tasty. Finally, he told Della he wanted to talk to me more about the school, just us, not with Mama and Daddy, at least for tonight. Della called up to the house and got permission for me to have supper with her and Alex.

And that was when it hit me. Everything was going so good—too good—that I had this funny feeling. Something about the way Alex and Della looked at each other and spoke quiet-like, almost whispering, gave me a chill.

Della locked the store's front door, Jake running like a dog let out of stir. But his happiness wasn't enough to stop me from worrying. I asked round a big lump in my throat, "Will you be here when I come back for weekends and holidays?"

Della smiled and took my hand. As we headed up the steps, Jake leading the way with Alex close behind, she said, "You know what Elbert says."

I had to think for a second, and then I started laughing, even before she added, "We're not moving. We're here to stay."

Read an excerpt from the next book in the Appalachian Mountain Mysteries series at the end of this book.

Your free book is "Waiting for You"

Want to know more about Abit and Della? Get your free copy of the prequel novelette, *Waiting for You*:

I've pulled back the curtain on their lives before they met in Laurel Falls—between 1981 and 1984. You'll discover how Abit lost hope of ever having a meaningful life and why Della had to leave Washington, D.C.

**Get your free copy of *Waiting for You:*
*https://www.lyndamcdanielbooks.com/free***

Dear Readers ...

I hope you've enjoyed Book 1 in my Appalachian Mountain Mysteries series. I sure enjoy writing them!

I've been a professional writer for several decades now, and it still thrills me when readers write to me. Sometimes they have questions about the stories and the characters. Other times they leave reviews and, well, make my day!

> "Reminds me of *To Kill a Mockingbird* ... finding your books is like finding a rare jewel."
> — J.M. Grayson

Before I started writing fiction 10 years ago, I wrote more than 1,200 articles for major magazines and newspapers and 15 nonfiction books, including several books on the craft of writing. I'm now working on my fifth Appalachian Mountain Mysteries novel.

Book Reviews ...

I'm touched whenever people post reviews on Amazon, Goodreads, book blogs, etc.

> "FIVE STARS! Lynda McDaniel has that wonderfully appealing way of weaving a story ..." — Deb, Amazon Hall of Fame Top 100 Reviewer

I'd really appreciate it if you'd take a minute or two to leave a review. (It's easy—just a sentence or two is enough.) Reader reviews are the lifeblood of any author's career. Often readers don't realize how much these reviews mean to the success of an author. In today's online world, reviews can make a huge difference—so thanks for posting a few sentences.

And Free Book Club Talks ...

I'd love to drop by your book club and answer your questions—whether about my books, what inspired them, or even how to write your own books. We can easily meet through **Zoom or other online meeting software**. To keep things lively, I've created an all-in-one Book Club Discussion Guides to download. Get your free copy on my website.

I get a kick out of hearing from readers, so don't be a stranger! You can contact me directly at *LyndaMcDanielBooks@gmail.com* or through my website *www.LyndaMcDanielBooks.com*.

Lynda McDaniel

P.S. I thought you might enjoy an excerpt from the next book in the series (following the book club questions).

A Life for a Life
Book Club Discussion Guide

1. What does the book's title refer to? How does it relate to the book's theme?

2. What do you think Lynda McDaniel's purpose was in writing this book? What ideas was she expressing?

3. What was unique about the setting of the book? How did the setting impact the story? Do you want to read more books set there?

4. What did you already know about the Southern Appalachians? What did you learn? Did you have misperceptions?

5. Did the characters seem believable to you? Did they remind you of anyone you know—even if they're from a different part of the country? To what extent did they remind you of yourself?

6. Abit Bradshaw is an outsider. Have you ever been excluded from something you longed for? How did you overcome this?

7. In Chapter 30, Abit Bradshaw says:

"I grew up with them dogs, and when they got old and died, I just about died right along with them. I swore I wouldn't get close to another dog, because you'd look in those big brown eyes and just knowed the pain that was waitin' down the road. ...

But after I thought about it, I decided it were a sin to do that. ... I only used that word when I needed the strongest word I could think of. Not like you were going to hell or nothin', just that what I was talking about was real serious. Like about it being a sin to avoid love because of the pain that surely laid ahead. Besides, I tried not to look too far into the future, because that's when I got myself in a terrible state. I tried to live one day at a time."

Have you ever avoided love or connection because of the pain you anticipated later on? Do you try to live one day at a time, or do thoughts of the future figure heavily in your day?

8. Why was Della Kincaid so determined to find the killer? What in her personal life and her professional life pushed her into difficult and even dangerous situations?

9. What are the major conflicts in the story?

10. What feelings did this book evoke for you? Could you relate to the sorrows and joys the characters experienced?

11. Were you surprised by any cultural difference you read about? Have you been to any of the places mentioned in the story?

12. In Chapter 57, Della Kincaid says:

"Community hadn't figured much in my life. Sure, I had friends, but everyone was always so busy. And neighbors? Forget it. We barely said hello as we passed in the hallways or at the front door. Not to mention I had a creepy security guard who kept asking me out and following me around. Abit was the best security guard I could ever have."

What does your community look like/feel like? Who's got your back when hard times show up?

13. How did Della Kincaid help Abit grow as a person? Have you ever taken someone under your wing and helped them, even in small ways? How did/does that feel?

14. Are there any characters you'd like to deliver a message to? If so, who? What would you say?

Excerpt from Book 2 in the
Appalachian Mountain Mysteries Series

The Roads to Damascus

October 1989

1

"Della, open up. I'm in a mess of trouble."

Jake was whining at the screen door, as happy to see me as I was him. While I was whispering what a good boy he was, I could hear Della in her office talking on the phone, so I figured she didn't hear us carrying on.

I couldn't talk too loud, since I didn't want Mama or Daddy to know I was back in Laurel Falls. At first when I went off to school about four year ago, I'd come home most weekends. (The school was a ways up the road in Boone, N.C.) But as I got to liking what the school offered, I rarely came home more than oncet a month.

I'd've visited more if I could've just hung out with Della Kincaid (who owned the store next door to my family's house), but I had to stay with Mama and Daddy. Mama fussed over me and worried about what I was getting up to in the "big city," and Daddy still ignored me. Not so much out of disgust, more like habit.

"Della!" I said as loud as I felt was safe. "It's me, Abit."

She came into the living room all smiles, her arms wide open, ready for a big hug after she unlocked the screen door. "Hey, honey," she said, throwing her arms round me. "I was on the phone with Alex. He had to go back to D.C. to meet with one of his editors. What brings you here at this hour?"

"I guess you didn't hear me. I got thrown out of school, and I need your help."

2

My troubles started about four months earlier when a girl came skipping over the mountainside where I was tending the cows. She'd put some violets in her long blond hair, and they matched the flowers on her gauzy dress. Truth be told, I thought I was seeing something from the spirit world. I blinked a time or two, not believing my eyes, but she was still there.

I was at the Hickson School of American Studies in a work/study program, something they offered folks like me who had a "learning disability"—a couple of words they drilled into us instead of *stupid* or *retard*. The school was part of the university in Boone and named after someone who'd given it a bunch of money. Too bad about his name. The way things like that went, the

301

school's long name kept getting shortened until it was known as simply The Hicks.

For one of my jobs, I tended the cows that were in season at the school dairy. They liked to graze on a grassy slope that faced west toward Beech Mountain, and every Tuesday and Thursday afternoons I kept check on them. I wasn't sure what was the prettiest—the view of the mountains or them Jersey cows with their dreamy brown eyes and long lashes. Mama had a cow for a while, but it was a Holstein, and while they're a fine-looking breed, they aren't gorgeous like these girls. I'd sit among them, not shepherding or anything like that, just keeping an eye out to make sure they were safe. I'd found a good place to sit, where the rocks formed a natural backrest, and I'd lose myself in the gentle lowing from the herd.

So that day, a particularly warm spring day, I was in a kind of daze when that girl appeared. She settled down next to me like an apple blossom fluttering to the ground.

"Hello! I'm Clarice. Who are you?"

"Uh, hi." I felt all tongue-tied, but pretty girls did that to me. I hadn't really had a girlfriend yet—no one back home would give me the time of day, and at The Hicks, there weren't that many girls. Besides, I couldn't imagine anyone would say yes if I asked her out, and I just wasn't up for more rejection.

"I said, who are you?"

I nearabout said Abit, but caught myself. "V.J."

I got that nickname Abit because Daddy told everyone, "He's a bit slow." That made him feel better, letting the world know that he knew he had a retard (his word). Turns out I'm not the sharpest saw in the tool chest, but not the dullest, neither. My teachers have showed me lots of things and helped me appreciate other qualities I have. I just needed someone—make that several someones—to believe in me.

Thing was, that school was everything I'd hoped it would be. I hadn't done so well in public school back in Laurel Falls, so again, to make himself feel better, Daddy took me out of school when I was twelve. But after that summer of 1985, Alex Covington (Della's ex-husband and later her boyfriend) and Della's best friend Cleva Hall pulled some strings and got me in The Hicks. Alex had even written a book about the place—more like one of them coffee table books with lots of pictures and some stories. (Thank heavens it ended up *not* featuring me, the way he'd threatened.)

"V.J. what?" she asked, snuggling kinda close-like.

"Do you mean what does V.J. stand for or what's my last name?"

"The latter."

That was a relief because I didn't have to tell her V.J. stood for Vester Junior. I hated Daddy's name, and I didn't even want to say it out loud. "Bradshaw. V.J. Bradshaw. What's yours?"

She frowned at me. "Clarice, as I said earlier." I guessed she was just so, well, different lookin', I'd been studying her rather than paying attention to what she'd said. "Ledbetter. Clarice Ledbetter," she added.

We started in talking and oncet we got warmed up, we carried on like old friends. I couldn't believe how much we had in common. When I told her I liked her blond hair, she said she liked my red hair. When she shared how much she loved dogs, I raved about them, too. But when I asked if she'd come for the Dance Week starting tomorrow—I could already see her dancing in that beautiful dress—her pretty face changed in a flash.

No, she said, her chin quivering, she was here because her mother was dying and the school had been nice enough to rent them the Gate House for the duration. Seemed her mama grew up round the school and wanted to die nearby. Clarice told me all about what medical things were happening to her mama (in more detail, to be honest, than I cared to hear). It was one of the saddest stories I'd heard in some time. No longer killing time out front of Della's store meant I didn't hear all the tales of woe from my fellow bench-sitters.

I wrestled with the fact that Clarice was living with so much sorrow, while I was feeling so happy that such a pretty girl was paying attention to me (even though I figured she just needed someone to talk to). And I liked the idea that she wouldn't be leaving after Dance Week (not unless her mama took a quick turn for the worse).

Too often people I enjoyed left after only a week or two; they came for just a short time to learn some of the art and music of the mountains. Way back, the school had started as a settlement school to teach mountain people the ways of the world. Then about thirty year ago, it turned into a place for city folks to come learn *our* ways.

Before long, the sun had slipped behind a mountain. Sunset came early there, the mountains stealing a good couple of hours from our days. Even the swallows were fooled, swooping and soaring as though it were time for their bedtime snack. As much as I wanted to stay (and not because of that sunset), I had to get down to the school kitchen to help the cooks, Lurline and Eva. "Do you take any of your meals with us at the school?" I asked. "I also work in the kitchen, and I could get you some extra helpings." I felt silly as soon as those words were out of my mouth. Even I knew I was groveling. But she smiled and seemed to take it in the right way.

"Thanks, but we can't afford the school's meal plan. I do most of our cooking now."

"Gosh, I'm sorry. I bet I could wrap up some leftovers for you, from time to time. We usually have a lot extra. Lurline and Eva always cook too much, just in case more people show than they expected. And it's a shame for it to just go to the pigs."

"That's real sweet of you, but I wouldn't want to deprive the pigs!" I was about to explain myself when she smiled and kissed me on the cheek. Just then one of them Jerseys let out a big fart, and we both started laughing. I don't know when I've appreciated a fart more, because otherwise, I'd have been sitting there like a fool, dumbstruck by her kiss.

We both stood up, and she brushed some leaves and stuff off her skirt—and my behind! She sure looked good standing there, the breeze catching her hair and rippling that gauzy skirt. "I knew what you meant, V.J., but you don't have to do us any favors. I wouldn't want to get you in trouble."

"Oh, you couldn't get me in trouble," I said. "Besides, I'm sure everyone wants to help you out. We take care of our own."

"But we're outsiders."

"Yeah, but you said your mama was from the area. So that's good enough for me." She smiled again, and I paused for a moment before adding, "I gotta get going. You comin'?"

"No, that dark old cottage depresses me. I believe I'll sit here a while longer and drink all this in," she said, sweeping her hand in the most graceful way.

I loped off, wishing I didn't have to leave. But it would be too obvious to suddenly say *Oh, I don't need to go, after all*.

I met a fair number of people who struck me that way—folks I'd like to know better—but most times they didn't want to know me. Like when I'd call someone and leave a message, but they'd never call back. Sometimes I'd check to see if there'd been an electrical storm that'd turned off my answering machine. Or I'd think maybe the tape had run out. Most times, it hadn't even started.

Other times, I'd see all these folks with big groups of friends, laughing and carrying on, piling into a car to go to the movies or a music gig. They'd wave at me, and I'd wave back, acting like I was real happy for them, heading off to have fun. And I guess I was. I just couldn't figure out why I was only good enough to wave at.

I always saw friendship—like me and Della had—as about the finest thing in the world, and I wanted as much of that as I could get. *Maybe I was trying too hard*, I'd tell myself when things didn't work out. Or, *maybe I said something wrong*.

No wonder, then, I was tickled that Clarice had taken a liking to me. After that first time, I saw her a bunch more at school. We hung out sometimes and had meals together, especially when her brother, Clayne, weren't round. They took turns taking care of their mama back at the cottage and, like Clarice had told me, cooked their own meals, most times. Later on, Clarice worked out some kind of deal doing odd jobs for the school in trade for some meals. "I just *have* to get out of that cottage, sometimes," she whispered oncet when we was sitting next to each other at dinner.

Even though Alex had warned me that Lurline and Eva weren't as good cooks as Mama, I loved those meals. Chicken and dumplings. Macaroni and cheese. Pork chops that weren't cooked to shoe leather. And with Clarice sitting with me, I felt like somebody. Out of all them guys, she chose me. Not that the competition was that stiff. Some of the guys were kinda scruffy and some were too shy to even look at her. But for a while, I felt like the luckiest guy at the school.

3

"Well, Mister, I hate to break up this lovefest, but it's getting late," Della said, carrying in a tray of cold chicken sandwiches, potato salad, and coconut cake. She set it on the coffee table.

Jake and I had been tussling on the floor on an oval braided rug she'd added since I was there last. Whenever I came home from The Hicks for a weekend, I tried to spend plenty of time with Jake. I'd trained him to dance on his hind legs and speak for treats, and we'd go for long walks into the woods. Whenever I'd see him after a spell of being away, I noticed how my heart felt fuller when we were together. It felt good, and I found myself wondering what happened to all them feelings when I wasn't with Jake. Were they in there, kinda dormant, like them noisy cicadas that wait seventeen years before they come back? Did the feelings build up between visits and come roaring out when we were reunited? I didn't know the answer, but I wanted them to come out more, even when Jake weren't round.

I sat up, tucked my legs under the coffee table, and started chowing down. I could've eaten every one of them sandwiches, I was so hungry. Della kinda nibbled on one, but she'd probably had her dinner earlier. She let me eat for a while before asking more about what'd happened at the school. I thought for a minute about how to answer her. There were things I wanted to share, and some I just couldn't tell her. Not yet, anyways.

"It started when some people came to the school—a mother, son, and daughter," I said with my mouth full, but Della didn't seem to mind. "The mother was dying, and the two kids were looking after her. They'd moved to the school because they were evicted from somewhere in Virginia 'cause she was too sick to work, and what her son earned wasn't enough to live on." I stopped to eat for a minute, and then added, "She'd growed up nearby our school and wanted to die as close to her family's home place as she could. I remember how tore up we all were listening to her story. A bunch of us had gathered on the front porch of Gate House, where she sat, talking and taking in that heavenly mountain view. It was like she was looking into her future."

While she listened to my story, Della didn't look all that sad. "Let me guess," she said after a while. "They got you to part with some of your hard-earned savings."

"Aw, come on, Della. It wasn't that obvious. You had to be there."

"Okay, you're right. It just pisses me off that they took advantage of you."

"It wasn't just me," I said through another mouthful—this time her homemade coconut cake. "A bunch of us were taken in. But that wasn't the half of it. Most people at the school don't even know what else happened. At least not about them stealing so much money. We all lost some, but old man Henson, the director of the school, lost a lot, and the money wasn't just his. It was the school's, too. At least that's the story goin' round. When someone said we should call the cops, he piped up that it wasn't worth it—crooks like them are next to impossible to catch. Besides, he said he didn't want to shame the school. I think he just didn't want people to know how stupid he'd been with the school's money."

"So, why are *you* in trouble, Abit?"

"Because before they left, they put $2,000 *into* my savings account! I know that sounds even weirder, but it's a long story." I don't know if it was because of the food or the time of night or the fact that I was unloading this burden on my best friend, but I suddenly felt so tired I could hardly finish my cake. I yawned real big, and Della noticed.

"You can tell me more tomorrow. For now, hop into bed in the guest room. It's all made up for you." She hugged me and said goodnight. She closed her bedroom door but then came right back out. "You'll need to clear out by noon tomorrow. I don't want to be sneaking behind Mildred and Vester's backs. You can go home and make it look as though you just walked from the bus station."

"What will I tell them?"

"We'll figure that out in the morning."

Della woke me up with breakfast in bed. I had no idea what that was like, though I'd seen it on TV. (And I sure was glad she'd left off the rose in a vase.) At first I felt like a fool with a tray in my lap, but I had to admit, I got accustomed real fast. She helped me get the pillows right behind my back and arranged the tray just so before pulling up a chair nearby. "I called Alex, and he wants to see you."

"OK, when's he coming back? I've got all the time in the world."

"He can't get away. He wants you to come to D.C."

I couldn't speak, and not because I'd just taken a big bite of one of Mrs. Parker's cinnamon rolls. I gulped it down, took a swallow of coffee, but I still couldn't get a word out. I'd never been out of North Carolina, let alone to the nation's capital.

Della chuckled. "Jake and I were already heading up that way in a couple of weeks. I checked with Billie, and she can keep the store sooner, rather than later. We can leave Monday."

"How will we go?"

"I'll drive us up there. Now that I traded in my truck for a bigger vehicle, we can all fit. You can have your lovefest with Jake the whole way up."

I nearabout started crying. Having friends help you out *and* a trip to Washington, D.C. bordered on a miracle. But then I thought about what a sight that would be—me with this tray in my lap and flowerdy pillowcases behind me, bawling my eyes out. That made me start chuckling. Della looked puzzled as she stood up to leave. Then she turned and added, "I don't feel good about tricking your mother. Can you tell her what's going on?"

"No!" I said, nearly upending the tray. "Really, let me have a couple of weeks or so. They won't miss me. I need to figure more of this out before I tell them anything. They'd be so ashamed of me." She nodded and let me be.

I went back to eating my breakfast. Damn, Della was a good cook. Mama worried about germs and such, so she cooked her eggs dry, but Della's were creamy and her bacon weren't burnt to a crisp. (Mama had a thing about pork and needing to cook it so she didn't give us ptomaine poisoning or something like that beginning with a T.) Just as I was thinking about that, Della stuck her head back round the door.

"They will—*do*—miss you, but I see what you mean. You've been gone a month before. But you have to go home now and spend a weekend with them. And kiss them goodbye!"

I was dreading that weekend with the folks, so I ate real slow (something I never did). I dawdled over getting dressed, too. It was well after noon when Della practically pushed me out the door.

**The Roads to Damascus and other books
in the Appalachian Mountain Mysteries series
are available at book retailers.**

Books by Lynda McDaniel

FICTION
A Life for a Life
The Roads to Damascus
Welcome the Little Children
Murder Ballad Blues

NONFICTION
Words at Work
How Not to Sound Stupid When You Write
How to Write Stories that Sell
Write Your Book Now!
(with Virginia McCullough)
Highroad Guide to the NC Mountains
North Carolina's Mountains
Asheville: A View from the Top